THE PATIENT'S SECRET

S.A. FALK

Storm
PUBLISHING

Ebook ISBN: 978-1-80508-183-8
Paperback ISBN: 978-1-80508-185-2

Cover design by: Lisa Brewster
Cover images by: Shutterstock

Published by Storm Publishing.
For further information, visit:
www.stormpublishing.co

ONE

The execution chamber at the Wyoming State Penitentiary is a long walk from my cell on death row. This is by design, I imagine. It forces men like me to reflect on our crimes and the punishment that we are about to receive as a result of those crimes.

I remember how, as my execution date approached, reporters wanted to know how I felt about my upcoming death. How I coped with the finality of it all. How I repented for what I had done and reconciled with those whom I had wronged.

I told them that every person has a death sentence. The only difference between me and everyone else is that I have the luxury of knowing not only *when* it will happen, but also *how* it will happen. Such knowledge allows you to savor the small things in life. A pleasant odor. The taste of a decent meal. The nostalgia of a fond memory.

As for repentance and reconciliation? Well, I told them, those two yokes are the burdens of the guilty and the remorseful. I feel neither guilt nor remorse. If I had to do it all over again, which I would in a heartbeat, incidentally, the only thing

I would change is getting caught. But, as the saying goes, all good things must come to an end eventually.

People have challenged me on this over the years, begging to know why I did what I did. Was I abused as a child, or molded by some traumatic experience? Did I suffer from mental illness? Sexual deviance maybe? Anything that could explain the inexplicable.

No, I told them. Killing was an instinct as innate and subconscious as hunger.

The guards lead me into the execution chamber. The room feels like the air has been sucked out of it, leaving a quietness caused more by nervous anticipation than respect for the occasion. I myself am not nervous though. I am as tranquil as a monk emerging from a long, enlightening hermitage. I glance casually into the witness viewing room, which is standing room only by this point. Every single witness invited by me personally in accordance with Wyoming state policy. Most notably the former Peak County Prosecuting Attorney, Kim Matthews, and my friend, Dr. Sharon Stevenson.

I make eye contact with Dr. Stevenson and smile. She does not smile back, although I can tell her lack of a response is more from surprise than apathy. She could have refused my request to see me off. Refused the burden of watching one of her friends being put to death. But she didn't. She's here because she still cares about me in spite of everything that has happened.

Poor thing... I almost feel bad for her.

The eyes of the other witnesses burn holes through her when I smile at her. A sort of guilt by association because the convicted serial killer has just made a human connection with someone. You see, we all start out as human beings. Even me. We don't want to believe this, but it's true. People like me don't just appear out of thin air, nor am I some monster who crawled out of the depths of a forsaken cesspool. A thing created for death and destruction. I was molded by experience and circumstance the same way we all are, and *that* is what caused me to be who I am and do what I did. And *that* is the thing that cripples society with terror: knowing that there are more men like me out there. Lurking in the shadows undetected. Living a Jekyll-and-Hyde existence unbeknownst to everyone, even those closest and dearest to us.

Of course, every one of the witnesses knows who Dr. Stevenson is because of all the news stories over the years. Her early involvement in the Blue River Strangler trial as the forensic psychiatrist who was hired by Kim Matthews to prove that the accused was both competent to stand trial and culpable for his crimes. The controversial diagnosis that made everyone question her expertise, not to mention her own sanity. Her testimony during the trial, not on behalf of the prosecution, but in support of the accused and his defense. The fallout after the conviction and sentencing, namely the destruction of Stevenson's own reputation.

Reputation. To most people, this is the immortal part of ourselves that, when lost, causes us to lose arguably the most important element of who we are as human beings. Dr. Stevenson is certainly this way. Without reputation, she's nothing more than a cracked, empty façade. A frail old woman who got the wool pulled over her eyes by me, a wolf in sheep's clothing.

The people who criticize and ridicule her fail to realize that it wasn't any fault of hers. She's certainly not weak or stupid or gullible. She's one of the most brilliant people I've ever known and the best at what she does. No, the fault does not lie with her; the fault lies with me. I was just that good, and nobody, not even Dr. Sharon Stevenson, stood a chance.

The guards unshackle me and guide me onto the padded crucifix. I'm sure the design of the table is strictly practical, but it's hard to ignore the irony. Not that I see myself as a martyr in any way, although I'll bet some activists will try to use me as one.

I make myself comfortable on the death bed, and they strap my arms and legs and chest down with leather belts. An experiment gone horribly awry and needing to be returned to its original state of inanimation. A modern Prometheus, of sorts.

"You think I'm going somewhere?" I mutter snidely to the guards, as they secure the belts tighter than is necessary.

The guards are stoic and say nothing in response. Hardened by their tasks and hateful of men like me. Fulfilling whatever moral duty it is that they think they're fulfilling. They're no better than me, though. No better than accomplices to my murder. They may not be wrapping their hands around someone's neck and squeezing the life out of them the way I did, but they're still aiding the process. The only difference is that society gives their murder a nod of approval. At least in a state like Wyoming.

I remain calm, serene even, as one orderly attaches heart monitor nodes to my body while another shoves IVs into each of my forearms. One for the sodium thiopental, the pancuronium bromide, and the potassium chloride. A second one just in case the first one fails. After all, you can't be too careful when killing someone. A lesson that Dr. Stevenson learned first-hand from me.

Psychiatry professors warn their students about transference all the time. Oftentimes, patients will project emotions they've had toward those closest to them onto the psychiatrists themselves. Love. Anger. Sadness. Hatred. The whole gamut of emotion vomited uncontrollably onto the psychiatrist.

Transference in and of itself is not a bad thing. Stevenson even found it to be quite helpful in the treatment process. It exposes subconscious motivation and repressed experiences. It can provide a microscopic looking-glass into a man's tormented soul.

Countertransference is when things become dangerous; when the psychiatrist projects her own emotions and regrets onto the patient. The cardinal sin of any psychiatric practice, but correctional psychiatry in particular.

It got an early colleague of Stevenson's stabbed to death. The countertransference caused him to let his guard down and the patient took advantage of it. Shoved the business end of a smelted toothbrush into his carotid a few dozen times.

That's the occupational hazard of working in correctional psychiatry though. Stevenson and her colleagues often joked that prison psychiatrists were just as crazy as their patients. And the way things have panned out these last five years, some of them really *are* just as insane.

A man in a suit enters the execution chamber. I recognize the man immediately from all of my unfortunate interactions with him. The warden of Wyoming State Penitentiary.

The warden looks at the guards who, after a few moments, give him a nod of approval.

Then the warden asks, his voice hollow within the chamber, "Do you have anything you'd like to say before your sentence is carried out?"

I've had a long time to prepare for this moment, yet now that I'm here, the statement I was planning on making feels too sterilized, too uncharacteristic of me.

I nod at the warden and glance over through the glass, my gaze locking on Dr. Stevenson. Then suddenly, the words just come to me as if whispered into my ear by a muse.

"Don't feel bad that it took you so long... Even *you* aren't that good, old friend."

Stevenson holds my gaze no matter how hard she probably wants to break it. To dissociate herself from me and her humiliation. But she can't help it. The countertransference she feels toward me is too strong. The affection, in spite of it all. The betrayal. The manipulation.

The word *friend* lingers in the air of the viewing room. I can see the other witnesses glowering at her. Kim Matthews in particular. How she has come to hate her over the years is breathtaking. A true testament to the human spirit, if you ask me. That's the real reason I invited her here. Not because I give a damn about her seeing me off, but because I knew how torturous it would be for the two of them to be in the presence of each other again. Each a caustic reminder to the other that the past and the pain that it caused was real. That I got the best of both of them when all was said and done. That's the thing that imprisonment and death will never take from me: the knowledge that *I* was ultimately victorious.

Dr. Stevenson refuses to look at any of the other witnesses though. Refuses to acknowledge their anger and absorb their hatred. She has always been the better person—even now when she has nothing more to lose.

After savoring the comedy within the viewing room, I finally turn my head and nod to the warden, who then motions to the orderly in the control room.

The thing about lethal injection is that the means can be rather anticlimactic given the triumphant nature of the end. It's not like the gas chamber where you hear the fumes race into the steel canister, or the firing squad where you see the sharp-shooters hone their muzzles on the prisoner's heart.

One moment a man is awake; the next he isn't. One moment his chest heaves with breath, the next it doesn't. This is all theoretical, of course. There are always outliers. Sometimes the orderlies don't insert the IVs correctly, so the lethal cocktail is pushed into the muscle instead of the bloodstream. An agonizing process of paralysis that eventually, but very slowly, induces infarction of the heart. A vice clamping around it ever so slowly as the atria gasp for fluid.

As much as I don't want to endure that kind of pain in my last moments, it would be quite a final impression to leave upon the witnesses. I'm sure they think that they can stomach watching a man die in agony—they may even *hope* for it in some sadistic, retributive way—but I know they can't. I know that bearing witness to something like that will haunt their dreams for the rest of their lives. And isn't that all a man can really ask for? Isn't that the closest thing that a man can get to immortality? To be remembered by those he cares about?

I turn my head toward Dr. Stevenson again and I feel my eyelids droop as the sodium thiopental enters my system. My gaze locks with hers, and I can see her tears pooling before the slightest hint of a smile forms on her lips.

Moments before my eyes shut for good, I wink at her: my dear friend. One last time.

TWO

I met Kevin Blackford in the spring of 1998 at the Peak County Prison in Park City, Wyoming. The prison was hardly equipped to house a handful of town drunks let alone an alleged serial killer, but Peak County worked with the resources they had.

As the guards led Kevin into the interview room and sat him in the chair across from me, I took note of his physical appearance. He wore a jumpsuit the color of pistachio ice cream and white slip-on shoes that shuffled along the concrete floor as he walked. The hair on his head was disheveled and his facial hair was patchy. His eyes looked exhausted. To be honest, I had a hard time imagining the man before me being responsible for twenty-eight grisly murders. I had imagined a maniacal expression like Manson's or an embittered tone like Ridgway's. I saw nothing of the sort in Kevin Blackford though. Just a miserable, deflated form of a man.

"Could you get us some coffee?" I asked the guards.

The guards glanced between me and Kevin, confused as to why a man accused of his crimes would be granted the luxury of a cheap cup of coffee.

"Do you take cream or sugar in your coffee?" I asked Kevin.

Kevin looked surprised by the question. "Hmm?" he mumbled.

"Cream or sugar in your coffee, Mr. Blackford?"

"Umm..." He glanced at the guards. "Sugar?"

"Sugar for him," I said. "Just black for me, gentlemen."

The guards continued to look at me skeptically before leaving the interview room.

"Now then," I said, finishing the note I was making in the file. "Do you know who I am?"

Kevin shook his head.

"I'm Dr. Stevenson," I said. "I'm a forensic psychiatrist, here to assess your competency to stand trial and your culpability for the charges against you."

"My competency and culpability?" he asked, sounding the words out by their syllables.

"Yes. Do you understand what those mean?"

"Umm... I think so. It has something to do with my insanity plea, right?"

"Sort of," I said.

"So... you're trying to decide if I'm crazy or not?"

"I wouldn't say it quite like that. It's more to decide how capable you are of understanding your actions, the charges against you, the role of your lawyer and the prosecution, that type of stuff."

"Oh." Kevin's tone made him seem unsure.

"I've spoken with the prosecuting attorney, and she says that you have no recollection of the crimes for which you've been charged."

Kevin shook his head. "What's recollection mean?"

"Memory," I said. "She said you don't remember the crimes."

"Oh... No..."

"Yet your DNA was found on several of the victims and

your handwriting matches that of the letters that were sent to the editor of the *Courier*. Is that correct?"

"That's what they've told me."

"I see. Do you know what transient global amnesia is, Mr. Blackford?"

"My lawyer has mentioned it before. He thinks I might have it."

"Yes. You were evaluated by the neurologist last week, is that correct?"

Kevin nodded. "I think so..."

I flipped through the case file in front of me, searching for the neurologist's report.

"Can you tell me a little bit about these moments of memory loss?" I asked.

"What do you mean?"

"Well, have you had any recently?"

"Umm... a handful, I guess?"

"How many is a handful?" I asked.

He shook his head. "I dunno..."

"How long would you say they typically last?"

"A few minutes most of the time. Some a few hours."

"I see. What's the last thing you remember before these moments occur?"

Kevin shrugged. "Nothing really. Most of the time it feels like I just zone out. Like I'm hypnotized or something."

"I see," I scribbled a note in the file, then glanced at the neurologist's report, noting the absence of seizures or strokes in Kevin's evaluation. "Have you had many seizures in your life?" I added.

Kevin looked confused by this. "Seizures? I... I haven't had *any* seizures that I know of."

"Oh, you haven't? It's just that a seizure disorder is common in people with your symptoms."

"Oh..." Kevin trailed off as if contemplating what I had said.

I watched him intently, trying to see if he knew enough about transient global amnesia to know that epilepsy would actually rule out a diagnosis for it.

"Seizures are when you shake, right?" he asked.

"Some types make people shake," I said. "Other types make them freeze up. Almost like they're paralyzed temporarily."

Kevin thought about it more before shaking his head. "No. I can't say I ever remember doing something like that."

"I see," I said, making another note in the file. "I noticed in your file that after you had been arrested and brought to the jail, you asked the officers where you were even though they had already told you when you were first arrested."

"Yes... I've had girlfriends tell me I don't listen too good. I guess I just didn't listen to the officers at first. I was pretty freaked out by the whole thing."

"I can imagine. Can you tell me what you *do* remember from when you were arrested."

"Well..." Kevin trailed off, scratching his head. "I remember being at work at the community college. I was waxing the floor, I think. I was listening to some music while I was working and I was singing along. I must've been loud because one of the professors came out of his office and yelled at me. Then things get fuzzy after that. The next thing I remember is when I was in the back of the police car."

"So you don't remember how you got into the police car?"

"No."

"Do you remember what song you were listening to or who the professor was who yelled at you?"

"Yeah," Kevin said, smiling, "I remember I was listening to Vermillion's 'BTK'."

"And the professor?" I asked.

"I remember his face, but I don't think I ever knew his name. He was an older, chubbier guy."

"Was he clean-shaven or did he have a beard?"

"Beard, I guess."

"Okay. And what did the officers say to you when they first arrested you?"

He looked at me with confusion. "Didn't I already tell you that I don't remember that?"

"Yes, you did. Just want to make sure I'm getting the details right."

The door to the interview room opened and one of the guards entered with two Styrofoam cups of coffee. The guard placed each cup on the table and glowered at me before leaving.

"I don't think they liked being treated like baristas, Doc."

I smiled. "I think you're right."

I watched Kevin lift the cup of coffee to his nose and breathe the aroma deeply.

"I haven't had coffee since I've been here," he said.

"Were you much of a coffee drinker before?"

He nodded. "Just the cheap stuff from the gas station. I can't afford Starbucks or nothing like that."

"You're not missing much anyway. Their coffee is terrible."

Kevin grinned.

"What can you tell me about the charges against you?" I asked.

"Well, as my lawyer says, they're charging me with twenty-eight counts of first-degree murder and a bunch of other stuff about messing with the bodies, or something like that." Kevin said this in a very matter-of-fact manner, as if the charges were nothing more than trivial items on a grocery list.

"Do you understand the difference between first-degree and second-degree murder?"

Kevin considered the question briefly before shaking his head.

"Do you know the possible consequence of first-degree murder in Wyoming?"

"Umm... It's the death penalty, right?"

"Yes, it is."

I paused to see if Kevin reacted in any way to this, but he did not.

"So, if you're found guilty of even one of those charges," I added, "the jury could sentence you to be executed."

"Yeah," he said, "I remember my lawyer saying something like that."

Again, Kevin said this with little emotion or inflection.

"Does that scare you?" I asked.

"I guess," he said with a shrug. "I mean, I don't want to be killed for something that I don't remember doing."

"Do you think it's possible to do something like kill someone and not remember it though? That seems to me like something you don't just forget."

"Probably not. Killing someone has to be pretty memorable."

"But you've never killed anyone before?"

Kevin shook his head.

"How do you suppose your DNA got on some of the victims that the police found?"

"I dunno..."

"Did you know any of the victims?" I asked.

"Umm... I remember seeing the two girls from the community college a few times."

"Amanda Hatcher and Tracy Malvar?"

"I guess so," he said. "I never met them or nothing. Just saw them on campus a few times."

"So you don't remember abducting either of them?"

"Abducting?"

"Kidnapping, Mr. Blackford."

"Oh... No."

"And you never spoke to either of them ever?"

Kevin shook his head.

"And yet your DNA was found on both of them. How do you suppose that happened?"

He shrugged. "The detectives asked me the same thing. I wish I knew, then I could clear all this up."

I wrote several more notes in the file. It was hard to believe that someone as simple as Kevin had eluded and taunted investigators for nearly ten years. Of course, there was always the chance that Kevin was a sociopath pretending to be an imbecile. Lord knows I had encountered my fair share of those in my thirty-year career.

"Do *you* think I did those things, Doc?"

The question surprised me a bit, but I was pretty good at hiding my hand.

"What do you mean by 'things'?" I asked.

"The murders... Do you think I murdered all those women?"

"I don't know. My opinion on that doesn't really matter. My job isn't to decide if you did or did not commit the crimes. My job is only to decide if you're of sound enough mind to stand trial."

"Oh. What happens to me if I do have this *trans...* amnesia thing?"

"You'll be committed to a psychiatric facility most likely," I said.

"For how long?"

I waited to respond, staring at Kevin briefly. Over the course of my career, I had developed an ability to read people's expressions to sense how truthful they were being. Kevin gave the appearance of confusion, but it was difficult to tell how genuine that confusion really was.

"For your entire life, Kevin," I answered.

Kevin became even more perplexed by my response, and I wondered if it had yet to dawn on him that he would never be set free regardless of his plea. But Kevin was confused for a different reason.

"Who's Kevin?" he asked.

The question caught me off guard again and I didn't respond for several moments.

"My name's not Kevin," he added. "It's Robbie."

"I'm sorry?" I said. I had to check my tone to keep from sounding condescending. "What are you talking about?"

"My name is Robbie," he answered. "You called me Kevin by accident."

"I'm sorry... You mean you *go by* Robbie?"

"No, I mean my actual name *is* Robbie. Robbie Blackford."

I remained silent, becoming even more skeptical of the situation. I sifted through the file and found the photocopy of Kevin's driver's license.

"Is this your driver's license?" I asked.

"How could it be?" he asked. "I can't drive yet."

"Excuse me?"

Kevin leaned forward and took a closer look at the paper. "This Kevin guy *does* look like me, I'll give you that."

I pulled the photocopy away. "So you're saying you're not Kevin?" I asked.

Kevin shook his head and sniffed the cup of coffee. "This coffee is gross, isn't it?" he said.

My eyes narrowed as I considered the situation. I was genuinely lost by that point. I didn't know if Kevin's confusion was legitimate or if he was just trying to screw with me, so I decided to play along to see if he was working to trip me up somehow.

"Do you know where we are, Robbie? Or what you're doing here?"

Kevin glanced around the room as if his surroundings were totally new to him. Then he realized his wrists and ankles were shackled and he started to panic.

"What the hell's going on?" He looked around the room frantically, breathing heavily.

"You're at the Peak County Jail, Robbie. Remember?"

"Remember? *No*, I don't remember." He continued to pant uncontrollably. "Seriously, what the hell?"

"Try to calm down," I said, continuing to play along for the time being. "I'm a psychiatrist. What's the last thing you remember?"

Kevin continued to breathe heavily as his eyes searched the room for an answer.

"Uhh... I was... I was playing video games, I think."

"What video game?"

"*Resident Evil* maybe?"

"I'm not familiar with that game. Can you tell me about it."

Kevin's breathing slowed a little.

"Well, it's like a zombie-killing game. The Umbrella Corporation has released some kind of virus that's turning people into zombies, so the point of the game is to kill the zombies and stop the Umbrella Corporation."

"It sounds complicated. I'm not very good at video games."

"It's not too hard once you get the hang of it. The hard part is finding all the clues and tokens that are hidden in the levels."

"Oh?"

"Yeah, each level is like a big riddle that you have to solve."

"That's interesting."

In my experience, I've found that the best way to expose a lie is to probe constantly for details. I've had lies continue for weeks on end, but eventually, the details begin to contradict themselves and the lies inadvertently poke holes into each other. It's all about patience and the long game in these cases.

I pretended to write notes down in the file. A useful technique to break the conversation and inspire something new to surface.

"What are you writing?" he asked. "That's a big file."

"It's *your* file, Robbie."

"*My* file? What's in it?"

I stopped writing and looked at him. His eyes somehow looked different to me, although I couldn't explain what it was exactly.

"It's the reason you're here, Robbie," I said. "You strangled twenty-eight women over the last ten years."

"What!?" he exclaimed. "You're jacking with me, aren't you? You're telling me that I *killed* people? *Twenty-eight* of them?"

I opened the file and found the crime scene photos of Denise Chapman, a young transient woman who was the first confirmed Blue River Strangler victim. The photos showed her naked body ensnared in the limbs of a tree that had fallen into the frigid water of the Blue River. She was only nineteen years old.

Kevin gasped when he saw the photos.

"Jesus..." he said, "they think *I* did that?"

I nodded. "They found *your* DNA on her. The same DNA as Kevin Blackford."

"I swear to God I had nothing to do with that. I don't even know who this Kevin guy is!"

"You *are* Kevin, Robbie."

"Stop saying that! I'm not!" Kevin slammed his fists on the table and tears formed in his eyes. "I'm telling you, that's not me!"

Kevin cried more freely at that point. I was amazed at how convincing he was. I had seen similar behavior in inmates who had borderline personality disorder, so at that point I wondered if Kevin's current ruse wasn't the result of a similar condition.

Kevin's fit of crying ended abruptly though. Through the tears that lingered, his eyes took that exhausted look that I had seen when I had first entered the interview room.

"Why are my eyes wet?" Kevin asked, wiping his face with the backs of his shackled hands.

I did my best to hide my own confusion.

"You don't remember that you were crying?" I asked.

Kevin shook his head.

"Would you mind telling me your full name?" I asked.

"Kevin Robert Blackford."

"And what do you go by?"

Kevin looked puzzled. "Kevin, of course."

"Do you know where you are?"

"Peak County Jail..."

"And why are you here?"

Kevin looked at me like I was a moron. "Because I'm being accused of murdering twenty-eight young women. They think I'm the Blue River Strangler."

Part of me was relieved, yet another part of me was equally disturbed.

"Does the name 'Robbie' mean anything to you, Kevin?" I asked.

"My mom used to call me that when I was a little kid, but I've never had other people use it."

"And you don't know anybody else by that name?"

"No... Why?"

"What's the last thing you remember me asking you? Before you realized you had been crying?"

Kevin shrugged. "I guess you were telling me about what you're doing here. That you're trying to find out if I have that amnesia thing my lawyer was talking about."

"But that's it?"

"Yeah... What else would there be?"

"Do you remember feeling anything right after I told you what I was doing here? After I told you that you'd be committed to a psychiatric facility if I found you did in fact have transient global amnesia?"

"I guess I felt tired? You know, like that feeling you get right before you fall asleep? Where things get kind of fuzzy and you can still sort of think but not actually do anything?"

"Yes," I said, making a few more notes in the file, "I know what you mean."

Kevin took a slow drink of the coffee in front of him. "Why do you ask?" he said.

I shook my head, my eyes fixed on the cup of coffee in his hand.

"No reason," I muttered.

THREE

The Blue River is the major artery of Peak County, providing over one hundred miles of gold medal trout fishing and renowned rafting to central Wyoming. The Rocky Mountains that give life to the Blue River are a haven for trophy sport hunting and, as such, Peak County is mainly known across the country as a sportsman's paradise.

Then, in March of 1989, a group of hunters found the body of Denise Chapman on a section of the Blue River near the town of Sweetwater. Over the course of the next decade, the Blue River Strangler left the remains of twenty-seven other young women along the banks of the Blue River and throughout the surrounding Griffith's Peak Wilderness.

The Blue River Strangler left investigators bewildered. Although DNA had been recovered from several of the victims, investigators could never match it to any suspects or past offenders. To add to the frustration, the editor of the *Peak Courier* began to receive letters from the Blue River Strangler after the sixth victim was discovered. Some letters revealed the locations of his newest victims, while others simply taunted the investigators who were trying to hunt him down.

It seemed the Blue River Strangler's reign of terror would go on endlessly until the editor of the *Peak Courier* received a final letter containing a photocopy of a driver's license and a Styrofoam cup in a plastic bag. The note accompanying the items read: *Your incompetence bores me. Let's see if you can find me now. Edward, 86911*

When investigators ran the DNA from the Styrofoam cup, they found a perfect match to the DNA found on the victims.

Investigators were unsure of the significance of the number following his signature, but to them it was irrelevant because it took the Blue River Strangler Task Force less than an hour to find the man from the photocopied driver's license: Kevin Blackford.

Kevin's DNA came back as a perfect match to that on the Styrofoam cup. However, when asked why he turned himself in, Kevin said he had no idea what the investigators were talking about.

At the time, the Peak County Prosecuting Attorney Kim Matthews had yet to try a murder case in her two years as lead prosecutor. As an assistant prosecutor, she mostly dealt with petty felonies. The largest trial of her career was for an involuntary manslaughter charge by a drunk driver.

Not only was Kim the first female prosecuting attorney in Peak County's history, she was also the youngest at thirty-two years old.

Born and raised in Laramie, Kim Matthews attended the University of Wyoming College of Law and graduated at the top of her class. She didn't have her sights set on private practice upon graduation, though. Her father was a veteran officer with the Laramie Police Department, and growing up under his roof, there was only one pathway she wanted to pursue: criminal law. Struggling to find a job in Laramie or Cheyenne, she was hired as an Assistant Prosecuting Attorney in Peak County, a role she served in for six years until the Prosecuting Attorney retired and she won the seat by a narrow margin.

The investigation into the Blue River Strangler had been nothing short of a disaster. With Kevin's own help though, Matthews eventually had all the evidence she needed to bury him under ten life sentences.

But she wanted more than that. From her perspective, she knew the never-ending torment that he had inflicted upon the families of the victims; she felt it was her duty to get nothing less than the death penalty for a monster like Kevin Blackford.

Kevin's only shot of avoiding that was an insanity defense.

Transient global amnesia. A sudden, temporary episode of memory loss that can't be attributed to a more common neurological condition, such as epilepsy or stroke.

That was what his lawyer, Arlo Braddock, tried to claim at least. Matthews didn't buy it for a second.

According to the FBI profiler assigned to the Blue River Strangler Task Force, Kevin was a once-in-a-lifetime type of murderer. The intellect of the Zodiac combined with the savage impulsivity of Ted Bundy.

As Matthews saw it, a man like Kevin Blackford didn't deserve to live out his remaining years in the comfort of a psychiatric facility; he deserved a death twenty-eight times more brutal than the ways he took the lives of his victims.

The Wyoming Attorney General at the time gave the judge my name when he asked about a forensic psychiatrist to evaluate Kevin's competence to stand trial and to disprove his insanity plea when the trial actually began. With nearly thirty years as a correctional psychiatrist, I had personally evaluated the competency and insanity defenses of eighteen high-profile criminals, and I served as an expert witness on dozens of other trials. I had sat nose-to-nose with six serial killers before, not to mention dozens of sociopaths. I certainly had the credibility that was incontrovertible but that wasn't the main reason the judge wanted me to evaluate Kevin. Based on my reputation, he knew I was one of the best at sifting through the bullshit that even the worst criminals could muster.

I was hesitant to call the prosecuting attorney on the evening following my first interview with Kevin. I knew she wasn't going to be pleased about my findings.

I pored over Kevin's file and the notes I had taken during the interview just to be sure I wasn't jumping to conclusions too quickly. There's so much at stake with these high-profile cases. On the one hand, the prosecutor and the families of the victims want justice to be served as appropriately and swiftly as possible; however, my duty as the evaluating psychiatrist was to expertly and *objectively* determine the culpability of the accused regardless of the nature of his crimes.

I knew one interview with Kevin wasn't going to be enough to fulfill that duty.

Matthews must've been eagerly awaiting my call because she answered after the first ring.

"Hello?"

"Good evening, Ms. Matthews. This is Dr. Stevenson."

"Yes, Dr. Stevenson. Thanks for calling." She paused, trying to get a bearing on things from my tone, I imagined. "How did it go today?" she added.

"Well..." I began, "I don't think he's suffering from transient global amnesia. The neurologist's report *does* rule out epilepsy and stroke, but his psychological symptoms show few signs of the condition as far as I can tell."

Matthews sighed with relief. "That's good news."

"Don't get too excited," I said. "Although I'm pretty sure he doesn't have transient global amnesia, I'm still not ready to sign off on his ability to stand trial."

"Oh..." she said. "Why is that?"

"Something happened during the interview today that left me very... perturbed."

"How so?" she asked.

Rarely am I at a loss for words, but I found it difficult to describe what had happened. "Well," I said, "there was a point during my conversation with him that he suddenly lost any recollection of who I was or what I was doing there. During that time, he also claimed that his name was Robbie, not Kevin."

"Is that something you've ever seen before?"

"I've seen a number of criminals try to pull some type of ruse during an evaluation before, yes. They think that bouts of confusion or disorientation will make me think there's something wrong with them when in reality they're making it all up."

"From what I've observed, Blackford knows nothing but dishonesty and manipulation."

"I'm not surprised," I said. "Most in his position are the same. But I must admit, he's one of the most convincing I've ever encountered in my career. Something about the transition from his state of awareness to his state of disorientation was fascinating. Completely imperceptible. Most of the time, criminals think it's like the movies where their face twitches or their bodies convulse like Jekyll transforming into Hyde or something. It's actually quite laughable how ridiculous some of them look. But Blackford did none of that. If he's lying, he's quite good at it."

"And if he isn't lying? What do you think it could be?"

"Could be any number of things," I said. "Borderline personality disorder or schizophrenia, most likely. I'm going to need more time with him. Those conditions require extensive observation over the course of several sessions. I'm not saying that it's likely that he has one of those conditions, but in order to make the best case possible for the state, I have to be completely sure that his only affliction is sociopathy."

"I understand. Please do what you need to do to make sure we can serve justice."

"I will," I said. "I'll keep you posted on what I find out tomorrow."

"Thank you."

I hung up the phone and sighed. Cases like these were always challenging, but something about Kevin told me this would be tougher than usual.

I was intrigued by him from that first interview though. It wasn't just the matter of him toying with me either. It was his demeanor. A sort of Dahmer-like innocence that made his impulsivity that much more terrifying.

Either he was a complete monster or a rare psychiatric case study. Regardless, I looked forward to speaking to him again.

FOUR

"Why'd you come back?" Kevin said to me after the guards left the interview room.

I looked at him as sincerely as I could. "Because I'd like to learn more about you. To see if I can understand you better, maybe find out an explanation for everything that has happened."

"I don't know how you expect to understand me better. *I* don't understand me."

"Well then, maybe we can figure it out together."

"I don't get it... Aren't you trying to prove that I'm not crazy?"

I shook my head. "My job is to evaluate you in the most unbiased way possible. My job is to treat you the way I would treat any other patient."

"So you're not... you know... afraid of me?"

I've heard this question hundreds of times before, and despite the terror that you may feel from sitting across the table from an accused murderer, you have to do everything you can to hide it.

"No," I answered. "Your crimes frighten me, sure. But you

as a person do not."

Kevin glanced down. "Everybody else is afraid of me. I didn't do anything though, I swear."

"I know you believe that, Kevin. What if we don't talk about the case for the time being?"

"What will we talk about?"

"Oh, I don't know. Maybe tell me about your work at the community college. How long have you worked there?"

He shrugged. "Twelve years, I guess?"

"That's a long time," I said. "Do you enjoy the work?"

"Sure... I mean, as much as someone can enjoy cleaning floors and toilets for a living."

"Did you usually work by yourself?"

"Most of the time, yeah."

"That must've been lonely," I said.

"I didn't mind it too bad. I like being alone."

"Have you always liked being alone? Like when you were younger?"

"I don't remember much about when I was younger. The pieces I do remember I try to forget."

"I see. I'm sorry to hear that."

"It's fine. I'm still here, right?"

"Sure," I said, "but just because wounds heal doesn't mean they don't leave scars."

"Scars? What do you mean?"

"What I mean is that things that happened to us ten or twenty years ago can still affect us today."

"Like what?"

"Well, I had a patient a while ago who was beaten by his father as a child, and when he became an adult, he too was very angry and abusive."

"Oh..." Kevin trailed off as if he had something more to say, but he didn't.

All the while, I passively scrutinized his every move. Even the most subtle tic could indicate deceit.

Kevin's expression slowly changed and I wondered if "Robbie" was going to magically appear.

"You alright, Kevin?" I asked.

Kevin shook his head slowly and his eyes became distraught.

"My father left before I can remember," he said. "It was just me and my mother and whatever boyfriend she had at the time..."

"I see. How did they treat you?" I asked.

"Some pretended like I didn't exist. Others just *wished* I didn't exist. My mother included."

"That must've been hard," I said.

Kevin nodded, his eyes fixed on his shackled hands. "Can we talk about something else?" he asked.

"If you want to. But I'd be interested in learning more about your childhood, if you're willing to talk about it?"

"There's not much more to say other than a couple of her boyfriends hated me more than the others."

"Were they ever tough with you?"

"What do you mean, tough? Like, did they hit me? Of course." He said this very matter-of-factly as if everyone was beaten as a child. "But I got over it eventually."

"So you're not angry about it?"

"I hate my mother for letting them do that to me, but I wouldn't say I'm an angry person because of it."

"Did your mother by chance ever call you 'Robbie'?"

"I don't remember," he said.

"Really?"

"Yeah, why?"

"I was hoping I could figure out why you wanted me to call you that when we talked yesterday."

"I really don't remember that."

"You're sure? Nothing at all?"

"No. Why would I lie to you about that?" Kevin's tone became more irritated.

"Well, part of my job is to make sure you're *not* lying to me, Kevin."

He scoffed at this. "*Everyone* thinks I'm lying."

"Who's 'everyone'?"

"The detectives, that prosecutor—even my own lawyer thinks I'm lying..."

"Can you blame them though? I mean, how can your DNA be on all those victims if you didn't do it?"

Kevin became more flustered and I braced myself for the worst.

"I told you, I don't know..." he said.

"But you've got to admit that it's pretty coincidental."

"Yeah, but it doesn't mean I'm guilty."

"It kind of does, Kevin."

Kevin hit the table with his fists. "How can I be guilty of something I don't remember doing?"

"What about the stuff from your childhood that you've forgotten? Just because you forgot about it doesn't mean it never happened."

"It's not fair..."

Kevin shook his head and I waited for him to add anything further. He said nothing.

"I'll be honest with you, Kevin. I don't think you have transient global amnesia."

"So you think I'm lying?"

"I'm not saying that. I think that these crimes affected you in a way that means you forced yourself to forget them the same way you've forgotten the trauma from your childhood. But that doesn't make you innocent nor does it mean you have a mental illness."

"Mental illness?" Kevin asked, confused. "What are you

talking about?"

"What do you mean, what am I talking about?" I answered. "I'm talking about your case, Kevin."

"This shit again?" he said, rolling his eyes. "How many times I gotta tell you it's Robbie?"

"Robbie?" I said.

"Yeah, Robbie," he answered mockingly, as if *I* were the one losing my mind.

"I have a very stupid question to ask you," I said. "What year do you think it is?"

Kevin rolled his eyes. "Uhh, 1989."

I fought to hide my skepticism.

"What? You gonna tell me that's wrong too?" Kevin asked.

"Robbie," I said. "It's 1998."

Kevin broke into juvenile laughter. "Shut up. No it's not."

I removed a copy of the newspaper from my bag and showed him the date printed on the top of the front page.

"You're screwing with me again," he said.

"*I'm* screwing with *you?*"

"Yeah. I may be dumb, but I know what year it is."

"Okay. Has anything like this ever happened before?"

"Anything like what?"

"A moment where you're really confused or you interact with someone who is really confused by what you're saying to them?"

Kevin shrugged. "I dunno... I guess. I always figured that people were acting weird because of how I dress or something."

"When people act weird toward you, what do they say or do?"

"They usually don't say anything to me. They just give me a weird look and walk away. People are shitty, aren't they?"

"So what year do you think it is?"

"Nineteen eighty nine, like I said."

"What new music are you listening to?"

"There's this metal band called White Zombie that just came out with their second album. It's crazy good."

"I'm not familiar with them."

"For real? They're legit," he said.

"Who else do you listen to?"

"Black Sabbath, of course."

"What was their most recent album?"

"*Headless Cross*. Of course, Ozzie went solo about ten years ago."

"I see." I wrote these names down in Kevin's file so I could check them out after the fact. Like I've said before, deceit falters with the details. If the details didn't pan out, then it was a good indication that Kevin was screwing with me.

"Why did you come back anyways?" asked Kevin.

"What did I say earlier, Robbie?"

"What, like yesterday?"

"No. Earlier today."

Kevin shook his head. "I don't remember."

"Then what did I say yesterday?"

"That you thought I was some serial killer or something."

"Correct. That's why I'm back here."

"I swear to God, I don't know anything that you're talking about."

"Have you ever been seen by a psychiatrist before, Robbie?"

"What, a shrink?" Kevin asked, laughing in a mocking way. "Yeah, my mom made me go once last year because the school said I couldn't come back unless I did."

"Couldn't come back?"

"Yeah. I got accused of doing something."

"Doing what?" I asked, vaguely remembering something I had read in his case file.

"Man, what difference does it make?"

"I'm just curious." I flipped through the file in front of me until I found the report I was looking for. "Was it because your

Biology teacher caught you torturing a frog during a dissection?"

"How the hell do you know that?"

"It's in this file, Robbie."

"Yeah, well, Ms. Shannon is a bitch. She's had it in for me since I first walked into her class."

"So you didn't torture the frog?" I asked.

"No, the damn thing was dead already. I don't know what she thinks she saw, but she's lying."

"And why do you think she's had it in for you?"

Kevin shrugged. "I dunno. Maybe she's threatened by me or maybe she's got a thing for me. Maybe she's one of those weirdos who likes teenage boys. Maybe you should be talking to *her*. Can't have pedophiles for teachers."

"I'm busy enough with you, kid."

"Kid?" Kevin's eyebrows wrinkled. "Why are you calling me 'kid'?"

I looked up from the file and watched him briefly. No facial tics or any indication of deceit. I was hesitant when I asked, "...Kevin?"

"Yeah?"

FIVE

"There's a chance Blackford might have dissociative identity disorder," I said into the telephone.

My friend from medical school, Dr. Wendy Newcomb, was on the other line.

"Come on," she said. "You know how rare that is?"

"I know. I'm not saying it's a good chance, just that it's a possibility."

"That's what those doctors thought when they evaluated Bianchi."

"I know, I know," I said, recalling the controversy that Kenneth Bianchi created during the Hillside Strangler trial. "I'm not saying I believe the guy, but the way he switches between these personas is impressive."

"I don't know..." she said. "He sounds like a borderline to me."

"I admit that *that* is a more likely possibility. At first I considered schizophrenia because of the obvious delusions, but that's really the only criterion he meets. I mean, he's said nothing about hearing voices or having other types of hallucinations. And he's managed to keep the same job for over a decade without a single complaint."

"I agree, schizophrenia is highly unlikely," she said.

"But so is the borderline personality disorder."

"Yeah... I mean, it's unusual that his professional life appears to be as stable as it was. But DID? I just think there is such a high chance that he's faking it."

"I know there is," I said. "That's why I'm not making any determinations until I've had a chance to interview him more and see if I can catch any contradictions."

"What of the 'Robbie persona'?" she asked. "You said he thinks it's still 1989. Was the information he gave you about the bands accurate for that time period?"

"Yeah, all of that checks out," I said.

"And neither of the personas appears to know about each other?" she asked.

"As far as I can tell, no."

"And he switches between them without any type of trigger or physical expression."

"None that I've noticed so far," I said.

"Have you thought about telling *him* that you think he has DID? Do like they did with Bianchi and bait him with a bunch of nonsense about the disorder. Tell him the personas have to at least know about the primary personality. If 'Robbie' magically has an awareness of Kevin, then you know there's a good chance he's making it up."

"That's not a bad idea, actually," I said.

"Have you asked the guards or the prosecuting attorney if these personas have come up during their interactions with him?"

"The guards said no. I haven't asked the prosecuting attorney yet. I would prefer not to mention it to her until I've interviewed him a few more times."

Silence fell between us for a moment before Wendy said, "You need to be careful."

"I know," I said, "but think of how many of these guys I've worked with before."

"It's just that this one seems... worse than the others, somehow."

"I agree. Regardless if he's lying or not, he's going to make for a fascinating case study."

"Well, just make sure *you're* controlling the interviews and not him. The last thing you want is him getting inside of *your* head..." She trailed off momentarily before adding, "I'm not trying to lecture you."

"I appreciate the concern," I said. "Really."

Wendy did have a tendency to do that though. She worked in private practice in Oregon, so she didn't know much about correctional psychiatry. She mostly spent her days prescribing antidepressants to teenagers, not dealing with the country's most violent criminals. I knew she had my best interest in mind though, and deep down, I also knew she was probably right about me needing to be wary.

"I know I'm stating the obvious, but just be careful," she said.

I knew how unlikely it was that Kevin legitimately suffered from dissociative identity disorder. The disorder was rare to begin with, and it was even more so in men. Plus, it was a major point of contention in the psychiatric and legal communities. The thing that was unusual was that neither DID nor multiple personality disorder were mentioned by Blackford or his attorney. In the cases where a criminal faked the condition, their defense was usually the first to bring it up as a possibility. If Blackford was truly faking it, he was banking on me suspecting it on my own; that was a risk that seemed just as unlikely as the condition itself.

At the same time though, I didn't know what else to think. DID was the only thing that made sense.

I knew I would have to be absolutely positive that Kevin's DID was legitimate. My reputation depended on it. But if it *was* in fact legitimate? Kevin Blackford could be the career-defining case study I had been looking for.

SIX

When I went to see Kevin that following morning, the guards told me that he was refusing to come out of his cell.

"Fine," I said. "Take me to him instead."

The guards glanced at each other skeptically. "I don't think we can do that," they said.

I smiled. "With all due respect, Blackford isn't the first murderer I've shared a room with. Take me to him, please."

The guards nodded hesitantly.

The Peak County Jail was small, outfitted with only five cells. The first four cells were empty.

Kevin was curled up on the cot in the fifth cell. He looked overgrown, like a young man trying to fit in his childhood bed.

One of the guards grabbed a folding chair and placed it next to the cell for me. I nodded my thanks and sat.

Once the guards left, I said, "Kevin? It's Dr. Stevenson."

Kevin hardly budged. Only his back rose and fell gently as he breathed.

"I know you're not asleep," I added. "I know you can hear me."

But Kevin still did not move.

"In that case, I'll talk until you're ready," I said.

Kevin's head moved as if nodding slowly.

"Have you ever heard of dissociative identity disorder or multiple personality disorder, Kevin?"

His head shifted on the pillow, but it was hard to tell if he was acknowledging what I was saying.

"Well, it's something where people can have several personas. Do you know what personas are?"

Kevin shook his head.

"They're like identities. As if there are several different people in one body. Do you understand?"

He nodded.

"In my conversations with you, I've interacted with two distinct identities: Kevin and Robbie. Do you remember this?"

Kevin shook his head again.

"In legitimate cases of dissociative identity disorder, the identities are aware of each other," I said.

Kevin did not respond or move.

"I'm going to have to speak with you more to figure out if this is what you have, Kevin. If you don't talk though, I can't do that."

His back continued to rise and fall with his breathing, but he said nothing.

"I'll just sit here for a while. Until you're ready."

I ended up sitting with him for over three hours that morning, during which time he didn't utter a word to me.

Depressive episodes can do that, so his lack of responsiveness didn't necessarily surprise me. What did surprise me was that he was completely disregarding the new defense that I was handing over to him. If he was trying to play me, it was reasonable to expect him to jump all over my suspicion of his condition. He wasn't, though. It was almost as if he didn't care at all.

It was fascinating really. His dedication to the long game.

His commitment to convincing me that he really was mentally ill. Assuming that he really was faking it.

I left the prison for a while and returned later that afternoon with the hope that Kevin would be more responsive. The guards told me that he still did not want to leave his cell, but he did at least want to speak with me.

Kevin was sitting on the floor against the side of his cot when the guards led me back to him.

"Hey, Doc," Kevin said, staring across the cell at the brick wall in front of him.

I took a seat in the folding chair and motioned to the guards that they could leave. He looked even more disheveled than the day before.

"How are you feeling?" I asked.

"Fine," he said flatly.

"Do you remember me stopping by this morning?"

He nodded, his gaze still fixed on the wall.

"Does that happen often?" I asked.

"Does what happen often?"

"The depression."

He shrugged. "It depends..." he said.

"What does it depend on?"

"If I feel like dying or not..."

"I see. Do you want to die *now*?"

He didn't respond for several moments as if considering the question.

Finally, he said, "No."

"When you're in those moments, do you know how you would do it?"

"That's the thing... I don't want to kill myself; I just don't want to live." Kevin glanced at me, pain seemingly pouring from his eyes. "Does that make any sense?"

"It does," I nodded. "Do you recall what I told you earlier today?"

"That you think I might have some personality disorder thing... something about multiple personas?"

"Correct. What are your thoughts on that?"

"I know you're the expert and all... but I don't think that's what's wrong with me."

His response shocked me, so much so that I didn't say anything for a moment.

"You don't?" I finally said. "How come?"

"Because I have no... was it awareness, you said? Of these *personas.*"

"You sure?" I asked. "No recollection of this Robbie character?"

"Nuh-uh."

"I see."

I couldn't believe that he didn't take the bait. If he was still faking a condition, he was doing a hell of a job maintaining the lie.

"I *want* to remember these things you tell me..." he said, "but I just can't."

Kevin returned his gaze to the wall and stared blankly. After a few moments though, he started smacking himself on the side of the head over and over again.

"WHY!" he yelled. "WHY! WHY! WHY!"

I stood and went to the bars separating me from Kevin.

"Calm down, Kevin," I said. "It's alright."

"No it's not!" he continued, his hand striking his head with every syllable he screamed. "What's wrong with me!"

"Breathe, Kevin," I said. "Deep breaths."

"No! No! No!" he yelled.

"Close your eyes and breathe," I said. "Slow... In through your nose and out through your mouth..."

He eventually did as I said, and he was able to calm himself down after a few minutes.

"If we're going to talk, Kevin, you can't do that to yourself, alright?"

He nodded.

"Now I'd like to ask you something about when you were a teenager if that's okay?"

"Sure..."

"Do you remember seeing a psychiatrist once when you were in high school?"

He thought about it momentarily, then shook his head.

"What about a teacher named Ms. Shannon? Remember anything about her?"

"Did she teach English? Maybe it was Math. I don't really remember. That was so long ago, you know?"

"Yes. Do you remember what high school you went to?"

"Yeah, actually—West High in Denver." Blackford smiled as if pleased that he finally had a correct answer to one of my questions.

"If you don't mind my asking, how did you end up all the way in Wyoming?"

"I had a half-sister who lived around here. She let me stay with her until I got settled."

"Are you still in contact with her?"

Kevin shook his head. "Not for years."

"How come?"

"I dunno... just stopped talking, I guess. I always figured she moved away."

"What was her name?"

"Brenda... *Wexler*, I think?"

"Brenda Wexler?" I said.

The name sounded oddly familiar to me, but I couldn't remember from where. I got the case file from beside the chair and flipped through it for several minutes before I finally stumbled upon the name. The shock made me nearly spill the contents of the folder onto the floor.

"Something wrong, Doc?" he asked.

I glanced up, trying to hide my surprise.

"You said that Brenda was your half-sister?" I asked.

Kevin nodded.

"Would you excuse me for a moment?"

"Sure..."

I hurried down the hallway past the empty cells. A guard opened the door to the holding area.

"Everything okay?" he said to me.

"Yes," I said, "I just need to make a phone call. You mind if I use the one at the front desk?"

"Go ahead," he said, looking at me skeptically.

I grabbed the phone and dialed the number for Prosecuting Attorney Kim Matthews. She answered within a few rings.

"Hello, Ms. Matthews. This is Dr. Stevenson."

"Dr. Stevenson?" she asked. "I wasn't expecting to hear from you so soon. How are things going?"

"Well, I'm at the jail right now and Blackford mentioned something I wanted to check with you."

"What is it?"

"Blackford said that Brenda Wexler was his half-sister."

There was a brief pause before Matthews said, "Brenda Wexler, the ninth victim?"

"Yes."

"Jesus..." she breathed.

"Do you know if that's true?" I asked.

"I honestly don't know."

"Is there any chance you guys can find out? Run her DNA against his, or see if you can check their birth certificates? It's critical I know if he's being honest about this."

"Wait a second—are you telling me he knows he killed his own sister?"

"Not exactly."

"What do you mean, not exactly?"

"Well, he claimed that he lived with Brenda when he first moved to Wyoming, but he said they've been *estranged* for several years now."

"Estranged?"

"Yeah."

She scoffed. "What a bastard."

"Listen, I haven't told him that she's dead or that he's the one responsible for it. I'll see how he reacts when I tell him. You just find out if she is in fact related to him."

"Alright."

"Oh, before I forget," I said, "there was something else I've been meaning to ask you."

"What's that?"

"Is there anything you've noticed about his behavior when you've spoken with him? Or anything that the investigators observed during the interrogations?"

"Like what?"

"Anything that deviates from his soft-spoken, simplistic nature?"

"I mean, he claims he doesn't remember anything, but I wouldn't say there are any dramatic differences. Why?"

"No particular reason," I said. "Just trying to get an idea of any behavioral patterns."

"The only behavioral patterns we've noticed are deception. The guy lies about everything he can."

"Is there a chance I could get a hold of the interrogation tapes? I really want to see for myself what his behavior was like."

"Yeah," she said. "Drop by my office later and I'll have them waiting for you."

"Thank you. You'll let me know as soon as you find out about Brenda?"

"Yes."

I ended the call and remained out by the front desk to

gather my thoughts. The situation was only becoming stranger the deeper I dug.

When I was ready, I had the guards lead me back into the holding area.

Kevin was still sitting on the floor when I returned to his cell.

"Everything alright, Doc?"

"I'm afraid I have some bad news, Kevin," I said.

"What do you mean?"

"I'm not sure how to tell you this, but your sister is dead."

I was intentionally blunt when I said this because I wanted to see what his gut reaction would be.

Blackford's face looked stunned. "Wha... what do you mean?" he asked. "How?"

I examined Kevin's expression, looking for any indication of deception. A twitch of the brow or a minute curl of the lip. I saw nothing but sincere shock.

"She was the ninth Blue River Strangler victim," I said. "They found her remains six years ago in the Griffith's Peak Wilderness."

Kevin was so stunned that he seemed to stare directly through me.

"What are you saying?" he murmured. "They think... they think *I* killed her?"

I nodded, holding my gaze upon him.

He shook his head with confusion, then rose from the floor. He paced between the back wall and the barred entry several times. I watched him intently, unsure of what he would do next.

"*I* killed Brenda?" he added, continuing to pace.

Meanwhile, I waited. For what, I can't really say. By that point, nothing would have surprised me.

He stopped in the middle of the cell and locked his gaze upon me. Tears formed in his eyes.

"Are they sure it was me?" he added, choked up.

"Yes," I said.

"Maybe it's... a mistake..."

I shook my head. "It's not a mistake. Your DNA was on her."

"I swear to God," he said, his tone becoming more urgent, "I had nothing to do with that. *Why* would I do that? I loved Brenda. She was the only one who ever gave a damn about me. Why would I do that, Doc?"

"I don't know."

"Maybe my DNA was on her from before she died. You know, when I was living with her?"

"It doesn't work like that. You said it yourself, you haven't seen her in years."

"I didn't kill her, Doc, you have to believe me..." He paused, his face contorting with emotion. "*Plea-please* believe me..."

There was a desperation in his eyes that I've only seen a handful of times. The type of desperation that you might see in the expression of a deer as the glowing façade of a semitruck barrels down upon it. It's hard to imagine someone being able to fake that, yet Kevin probably saw such animalistic terror in the eyes of his own victims.

"I believe you," I said. "At least... I believe that you don't *remember* doing it. I believe that maybe you didn't do it on purpose."

"I didn't do it!" he screamed, rushing at the bars of his cell, and thrashing against them.

The guards must have heard, because they came racing down the corridor.

"What's going on?" they asked, batons drawn from their belts.

"It's alright," I tried to tell them. "He's just upset—"

"Step away," the other guard said, pulling me away from Kevin's cell. "Blackford, back up and sit down!"

"I didn't do it!" Kevin screamed through the bars. "I didn't do it!"

"Back up!" one of the guards yelled at Kevin, smashing his baton against the bars.

Kevin yelled and thrust his hand through the bars toward the first guard.

"Back off!" barked the guard, swinging his baton in defense.

The baton crashed into Kevin's hand. Kevin yelped and fell against the bars of the cell in a crumpled heap.

"Goddammit, Hank," said the other guard, "why the hell did you do that?"

"The piece of shit tried to grab me—you saw."

"You antagonized him," I said.

"*I* antagonized him?" he retorted. "You're the one who got him all riled up in the first place."

"You didn't have to break his hand in the process."

The guard scoffed at this. "I didn't break his hand, and even if I did, the son of a bitch deserves it after what he's done."

Meanwhile, Kevin remained curled up on the floor by the bars, whimpering.

"Not much of a tough shit now, are you?" the guard taunted. "Hard to believe you could even get your dick up for those girls."

"That's enough," I interjected.

The guard glowered at me, his face ruddy with hatred.

"Go on, Hank," said the other guard. "Take a break. Cool off."

The guard glanced back at Kevin, grumbled something, and stormed down the hallway.

"I'm sorry about him," the other guard said to me. "This case is straining all of us."

I knelt beside the cell and put my hand on Kevin's back.

"I wouldn't do—" began the guard.

"You wouldn't do *what*?" I snapped at him. "Treat him like a human being?"

"But he's—"

"A person," I retorted. "Accused of doing horrible things, yes. But a person all the same."

I returned my focus to Kevin, keeping my hand firmly on the back of his shoulder. I could tell the guard wanted to say more, but he didn't. He remained behind me momentarily before embarrassment or shame or whatever emotion overwhelmed him to the point of leaving the holding area.

"You're alright," I said to Kevin, all the while keeping a vigilant eye on him.

Even with a busted hand, there was no telling what a man like Kevin Blackford was capable of.

SEVEN

I first learned about the Blue River Strangler when the body of the seventh victim, Amanda Hatcher, was identified and the national media outlets began pouncing on the story.

Seven women had to die before anyone outside of Wyoming really knew what was going on.

Seven.

I don't know if you blame law enforcement for their lack of resources and humility or the media for their indifference toward the homeless, but in many ways, I'm not surprised that Kevin was able to get away with what he did for as long as he did.

I kept an eye on the story from Florence, Colorado. At the time, I was the lead psychiatrist for USP ADX Florence, otherwise known as "the Supermax". For those of you who don't know what this concrete Alcatraz of the Rockies is, ADX Florence is presently home to the Unabomber and the Boston Marathon Bomber.

Yeah. The worst of the worst. Bastards who haven't seen natural light since the moment they entered. Those were the types of patients I was treating.

I was eager to be involved in the Blue River Strangler case from the moment I heard about it. Serial killers really are a fascinating breed of criminal. They're not typically motivated by extrinsic factors like money or security. They're motivated by something that is buried deep within their being. Something that has taken years, possibly decades, to be sown and nurtured.

It's disturbing and intriguing all at the same time. Their minds are a convoluted riddle, an enigma that only very few can decipher.

It was obvious the Blue River Strangler would be one such challenge. Maybe the most difficult, in fact.

Professional curiosity wasn't my only motivation though. My daughter, Maddie, had run away from home when she was seventeen and I hadn't seen or heard from her since. She disappeared shortly before the Strangler victims began to emerge, and although Park City was over six hundred miles away from Florence, there was always that fear in the back of my mind that she would be identified as his next victim.

In the evening after that third interview with Kevin, I went directly from the prison to the county courthouse to meet with Kim Matthews. She had yet to confirm if Kevin was telling the truth about Brenda Wexler being his sister and I was eager to learn more.

The prison and the courthouse were both in Park City, the seat of Peak County. The town was microscopic by most standards with a population just shy of 5,000. Aside from a few chain restaurants, the only thing of particular note in the town was the community college.

It was a beautiful little community though. Alpine terrain protected the town with the 14,000-foot Griffith's Peak standing sentry to the southwest. Coming from Florence, which is a hideous little place, I found Park City to be a world-class mountain resort in comparison.

The courthouse wasn't much to write home about in terms

of its size, but it was a newer building at least. There was a bronze statue in front of the main entry. A gigantic replica of Remington's "End of the Trail" sculpture.

Most people had gone home for the day, so it wasn't difficult to follow the trail of lights that were still on in the hallways that led me to the prosecuting attorney's office.

When I walked in, Kim Matthews was at her desk, staring intently at a computer monitor.

"Ms. Matthews?" I said, knocking on the door.

"Yes?" she said, still transfixed by what she was working on.

"I'm Dr. Stevenson."

This immediately broke her train of thought, and when she realized it was me, she jumped from her chair.

"Hi. Please sit down."

"Thank you."

Kim Matthews was a sturdy woman, broad-shouldered with an abruptness to her tone when she spoke. The type of physique that caused people to wonder if she played a sport in college.

"I can't tell you how grateful we are for your help," she told me. "Truly."

"Of course," I said.

"Were you able to find anything else out today?"

"No, unfortunately. The guards threw a wrench in that plan."

"Let me guess. Hank?"

I nodded. "That's the one."

"What'd that jackass do?"

"Oh, nearly broke Blackford's hand."

"Figures," she said, shaking her head. "He was a prick to begin with, but ever since we've been holding onto Blackford, he's been especially difficult."

"He's itching for a lawsuit. He can't treat an inmate like that, especially unprovoked."

"Unprovoked?" Matthews asked, her eyes quizzical. "Let's not forget that we're talking about someone who strangled twenty-eight young women. I'm pretty sure he can handle some tough love every now and then."

I wasn't about to get into a debate with her over the civil rights of alleged serial killers, so I changed the subject.

"Were you able to get those tapes of the interrogation, by any chance?" I asked. "It would really help me see if these personas were observable before."

"I was," she said, reaching into her desk drawer and handing me a set of videotapes.

"Thank you," I said. "Any word on Brenda Wexler yet?"

"Yeah..." She paused, clicking her mouse several times before finding what she was looking for on the computer screen. "I had my investigators sift back through the public record to see if they could dig anything up. They tried to see if Brenda Wexler and Blackford shared the same address at any point, but both have always subleased, so their addresses have never been registered anywhere."

"What about his driver's license?" I asked. "Didn't he send the *Courier* a copy of his license and the Styrofoam cup with his DNA on it? The license would have had his address on it."

"Yeah. We checked with the DMV and he got that license a few weeks before the *Courier* received his package."

"He didn't have a license before?"

"Apparently not."

"So he finally gets a license only to use it to turn himself in?" I replied. "That seems odd, doesn't it?"

"You're telling me. So then our investigators dug a bit more, and they happened upon a photo of Brenda with a young man who looks an awful lot like Blackford."

Matthews turned the computer screen to show me the photo. It was blurry from a bad sun glare, but the young man standing next to the young woman did resemble Kevin. Lanky.

Spry. The lively version of the man I had sat across from for the last two days.

"Well, sister or not," I said, "he sure as hell knew her."

"Yeah. And as far as we know, she's the *only* victim he had a personal relationship with."

"Is there a time stamp on that photo?"

"Not that I could find," she said.

"He looks quite a bit younger than he does now. Brenda's remains were found six years ago, right?"

"Yeah."

"Did the coroner have any idea how long she had been dead?"

"Based on decomposition... maybe twelve to eighteen months? Hard to tell when you consider how harsh the winters can be out here. Why does that matter?"

"Well, I might be able to catch him in a lie if he says they parted ways earlier than seven years ago."

"You say that as if you haven't caught him in a lie already."

"*Caught* is the key word," I said. "I'm sure he's lying to me, but I have to catch him in his lies to be able to prove it in front of a judge. Especially when the death penalty is riding on it."

"I don't mean to question your ability," she said, "but how do you propose to do that, exactly? This guy dodged investigators for a decade before basically turning himself in. And not just our podunk deputies; state and federal investigators couldn't find this guy either."

"Time," I said. "If I can talk to him long enough, he'll eventually slip up on the details of his stories. Especially with these different personas, it's only a matter of time before I start to notice inconsistencies."

"Yeah," she said. "He never pulled that shit with me."

"That's what's making me think he's trying to play me," I said. "Otherwise, why else am I the only one who has encountered these other identities?"

"Well, hopefully those interrogation tapes will confirm that suspicion," she said.

"We'll see."

"I know you know this, but I can't tell you how critical it is that you deflate this insanity defense. I mean, aside from the pressure I'm getting from the community and the State Attorney General's office, a man like Blackford does not deserve to live. Period. I know that's probably wrong of me to say, but it's the truth."

"I don't disagree with you," I said. "But I've been involved in enough of these cases to know you've got to do it right, otherwise you risk the whole thing being thrown out. Besides, a life sentence is no cakewalk. I've spent most of my career around lifers and I'll be the first to tell you that those guys are living in a perpetual state of hell."

Matthews looked at me firmly for a moment before saying, "We're talking about a man who murdered not one, not two, but *twenty-eight* young women in the most intimate way possible. He cinched his hands around their throats and watched the life drain out of their eyes. He doesn't just deserve to die. Blackford deserves every punishment that hell has to offer."

EIGHT

You can tell when someone hasn't spent enough time around hardened criminals. Take Kim Matthews for example. She possessed a visceral hatred for Kevin based mainly on what she had read about him in his case file. Sure, she interviewed him a few times, but she didn't really listen to what he had to say. If she had, she might've gotten to know the man beyond the murders. Understood the early beginnings of what brought him to do such horrific things. I'm not saying guys like him deserve our sympathy, but taking the crimes at face value blinds us.

That's the problem with our justice system though. We only want to know who did what and how they did it; the only time we want to know *why* they did it is to prove premeditation so we can justify a harsher sentence. Our system seeks to blame and condemn and punish, not understand and reform and mitigate. Maybe if we took the time to understand why people do the hellish things that they do, we could prevent atrocities from happening in the future.

After meeting with Matthews, I grabbed dinner and went back to my hotel room to watch the interrogation tapes.

I admit I was pretty distracted. For one, I was mentally

exhausted, but as I watched the interrogations, I couldn't help but wonder why Kevin had turned himself in. I mean, he was invincible for a decade: why intentionally end his own reign of omnipotence? Because he was bored? Because he was satisfied? If there's one variable that is constant across serial killers, it's that their thirst to control is never quenched. The exhilaration of destruction never wanes. They don't stop because they're bored. They may pause, but they never stop. The only time they stop is when they're locked in a seven-by-twelve concrete box.

But Kevin? He *wanted* to be caught. He wanted it, despite apparently not remembering doing anything. Aside from figuring out why he killed all those women, *that* was what I wanted to discover: why did he allow himself to be stopped?

What I saw from those first interrogation tapes only confirmed what I had already seen in Kevin. Demure. Passive. Confused. Simple-minded. Watching the investigators interrogate him was as pathetic as watching an executive berate a dim-witted intern. I felt bad for him, honestly.

The investigators weren't cruel or unconstitutional in their tactics, but they were relentless in their questioning. And every time, Kevin answered with a childish shrug of the shoulders and a mumbled "I dunno..." Usually, those types of suspects will crack under such pressure. Even if they're innocent, they'll confess to the Kennedy assassination just to get investigators to leave them alone. But not Kevin.

It wasn't until one of the later interrogation tapes that I saw a change in Kevin's demeanor. From the moment the investigators walked into the room, Kevin was defiant. Belligerent even. His posture was different too. He remained in his chair, but he sat tall with a forward lean.

"What the fuck do you want?" he asked the investigators.

"You ready to tell us what we need to hear?" they asked.

"Go to hell."

The investigators left, and that was the end of the tape. Ten seconds long at most.

But I had never seen him behave like that. Not during the interrogation tapes and certainly not during my interviews with him.

Frustrated? Yes.

Angry? Sure.

But defiant? Never. He was relatively compliant, and if he wasn't, he was disoriented and confused.

He certainly didn't use profanity with me either. As if he was afraid that someone was going to make him toss a quarter into the swear jar.

I spent many more hours watching the tapes, ignoring the investigators' questions and focusing on Kevin's behavior and the tone of his responses to them. Passivity and confusion certainly dominated his demeanor, but there were several times when the defiance and confidence came out. Sometimes he began the interview that way, but other times he imperceptibly became this way. One moment he was withdrawn, the next he was boisterous. Outraged. No triggers or precursors. Just a seamless change in disposition.

Looking back through the investigators' notes in the case file, I saw that they too had noticed these changes in demeanor; however, they believed these instances of subversion merely proved his tendencies toward violence. That the interrogations were breaking him down, causing him to lose control of his deception.

They underestimated him though. They forgot that *they* didn't catch him; he turned himself in. He was caught because he *wanted* to be caught.

Why?

Why would a serial killer *want* to be caught, I wondered.

NINE

I went to see Kevin first thing that following morning. I slept awfully because all I could think about was why he turned himself in. But I knew I couldn't just ask him that. Whatever game he was playing, it was a game of finesse, a game that required the utmost patience. And if there was one thing he had proved during his decade of terror, it was that he was patient and disciplined. He didn't mind waiting months or years to make his next calculated move. *That* was what made guys like him so dangerous.

I would have to be just as cunning and disciplined as him. Time and details were going to have to be my means of dissecting him.

To be honest, such a challenge excited me.

When I entered the prison, I was met by the guard from the previous day, Hank.

"Back again?" he asked, in a somewhat reserved manner.

I nodded.

He radioed for the other guard to bring Kevin to the interview room for me.

"Follow me," Hank said, leading me back to the interview

room. "Look, about yesterday... I, uhh... I *might* have overreacted a bit."

"I would say so," I said.

"Well, for what it's worth, I'm, uhh... I'm sorry. It's just, you know how guys like that are. You give them an inch and they'll take ten miles, you know?"

"It's fine," I said. "I understand."

Of course, I didn't really understand, but I didn't care to get into that with him.

Hank's radio crackled with the voice of the other guard.

"Say that again, Shawn."

"Blackford's pitching a fit again."

"Keep him in his cell then," said Hank. To me he added, "You'll have to come back later."

"I'll go to him instead," I said.

"Sorry. Not after what happened yesterday."

"With all due respect, what happened yesterday was escalated by *you*, Officer. Take me back to him."

"No way," he said, his temper rising. "You think you can just come in here and do whatever you want? Who the hell do you think you are?"

"The one who stands between Blackford and the needle," I said firmly. "The one who can help guarantee that Blackford gets the punishment he deserves. If it were up to you, they'd be strapping him to the electric chair this very morning, right?"

"You bet your ass," he said with a glare.

"Then do me a favor and let me do my job. The less you get in my way, the closer Blackford's execution date gets."

Hank scoffed. "I thought people like you were trying to protect people like him."

"I have no interests in this other than doing my job. Whether Blackford lives or dies makes no difference to me. I'm doing what needs to be done and that's all. Now you can either take me back to him or I can have the prosecuting attorney come down here and escort me instead. Your pick."

I could tell by Hank's expression that he thought very little of Kim Matthews. Nonetheless, he said, "Fine. But I'll be watching the cameras."

As he guided me back to the holding area, I expected to hear Kevin thrashing against the bars of his cell or cursing the way he was the day before, but all I heard was sobbing. The other guard was standing in front of his cell, looking at us with confusion.

"I don't know what his deal is," the guard said. "I came back to get him and he started crying and asking why he was here."

I could see Kevin curled up on his bed, sobbing and muttering unintelligibly.

"He's full of shit, Shawn," said Hank. "Ain't nothing more to it than that."

"Pretty convincing if you ask me," Shawn said.

"Yeah, I bet all those girls said the same thing too. Probably how he lured them in."

"Thank you, Officers," I interjected. "I'll let you know if I need you."

"Good luck," said Hank, walking with the other guard out of the holding area.

When they were gone, I pulled the folding chair over to the edge of the cell and took a seat. Kevin's crying was slowing, turning into shallow, intermittent gasps.

"You alright, Robbie?" I said, assuming he was playing his adolescent persona for my benefit.

He didn't respond though; he just kept weeping.

"Robbie?" I said again.

Kevin rolled over and peered up from the ragged pillow he was clutching in his arms.

"Who are you?" he said. "Why are you calling me Robbie?"

I tried to read his expression briefly, but his disquiet

appeared genuine. I decided to push back against his guise anyway to see if I could catch him off guard.

"Then who the hell are you today, Kevin? Hmm? Maybe you're the CEO of Apple today."

Kevin's face contorted and fresh tears formed in his eyes. "Why are you being mean to me?" He said this like a child who's just had his feelings hurt by a classmate on the playground.

"I'm done playing along with your bullshit," I said. "You don't have DID. I made the whole thing up yesterday."

Kevin whimpered for a moment, but then confusion overcame his face as he looked about his cell. "Where am I?" he said. His eyes locked on the bars separating us, and his confusion transformed into panic. "*Where am I?*" he begged, tears forming in his eyes.

"Stop it, Kevin," I said, refusing to take his bait. "I know you think you had me going there for the last few days, but I know you're faking it."

"Faking what?" he muttered, his voice wavering with fright. "Why—why am I here? Who are you?"

I've seen just about everything you can think of in my profession, but this was a first.

"You're faking this whole thing," I answered, not giving in to his ruse. "These personas and the stories and the amnesia and everything. There's nothing wrong with you."

Kevin erupted into tears, burying his face into the pillow and shrieking like a toddler throwing a tantrum.

I decided to take a slightly different approach.

"I expected more out of you, Kevin. When I came out here, I was so excited to meet one of the most notorious men in modern history. You, though? You're pathetic. Curled up on your bed like a frightened little boy. What happened to the man who gave those women what they had coming to them?"

He gasped several times before he lifted his face from the pillow.

"But I *am* a little boy," he said. "I'm only eight."

I laughed. I know, I know. I told you I could squelch any reaction. But this was ridiculous. So pathetic. I just couldn't help myself. This is the moment, I thought. This is the moment I dismantle his little game.

"That's real funny, Kevin," I said. "I'll give it to you, you had me going with Robbie. But an eight-year-old boy? Come on. Certainly you don't think that that is going to work? Even *you* can't pull that off."

He stared at me for a few long moments. His gaze was puzzled, frightened. Tears continued to roll down his cheeks. His lips quivered.

"Why are you calling me Kevin?" he asked. "Kevin's my big brother. *My* name's Jackie."

"Enough," I said with finality. "Just cut the bullshit already. I'll tell you what: I'll diagnose you with borderline personality disorder if you give this whole thing up, Kevin. Borderline personality disorder will keep you off death row. What do you say?"

This was a lie, of course. Borderline personality disorder, while a legitimate psychiatric diagnosis, was not enough to fulfill his insanity plea. But as the saying goes, fight fire with fire.

Kevin's eyes became even more terrified. "What's death row?" he asked. "Is Kevin in trouble?"

I stared at him. I said nothing. Just stared. I figured the silence and the awkwardness would pressure him into slipping up.

"You're scaring me..." he said, tears clawing at his eyelids. "Who *are* you?"

I was at a loss for words. If Kevin was faking his condition, he was doing a marvelous job.

"I'm Dr. Stevenson," I finally said, deciding to return to my original approach of playing along. "You're at the Peak County Prison in Park City, Wyoming."

"Wh-what?" Kevin stammered, shaking his head. "*Prison?*"

"Yes."

"But why?" he asked, his tone desperate.

"Because you're being charged with twenty-eight counts of first-degree murder," I said.

Confusion and terror immediately washed over his face, and his mouth trembled as he tried to speak. Nothing came out though, and soon he buried his face in the pillow again and sobbed.

I too was speechless. The act was the most convincing I had ever seen. Three separate personas? I refused to believe such a condition was possible.

I figured there was no way he would be able to keep them all straight without inconsistencies appearing. It was just a matter of time before the whole thing unraveled around him.

I left the prison for a few hours to clear my own head and to give Kevin time to return to normal. Before I left, I told the guards to check in on him periodically and to let me know when his act was finally over.

I didn't receive a call from Hank for four hours.

When I returned, Kevin allowed the guards to escort him to the interview room without complaint.

"Have you been crying?" I asked him.

He looked at me skeptically. "I don't think so... why?"

"Your face," I said. "It's red and your eyes are all puffy. You sure you haven't been crying? You can tell me. It's alright."

Kevin wiped his hands across his face and felt the lingering moisture.

"I guess I have," he said. "Don't really remember though."

"So you don't remember why you were crying then?"

He shook his head.

"Do you remember me stopping by this morning?"

"Nuh-uh," he said.

"What *do* you remember from this morning?"

He shrugged. "I slept until noon I guess... I had a couple of dreams, but I don't remember nothing about them."

I stared at him. Silent. Waiting for him to continue with something. Anything.

"Why are you looking at me like that?" he asked.

"Because I don't like it when you lie to me, Kevin," I said, my tone firm but non-confrontational.

"What are you talking about? Why do you think I'm lying to you?"

"Because, Kevin, you didn't sleep until noon today. And you know that we spoke earlier this morning."

"I swear to God, Doc, I have no idea what you're talking about. Honest."

As was typical, everything about his response seemed genuine and truthful.

"Do you remember what I told you about diagnosing you?"

"About the dissoc... what did you call it?"

"No. Not the dissociative identity disorder. The condition I brought up this morning."

"Doc, I... I don't remember seeing you this morning..."

I smacked the table and he jumped back against his seat.

"Cut the bullshit, Kevin. This amnesia thing is over. I already told you, you don't have transient global amnesia."

"What about dissoc... identity...?" he stammered.

"No," I said. "You don't have dissociative identity disorder either."

"So there's nothing wrong with me then?"

"I'm diagnosing you with borderline personality disorder, Kevin." Again, a lie. "That's the only thing that explains your behavior."

"But I'm not—"

"Just stop already," I interjected. "It's over. Borderline personality disorder isn't enough to make you legally insane. I'm signing off on your evaluation, Kevin."

This visibly stunned him, and a quiet satisfaction overcame me. Finally, I thought, he's going to fold once and for all. He was crafty, but not crafty enough.

He shook his head slowly then said, "I'm not... I'm not lying to you, Doc. I have no reason to lie to you. I didn't do it. I didn't kill those women. I'm sorry you don't believe me... but that's God's honest truth."

"You're right, Kevin," I said. "I don't believe you."

I stood and gathered the case file from the table.

"I'm sorry..." he said to me.

"No need to apologize," I said. "I just wish you were honest with me. If you were honest, I might've been able to help you."

"But I *am* being honest," he pleaded. "I swear to God."

"You're not. You're trying to play me for a fool."

I pushed my chair toward the table and started walking toward the door. I expected at any moment for him to jump from his seat and beg me to reconsider my decision, but he never did. Even when I looked back at him before leaving the room, he had his head hung low, buried in his shackled hands. He didn't utter another word.

As soon as I left the prison, I called Kim Matthews to tell her what happened. She clearly had doubts about my plan.

"What are you hoping to accomplish by lying to him?" she asked. "You know he's going to have his lawyer up my ass in no time, right?"

"I'm counting on it," I said.

"Counting on it? What are you talking about?"

"If he really is trying to deceive me, he's not just going to give up. Not when his life is on the line. He's persistent, and he's going to have his lawyer call you to try to figure out why I've deemed him competent."

"What makes you so sure? Why wouldn't he just hire their own psychiatrist to evaluate him and dispute your findings?"

"Because," I said, "there's only a handful of forensic psychiatrists in this country who have the reputation that I do, and none of them are going to stick their necks out for a guy like Blackford. Trust me, if he's trying to play me, you're going to hear from his lawyer."

"Yeah..." she said, hesitant. "I guess... What if I *don't* hear from him then?"

"That's not going to happen. You're *going* to hear from him."

"I know, but hypothetically, what if I don't? What does that mean?"

I was so caught up in the plan to discredit Kevin's ruse that I hadn't even considered another possibility.

"Well..." I said, thinking about it, "I may have discovered a case of one of the rarest psychiatric disorders in the book."

TEN

Less than twenty-four hours passed before Matthews received a call from Kevin's lawyer. He told Matthews what I had told Kevin about being deemed culpable. The borderline personality disorder diagnosis and my less-than-professional outburst.

He wasn't calling about that specifically though. He was calling because Kevin wanted to speak with me again before I submitted my final evaluation.

I was almost overjoyed on my way to the prison. This was going to be Kevin's last-ditch effort to get me to reconsider his diagnosis and his competence to stand trial. I wasn't sure how he was going to try this, but it didn't matter. Just the fact that he would try to convince me was enough to prove to me that he had been lying all along. It seemed my plan had finally worked.

Hank led me back to the interview room and I waited impatiently as the other guard retrieved Kevin from his cell. I half expected him to pull some ridiculous antic like the one from the day before. A tantrum ten times worse, or the emergence of a new personality.

Kevin did nothing of the sort though. He walked into the

interview room without complaint and took his seat across from me.

I inspected his expression as he did this. He looked like he did the first day I met him though. Dejected. Defeated.

It was quiet as I watched him. I could tell he was anxious, uncomfortable. His eyes searched the room and his hands fidgeted.

But I refused to break the silence. He asked to see me; he was going to be the one who started talking. Plus, I wanted to see where he was going to try to go with the conversation anyways.

"Listen, Doc..." he began, still not making eye contact with me, "I uhh... I wanted to talk to you. You know, about yesterday..."

"What about yesterday do you want to talk about?" I asked, my tone flat, unassuming, lukewarm.

"You know... what happened."

"Which was what, Kevin?" I said his name almost as a way to bait him into switching to a different persona. "What happened yesterday that you want to talk about?"

"My uhh..." He rustled his hands and the shackles jangled.

"Your what?"

His eyes continued to search the room. "My behavior. The things I've been telling you..."

"Okay," I said. "What do you want to tell me?"

He sighed. "Just that... I'm sorry... for wasting your time, I mean."

"How have you wasted my time?"

"I dunno exactly. The fact that I'm too stupid to remember these things you tell me."

I looked at him quizzically. "I'm not sure I follow, Kevin."

"I swear to God," he said with more emphasis, "I'm trying to remember this stuff, Doc, but I can't. I just can't. I stare at the wall and try to remember, but nothing's there. It's just empty holes everywhere. Little bits and pieces that make no sense. I just... I dunno... I don't want you to hate me, is all."

He finally made eye contact with me. His gaze was distraught. Genuinely distraught. Or at least, that's how it appeared to me.

"I don't hate you, Kevin," I said. "Do I *trust* you? No. But I don't hate you."

"I don't know what to do to get you to trust me. Tell me what I need to do." He was frantic, desperate even.

I leaned forward and said, "You need to tell me the truth, Kevin. About everything. About these personas you've been using. About the lies of not remembering things."

"Doc," he pleaded, "I swear on my life that I don't know what these persona things are. Honest to God, I don't. Don't you think I would tell you I did if it meant that it would save my life?"

"I don't know, Kevin. I honestly don't know what to think anymore."

"You have to believe me, Doc. *Please* believe me. I don't know what these persona things are and I truthfully don't remember the things that I say I don't. *Please* believe me."

"Fine," I said.

I flipped through the case file until I found the document I was looking for. It was the photo of Kevin with Brenda Wexler that Kim Matthews had shown me the day before. I held it up for Kevin to see.

"Where'd you find this?" he said, reaching for the photo with his shackled hands.

The chain attached to his waist restraint stopped his hands mid-air, so I handed the photo over to him. He stared at the photo, stunned.

"Seriously," he added, "how did you get this?"

"Do you recognize these people, Kevin?"

"Of course I do. That's me with my sister."

"When was this taken?"

"Geez, I dunno..." he said. "Ten years ago, I guess?"

"Do you remember what you were doing that day?"

"We went to the lake. We used to do that quite a bit."

He continued to look at the photo in silence, nostalgic.

I removed several more photos from the case file and placed them on the table for him to see. The graphic content caught his attention quickly.

"Jesus..." he said. "What are those?"

"Crime scene photos, Kevin."

"Of what?"

"Look at them," I said, pushing them closer to him.

The photos showed human skeleton remains scattered across a frost-covered forest bed. A hand. A femur. A mandible. Several ribs. Everything that hadn't been destroyed by the elements or the wildlife of the Griffith's Peak Wilderness.

Kevin sifted through the photos slowly, shaking his head. "Did *I* do this?" he muttered.

I nodded. "Do you know who that victim was?"

"No..."

"That's your sister," I said. "That's all that was left of Brenda when they found her."

He looked up at me, horrified. "I... I..." he stammered, but before he could say anything else, emotion overcame him and he sobbed.

"Kevin," I said as compassionately as I could. "Just be honest with me. Did *you* kill Brenda?"

His sobs became heavier as he shook his head in disbelief.

"I can't help you if you don't tell me the truth," I said.

"I swear to God..." he said, his words muffled. "I loved her."

"Of course you loved her," I said, "but maybe it was an accident? Is that what happened? An accident?"

"No!"

"But your DNA—"

"I didn't do it!" he cried. "You have to believe me. I would *never* do that. She was everything to me."

His head fell into his hands and he wept uncontrollably.

If there was ever a moment when I started doubting my initial thoughts about him, it was right then. I mean, Tom Cruise couldn't have put on a better acting performance. And the fact that he was not reverting back to the other personas astonished me. If he truly was lying about his condition, he would have done everything he could to convince me of it. The only thing he was showing me though was despair. Raw, unmitigated despair.

But an enormous question still remained unanswered: was Brenda Wexler really his half-sister?

ELEVEN

From the summer of 1990 to the spring of 1993, the Blue River Strangler went inexplicably dormant. Investigators wondered if he hadn't gone elsewhere to escape the harsh Wyoming winters. They wondered if victims would start appearing in one of the southern states, perhaps Arizona or New Mexico.

But nothing came up.

He simply vanished.

Investigators speculated that either the Blue River Strangler was getting better at hiding the bodies of his victims, or worse, he was in total control of his compulsion to kill and would return soon enough.

Then in April of 1993, a hiker stumbled upon the remains of a human body that had been desecrated by wildlife a few miles from the summit of Griffith's Peak. Under normal circumstances, investigators would have assumed the victim was a hiker attacked by a bear or mountain lion. Considering the fact that the Griffith's Peak Trail was far from the Blue River, it seemed unlikely that it had any connection to the Strangler.

The autopsy, however, showed significant trauma to the victim's trachea consistent with strangulation. Dental records identified the victim as Lorie Woods, a teenager from Colorado who was reported missing the previous spring.

Investigators debated whether to consider Lorie as the Blue River Strangler's eighth victim or not. Despite the victim's general description and cause of death being similar to the other victims, the location of her body was atypical. There was a possibility that the Strangler left her somewhere else and a bear had dragged her up the mountain, but it seemed unlikely.

In an attempt to squelch panic in the community, the *Peak Courier* reported that Lorie Woods' death was not connected to the Strangler murders.

Two days after the story was published, the chief editor received the following note:

Give credit where credit is due. Take a closer look at the mountain. Ed

The editor didn't know if the note was actually from the Strangler or if it was from a disgruntled citizen posing as him. Regardless, the members of the Blue River Strangler Task Force went out to the Griffith's Peak Wilderness to see what they could find. Over the course of the next three weeks, the task force recovered the remains of five more victims.

One of these victims was Brenda Wexler.

Brenda was recorded as the ninth Blue River Strangler victim, however, the coroner believed that she was one of the first women killed considering the decomposition of her remains. Why investigators didn't look into her background more closely at the time is beyond me. Maybe they figured she was a transient like Denise Chapman and Cindy Nelson, and therefore looking into her background would have led them nowhere. Or maybe they weren't even sure she was a Strangler victim since they couldn't confirm her cause of death. Regardless, nobody ever stumbled upon the photo of her with Kevin at the lake or any other information that might have helped connect her with him.

After my interview with Kevin that morning, I called Kim Matthews to notify her of what had happened and to tell her that I still was not ready to deem Kevin culpable for his crimes.

"What do you mean you're not ready to sign off on the evaluation yet?" she asked. "I thought you said that him asking to see you again was proof enough that he was lying to you?"

"I know I did," I said, "but if you saw what I saw this morning, you would have doubts too."

"I *have* seen his behavior, Dr. Stevenson, and you wanna know what I see? A sociopath who will do and say anything to get what he wants."

Matthews sounded flustered, and to a certain extent, I couldn't blame her.

"Trust me," I said, "I'm not saying I believe his story. All I'm saying is I have reason to doubt, and I can't in good conscience sign away on his culpability without being one hundred percent sure. *Especially* if the stakes are as high as the death penalty."

Matthews scoffed at this. "Please don't tell me that *that* is what this is about."

"I beg your pardon?" I asked.

"Your personal stance on the death penalty," she said. "I've read several of your articles and case studies, and it sure seems like you oppose capital punishment."

"No," I said, taken aback by the accusation. "My personal opinions have nothing to do with this."

"I hope so. I would hate for that to get in the way of justice being served."

"Justice being served?" I said. "Last I checked, executing the mentally ill is neither just nor constitutional."

"Wow," she said. "The man is a cold-blooded monster and all you're worried about is protecting his constitutional rights?"

I didn't respond. The conversation had escalated and I needed to take control of the tone.

"You still there?" she asked.

"Yes, I am. But I'm not going to argue with you about this."

"But it's our duty—"

"*Our duty*," I interjected, "is to uphold the law and the processes governing it. Period. This man hasn't even had his trial yet and already you're concerned about making sure he gets the needle. I understand that the outcome of this case is very important to a lot of people, but do not mistake vengeance with justice."

"Try telling that to the families of the victims," she retorted. "Look, you don't know what it's been like for the last ten years here. I mean, people were terrified to leave their houses when he was on the loose. Tourists stopped visiting because they were too scared. This county can't survive without tourism. A lot of folks suffered because of it. Businesses folded. It wasn't just those young women who suffered; this whole county has suffered for a long time."

"I empathize with that," I said, "but vengeance isn't going to undo that damage the same way that it won't bring those girls back to their mothers and fathers. Trust me, putting Kevin Blackford to death is not going to be the end of this county's suffering. If anything, it's only going to make it worse."

"You don't get it..." She paused and I could hear her trying to recollect her composure. "There are some very powerful people behind the scenes who refuse to let Blackford live through this."

"What are you talking about?" I asked. "What people?"

"People who can destroy careers and reputations in the blink of an eye. People who want to maintain Wyoming's image as a no-nonsense state. People who hate the fact that the lead prosecuting attorney of this case is a young woman..."

"Integrity is more important than some job," I said. "*Trust me.*"

"Is it?" she said.

"Yes. At the end of the day, integrity is about all we have to show for ourselves."

"Well, for your sake and mine, I hope you're right." She paused briefly before adding, "You need to know that I've been given two more weeks to push this forward. That means I need your decision in no more than a week. And if you can't find him competent and culpable, then the powers-that-be will find someone who will."

"I can't tell you how much of a mistake that would be."

"It's out of our hands. Either you find him competent or someone else will. No matter what you or I do, the only way this ends is with Kevin Blackford dead. Integrity or not."

"I'll testify on his behalf if it comes to that."

"I really hope it doesn't come to that. Like I said, these are very powerful people that we're dealing with. Standing in their way is not something I would advise."

"That sounds like a threat—"

"Not from me it isn't. But from them? It's more than a threat; it's a guarantee."

Silence fell between us again, and for the first time, I started to doubt why I agreed to evaluate Kevin Blackford in the first place.

But then Matthews said something that made those doubts evaporate as quickly as they entered my brain.

"I almost forgot to tell you," she said. "My investigators found out more information about Brenda Wexler. She wasn't Kevin's sister—"

I don't know if it was relief or disappointment that came over me. I didn't know what to feel about anything at that point.

"She wasn't?" I asked, more to convince myself than anything else.

"No," she said. "Brenda was his girlfriend."

TWELVE

I returned to the prison shortly after my conversation with Kim Matthews. Although Kevin had technically lied about his relationship with Brenda Wexler, the fact remained that he had known her intimately. It also was not clinically unusual that his main persona had confused this. If anything, it made DID even more of a possibility because of the psychological fragmentation it causes. It is an extremely elaborate mechanism to protect the main persona from traumatic experiences, even those caused by the patient himself.

Unearthing the truth about his relationship with Brenda was a monumental finding. She was the only victim who had any personal connection with him as far as anyone knew, and given the approximate time frame of her death, she was likely one of the first of his victims.

I admit that my job was becoming more about the case itself than it probably should have been, but it seemed that *that* would help me figure out whether or not Kevin was faking his condition.

Regardless, I was running out of time. I had a week at most and

I just didn't see that as enough time to diagnose him with something as rare and unlikely as dissociative identity disorder. The thing that was in my favor was "reasonable doubt". As long as I had reasonable doubt about his sanity and culpability, then in the grand scheme of things it didn't really matter what his diagnosis was. It wasn't a strong evaluation by any means, but it would at least keep a potentially mentally ill man from being wrongfully put to death.

The guards had not moved Kevin from the interview room when I returned. I peered through the window in the door and watched him for a moment. I was curious to see what he was doing when he didn't know I was there.

He appeared to be less distraught than before. He was sitting up in his chair, but the expression on his face was frustrated—angry, in fact. His mouth was moving as if he was talking to someone. I looked around the little room, but nobody was in there except for him.

"Who are you talking to?" I asked as I entered the room, startling Kevin in the process.

"I'm sorry?" he said, looking at me as if he'd never seen me before.

"It seemed like you were talking to someone," I said. "I was just wondering who?"

"Why do *you* care?" he answered. "And where the hell am I anyways?" he added, glancing about the interview room.

"I beg your pardon?" I said before it dawned on me what might be happening. "What's your name?" I added hesitantly.

"Russell," he said. "Who the hell are *you*?"

"I'm Dr. Stevenson," I said. "You're at the Peak County Prison in Park City, Wyoming. I'm a psychiatrist. I've been evaluating Kevin Blackford."

"Kevin?" he answered. "What kind of trouble is that dipshit in *now*?"

"*Now?*" I asked. "You know him?"

"Unfortunately..." he said, shaking his head. "What'd he do, anyways?"

"Well," I said, "the police think he murdered twenty-eight young women."

"*What?*" Kevin said, the surprise almost knocking him off balance. "Wait a second... they don't think *he's* the Blue River Strangler, do they?"

"How do *you* know about the Blue River Strangler?" I asked.

"I wasn't born under a rock. Anybody who sees the news knows about the Blue River Strangler."

"And how do *you* know about Kevin?"

He rolled his eyes and motioned to his own body. "It's kinda hard to *not* know who he is," he said. "*He* created me."

"What?" I retorted, my own confusion getting the best of me. "So he knows about *you* then too?"

"Not exactly. Not consciously, at least."

"That doesn't make any sense," I said.

"You're telling *me*," he answered, almost laughing at the absurdity. "And yet, here we are, Dr. Stevenson."

"Explain that to me," I said. "How do you know about him, but he doesn't know about you?"

"*You've* talked to him, haven't you? The guy isn't the sharpest knife in the drawer. It should come as no surprise to you that he doesn't remember me or any of the others."

"The others?" I asked. "What do you mean, the others?"

"*The others,*" he said. "Jackie, Robbie, Eddie."

"Eddie? I haven't met any Eddie."

"Be thankful for that, trust me—"

"Why's that?"

"Because Eddie's fucking crazy," he said. "He'd kill me just for talking to you about him."

It was in that pause of the conversation that I remembered

the letters that the Strangler wrote to the *Peak Courier*. The name that the Strangler had given himself.

Edward.

Kevin must have seen my reaction because he asked, "Is everything alright, Dr. Stevenson?"

"No," I said. "Russell, what do you know about the Blue River Strangler?"

"Only what the news has said."

"Russell..." I probed, having the impression that he was hiding something.

"I can't tell you," he said, fright overcoming him.

"Why not?"

"Because... I promised Eddie I wouldn't..."

"But Eddie isn't real, Russell."

"*Real?*" he scoffed. "How do you even know which one of us *is* the real one? We're *all* the real one at some point. Besides, I promised I would keep my mouth shut."

"You can tell me, Russell. You can trust me."

"I can't..." he said. "I've tried before and he just does it again. I *can't* let it happen again. I can't."

"What do you mean, you can't let it happen again? What happened? What did he do?"

He shook his head saying, "No way. I'm not telling you a damn thing."

"Tell me, Russell. What does Eddie have to do with the Blue River Strangler?"

Kevin was silent, but I could see fear emerging in his face.

"Russell..." I added.

He lifted his head, and in that single moment, his expression had changed completely. The terror vanished from his eyes and he looked at me tranquilly.

"Miss," he said, "my name's Jackie."

"Jackie?" I asked, scrambling to keep up with the absurdity.

"Jackie, I was just talking to Russell. Do you know who Russell is?"

"Nuh-uh..."

"What about Robbie, or Kevin?" I asked. "Any of these names sound familiar?"

"Nope," he said.

"You're sure?"

"Uh-huh."

"You wouldn't lie to me, would you?"

He shook his head. "Eddie says it's bad to lie. Especially to grown-ups."

"*Eddie?*" I asked "*You* know about Eddie?"

"Yeah. He's my special friend..."

"Your special friend?" I said, perplexed. "What do you mean, he's your special friend? Like your imaginary friend?"

"No," he said, shaking his head and casting his eyes downward. "Eddie is *real*."

As bizarre as Kevin's transition from Russell to Jackie was, the discrepancy about Eddie had caught me entirely off guard and I struggled to try to piece it all together.

"I see..." I said, still trying to shake my own confusion. "Can you tell me what happens if you *do* lie, Jackie?"

"I get punished..." he mumbled.

"By Eddie?" I asked.

Kevin nodded, shifting his weight with discomfort.

"What does Eddie do?" I added.

"I don't want to talk about this no more," he said quickly.

I could tell Kevin was becoming upset, so I hoped I could needle something meaningful out of him.

"Jackie, does Eddie get aggressive with you?"

"I said, I don't want to talk about it..."

"But I need to know so that I can keep him from doing it again," I said.

"Nobody can stop him." Tears formed in his eyes. "If I tell someone, it'll just make Eddie mad."

"Does Eddie get mad a lot?" I asked.

Kevin shrugged. "I guess..."

"Is that why you have imaginary friends?" I asked, hoping I could get him to confuse his personas.

"Only babies have imaginary friends," he said.

"But I thought Russell and Robbie were your imaginary friends?"

Kevin shook his head. "Nuh-uh. I don't need no friends."

"What do you mean, you don't need friends? Everybody needs friends."

"Not me."

I quickly considered my next move, but I couldn't shake this new persona, Eddie, out of my head. The connection of the name to the Strangler's letters to the *Courier* was too convenient to be coincidental. I needed to find a way to get Kevin to talk more about Eddie, but I didn't know how.

"Jackie?" I asked Kevin. "Can I get your help with something?"

"Sure," he said, twiddling his fingers.

"I could really use your help finding Eddie."

He shook his head. "I don't know where he is."

"Are you sure?" I asked. "Do you know how I can talk to him, maybe?"

"Nuh-uh..." he answered. "You don't want to meet Eddie anyways."

"Yes, I do," I said. "Has Eddie ever done anything that got him in trouble? Like with the police?"

Kevin shrugged. "I dunno... maybe..."

"Because I think Eddie's done some very bad things, Jackie. Things that would get him in trouble with the police. Things that would make him go to jail for a long time and never be able to hurt you again."

He shrugged. "I dunno."

"You can tell me—"

"I don't know!" he yelled, clenching his fists. "I don't know! I don't know! I don't know!"

"Okay, okay," I said. "It's alright. Calm down. I believe you."

"I want to go home!" he shrieked.

"You know you can't go home."

"No!" he screamed, rushing over to the door. He crashed into the locked door with his shoulder, yelling, "Let me out!"

"I need you to calm down, Kevin."

"Stop calling me that!" he wailed. "I'm Jackie!"

Kevin let out a shrill cry, continuing to throw himself against the door.

The guards soon opened the door, batons ready.

"Jackie," I said, "you need to calm down or these men are going to take you away."

"No!" he screamed.

He rushed toward the open door in the midst of his tantrum, and one of the guards brought his baton down upon the back of Kevin's head. Kevin crumpled to the floor immediately, unconscious.

THIRTEEN

Kevin regained consciousness as the guards and I carried him back to his cell. He was disoriented, likely concussed from the impact of the guard's baton.

After getting Kevin back to the holding area, I sat in the folding chair outside his cell and watched him for a while. Hoping I would observe something that might give me some answers. The effects of the concussion made him nauseated, and he spent much of the day sleeping. As far as I could tell, he never switched from the Jackie persona in that time.

I asked that one of the guards sit with him all afternoon and watch his demeanor if and when he finally woke up. "If you speak to him, use his name as much as possible," I told them. "And if he disputes it, ask him as many questions as you can and notify me as soon as possible."

They looked at me like I was nuts when I told them this, but they agreed nonetheless.

After I left the prison, I called my boss, Deputy Warden Allen Kranick, to notify him that I would need to take at least another week to continue evaluating Blackford.

"What's wrong with him, anyways?" Kranick asked. "Besides being a complete psychopath, of course."

"You know I can't discuss that."

"Yeah, but rarely does one of these evaluations take you this long. You usually know pretty quick whether something's wrong with them or not."

"Just being thorough is all," I said. "There's a lot riding on this as I'm sure you can imagine."

Little did he know that it wasn't just Kevin's life potentially riding on my decision; my reputation was at risk as well. Dissociative identity disorder was so rare that I had to be absolutely certain about the diagnosis.

I spent much of that afternoon combing through the limited literature on dissociative identity disorder, trying to find evidence to prove that Kevin was in fact lying about his condition. The problem was that dissociative identity disorder had only become a recognized diagnosis four years prior. Its precursor, multiple personality disorder, was viewed by many psychiatrists as either hoaky or merely a symptom of some other condition. Borderline personality disorder most likely. Borderline personality disorder manifests itself through impulsivity and extreme shifts in temperament. Anger and depression mostly. Intense anger, in fact. I've treated countless inmates with borderline personality disorder, and the majority of them experience these bouts of spontaneous violence. Toward others and toward themselves.

But what really made psychiatrists believe that multiple personality disorder wasn't a stand-alone condition was that those with borderline personality disorder typically had a fragmented and unstable sense of self. They didn't necessarily give these fragments names, but working with people who are borderline often feels like you're working with completely different people depending on the day.

Much of the controversy associated with dissociative identity disorder revolved around the therapeutic techniques used to identify the various identities. Namely hypnosis. Hypnosis became more widely used during the Freudian era, and ever since, it's been as popularly synonymous with psychology as the padded leather couch. In reality, hypnosis has been discredited as an effective therapeutic technique for a while. It actually was how Kenneth Bianchi, one of the Hillside Stranglers, was able to fake multiple personality disorder as part of his own insanity defense.

Many psychiatrists, including myself, believed that dissociative identity disorder was the result of a therapist's own self-fulfilling prophecy rather than a legitimate psychological dysfunction.

What made Kevin different from Bianchi was that Bianchi had studied psychology prior to his crimes. He had attended college courses as a young man, and he even ran a fake and illegal psychiatric practice for a brief time. So in his case, it was clear that he had prior knowledge and understanding of multiple personality disorder. Kevin on the other hand had no such background as far as we knew.

What really forced me to second-guess my judgment with Kevin though was the fact that he exhibited all five criteria of the disorder without any apparent background knowledge of the disorder itself. He obviously presented several distinct personality states, but he also experienced amnesia, distress, and decreased cognitive functioning as a result of the condition.

When I searched through the few case studies that I could find, the majority highlighted childhood trauma as an inciting element of the disorder. Physical and sexual abuse being the most common. We simply did not know a whole lot about Kevin's personal history at that time because it wasn't necessarily relevant to the criminal case. I, however, wondered if I wouldn't be able to dive into this further, particularly with the Jackie and Robbie personas.

But again, would that be enough to confidently diagnose him with dissociative identity disorder? Would that be enough to justify not deeming him culpable for his heinous crimes?

I wasn't sure.

Then I started to wonder if I hadn't allowed myself to be jaded by the possibility of a rare psychiatric discovery, or worse, that I had allowed myself to be manipulated by an incredibly cunning sociopath.

Other than continuing to interview Kevin, the only other option I considered was calling a colleague up to Wyoming to get a second opinion. I thought about asking Wendy, but I didn't trust her inexperience with such severe conditions, nor did I want to expose her to someone like Blackford.

I also considered one of my colleagues at the Supermax, but our staff was stretched thin as it was. Kranick would have had a conniption if I pulled another psychiatrist away.

My contemplations were interrupted by a phone call from the Peak County Jail.

"Dr. Stevenson?" the guard asked. "You said to call if Blackford woke up?"

"Yes. How is he?"

"He's a little groggy, but seems fine otherwise."

"Is he responding to his name?" I asked.

"I honestly don't know..."

"Would you mind checking?" I asked.

"How?"

"Call him by name and see how he responds."

"Hold on..."

I waited a minute. Anxious.

"Doc?" the guard finally said.

"Yeah?"

"He responded to us."

"He did?"

"Yes." The guard sounded annoyed by this point.

"Did you call him Kevin or Blackford?" I asked.

The guard sighed. "Does it matter?"

"Yes," I said. "It matters. Trust me."

"We called him Blackford."

"Call him Kevin," I said. "Let me know how he responds."

"Fine..." The guard said, agitated.

Another minute passed before the guard came back to the phone.

"He said his name's not Kevin..." said the guard, his tone perplexed.

"What name did he give you?" I asked.

"Robbie."

"I'm on my way. Keep talking to him."

"What do you mean, keep talking to him? What the hell is going on?"

"Don't worry about it. Just keep talking to him and try to remember anything else he says. I'll be there in a few minutes."

"But—"

I hung up. I don't know if it was excitement or apprehension that flowed through my veins, but the fact that Kevin displayed one of the personas to someone other than me seemed to further support my suspicion that he legitimately suffered from dissociative identity disorder.

I couldn't get to the prison fast enough.

FOURTEEN

When I arrived at the prison, Kevin was in the midst of a screaming fit at the guards.

"What the hell happened?" I asked, rushing through the doors to the holding area.

"I just did what you asked me," the guard said. "All I did was talk to him."

"Get me out of here!" Kevin screamed from within his cell, shaking the bars that separated him from us.

"What did you ask him?" I said.

"Why he was using a different name."

"Shit," I said. "Why would you ask him that?"

"Why not? Was that wrong?"

"It wasn't good," I said.

"Well, how the hell was I supposed to know?"

"You weren't, I guess." I paused and watched Kevin thrashing about the cell like a rabid animal. "Both of you can leave us," I said to the guards.

"Not like *this* we can't."

"No! No! No!" Kevin howled, smacking himself on the forehead with his palm.

"Trust me," I said. "Just go. I might be able to get something out of him this way."

"Alright..." they said, glancing at me skeptically. They left a walkie-talkie on the folding chair, adding, "You call us if he gets worse, alright?"

"Sure," I said, waving them off. I went to the bars and said to Kevin, "Robbie, do you recognize me?"

Kevin growled with anger, continuing to hit himself.

"Robbie, I need you to stop and breathe. Remember what I told you a few days ago? Close your eyes and breathe. In through your nose and out through your mouth... Slowly... In through your nose and out through your mouth..."

He hit himself a few more times before closing his eyes.

"Good," I said, "now breathe. In through your nose. Out through your mouth."

He did as I asked, his fit slowing down the more he breathed.

"Nice and slow... Through your nose... Out through your mouth..."

His breathing continued to slow and he started to regain control of himself.

Finally, he said, "Doc, I—"

"Just breathe," I interrupted. "Don't talk. Just breathe..."

He followed my instructions and eventually calmed himself down. He took a seat on the floor afterward, leaning against the foot of his cot near the bars.

"Can you tell me what happened?" I asked him, taking a seat on the floor on the other side of the bars from him.

"I..." he began, thinking, "I just... I dunno... lost it... He kept calling me Kevin after I asked him not to and I just lost it." His eyes looked pained, frightened. "Doc... what the hell is happening to me?"

"I'm going to be honest with you, Robbie," I said. "I'm not entirely sure. But I'm going to do everything I can to find out."

"So... everybody thinks *I* killed those women?"

I nodded.

"Jesus—" he said, his hands trembling. "You have to believe me, Doc. I don't know who the hell this Kevin guy is and I don't know nothing about those murders."

"Do you mind if I ask you a couple things, Robbie? Things that might help us explain all of this?"

"*Please.*" He sounded desperate. Legitimately desperate.

"Does the name Brenda Wexler ring a bell?" I asked.

His brow furrowed. "Brenda?" he said. "What the hell does Brenda have to do with this, Doc?"

"So you know her?" I asked.

"Know her? Of course I know her. She's my girlfriend, for Christ's sake."

"Your girlfriend?"

"Yeah. How do *you* know her?" He stopped and looked at me skeptically. "Doc..." he added, his voice cracking with worry. "Please don't tell me something happened to her."

"No," I answered. I wanted to avoid upsetting him again, so I figured I'd lie. Plus, it could be a point of discrepancy if Robbie later said something about Brenda being dead. "Her name *has* come up a few times," I added, "but that's all. She's fine as far as I know."

He sighed, smiling. "Thank God. I don't know what I would do if I lost her..."

"Do you love her?" I asked.

He nodded, still smiling. "I'm going to ask her to marry me," he said. "When the time is right, of course. Gotta make some more money and get us out of that dump we live in."

"That's great," I said. "When was the last time you spoke with her?"

"I dunno..." He paused, thinking. "The morning before I got taken here, I guess?"

"She hasn't come by to see you?" I asked.

"I left her a message and told her not to come. I don't want her getting caught up in all this shit."

"I see." I paused before adding, "What about the name Eddie? Do you know anyone by that name?"

"Eddie?" he said, his expression turning to anger again. "Yeah, I knew someone by that name."

"You *did*?" I asked, thinking maybe I was finally going to get somewhere. "How did you know him?"

"He was a counselor at the Wadsworth Center. Supposedly he abused some of the kids when I was there."

"What's the Wadsworth Center?" I asked.

"Some group home for kids. A *residential treatment facility* they called it. It was a shithole. Not much better than where I was with my mom."

"Why were you sent there?"

"Probably because my mom was fucked up in too many ways to count," he said. "Tried to kill herself once even. I found her in the tub with her wrists slashed, so I called 911 and they saved her life. Barely. You wanna know what she did afterward? She handed me over to Child Services. Told me that everything was *my* fault. That *I* made her want to kill herself. That her life was just fine until I came along. You know she tried to get an abortion when she was pregnant with me?"

I shook my head. "I didn't. I'm sorry."

"Yeah. Bitch didn't even know she was pregnant until she was four months along. She tried to go to the clinic but they turned her away. Said it was too late. She was a junkie, so I was born addicted to meth." He shook his head, muttering, "Should've let her die in that goddamn tub…"

"I'm really sorry about that," I said, wondering how much of this was actually true. "When was the last time you saw her?"

"Around that time she abandoned me, I guess? I dunno if she's even alive anymore…" His gaze drifted toward the shadows of the cell as he ruminated.

"What happened to *you* afterward?" I asked.

"The court sent me to that group home with that piece of shit, Eddie."

"Did he ever try to abuse *you*?" I asked.

"Hell no," he said emphatically. "If he would've tried anything with me, I would've kicked his ass."

"Did anything ever happen to him? Was he arrested or anything?"

Kevin scoffed, "Arrested? They *protected* him. Said that the kids he was abusing were lying about it. For all I know, they were abusing kids too."

"Do you remember what year that would've been?"

"Mid-eighties, maybe? I honestly don't remember."

"What about Eddie's last name? Do you remember that?"

Kevin shook his head. "I've tried to forget as much about that shithole as I can. You know they had like twenty kids crammed into what was basically a prison block? Each of us stuck in a room just big enough to hold a little bed and an old dresser. A lot of the boys were older than me, so I got toughened up pretty quick when I first got there."

"What do you mean, toughened up?" I asked.

"How else?" he said. "They'd bully me, try to beat the shit out of me. Screw me any way they could. So I learned to fight back." He inspected his hands. I hadn't noticed it before, but his knuckles were permanently swollen. "Got to be a pretty good fighter too," he added, grinning.

"Where were your counselors when all of this was going on?" I asked.

"The *counselors*?" he scoffed. "They were a bunch of dipshit college students who didn't give a damn about any of us. They were trying to survive just as much as we were. They fucking hated us and we hated them."

"That sounds like a rough environment to grow up in."

"Yeah, well, story of my life..." he said.

In the midst of our conversation, I had opened the case file and jotted down the names and other details he mentioned so I could look into them later. If the stuff about his childhood ended up being true, then there was a stronger possibility that his condition was also true. If he did in fact have dissociative identity disorder, then his Jackie and Robbie personas were likely a manifestation of his childhood trauma. His way of coping with it and processing it. He also appeared to have a great deal of resentment toward his mother, so I wondered if that wasn't a driving force for his murders.

"Was any of that helpful?" he asked me as I finished my notes.

"It very well could be," I said.

He didn't respond for a moment, but as he looked at me anxiously, I could tell there was something else on his mind.

"Can I ask you something, Doc?" he finally said.

"Of course."

"Why are you helping me? I mean, everybody else here has treated me like I'm a monster, but not you."

"Well..." I said. "It's partly because it's my duty to give you the benefit of the doubt."

He shook his head with confusion. "I'm not sure I know what you mean?"

"To give you a fair shake. You know, assume that you're innocent until proven guilty. The way the justice system *should* operate."

"Yeah... but why?"

"Because despite the things that you're accused of doing, I believe you should still be treated like a human being, Robbie."

He looked at me with gratitude, and for a moment, the bars between us dissolved and he ceased to be the Blue River Strangler. He became a patient. A deeply afflicted one. But a patient all the same.

FIFTEEN

The more I learned about Kevin's past history, the more I became convinced that he did in fact suffer from dissociative identity disorder.

Was it unlikely? Yes.

But was it impossible? No.

It was at that point that I decided I needed a second opinion.

I called Dr. Georg Edmund at the Oklahoma State Penitentiary a.k.a. "Big Mac". Georg and I had worked together at Custer Correctional before I transferred to the Supermax and he went on to work at Big Mac. He had a great deal of experience working with Class B and Class A felons, so I knew he would be able to give me an honest opinion about Kevin.

Georg's introduction to the field of psychology was his participation in the notorious Stanford Prison Experiment in 1971. He served as an inmate in Dr. Philip Zimbardo's fictional prison. Zimbardo was a social psychologist who wanted to explore power roles and group identity in the context of a simulated prison, so he built a makeshift prison in the basement of Stanford's psychology building, and he recruited twenty-four undergraduate men to participate. The plan was to essentially "play jail" for two weeks and record what happened.

What happened was nothing short of a disaster.

Within a day, the prisoners became non-compliant, and as a result, the guards became autocratic. Tyrannical in fact. Despite the instruction at the beginning of the study to not physically harm the prisoners, the guards tortured their fictional inmates with physical exercise, food deprivation, and psychological manipulation. Even Zimbardo got caught up in the craze.

Zimbardo did however shut the study down after six days. He recently published a book about the experience.

The Lucifer Effect.

While the experience traumatized most of the participants, Georg was inspired by it. Captivated even. As he described it, "Golding's *Lord of the Flies* came to life before my very eyes. The only difference was that our deserted island was in a basement at one of the most prestigious universities in America. I saw regular boys become monsters and savages in the matter of a few days." From that moment onward, Georg became infatuated with the psychological underpinnings of evil and wickedness. And what better field to explore this than correctional psychiatry?

It took little effort to convince Georg to catch a flight out to Wyoming to help me. Excited to sit face to face with the Blue River Strangler, he told me he would fly out the following day.

In the meantime, I needed to avoid Kim Matthews as much as I could until I could confirm what Kevin had told me about his childhood. There was little in the case file about Kevin's history though, so I needed to find the information elsewhere. The problem was that it would require time that I didn't have to spare.

That's when I called Wendy.

"I could really use your help," I told her. "I could have the investigators here look into it, but I don't trust them. Everybody here is frothing at the mouth to give Blackford the needle."

"Can you blame them?" she said. "After what the guy did, he probably deserves it."

"*Deserves it*?" I said, shocked by her callousness. "How can you say that? He hasn't even been convicted yet."

"You said it yourself, didn't you? The evidence so obviously implicates him."

"Yes, but this is about his culpability, not his guilt. If he suffers from this condition, it's morally and ethically wrong to put him to death for it."

I heard her sigh over the phone.

"What?" I asked, irritated.

"What is this really about?"

"What do you mean, what is this about? It's about a man's life, for Christ's sake."

"Alright..." she said, trailing off.

"What?" I asked.

"It's just... This seems more personal for you. More so than any other patient you've told me about."

"It isn't," I said. "He's no different than any other patient."

"Okay. Then why were you so interested in his case before you started working with him? Before they even knew who he was?"

"What are you implying?" I retorted, knowing full well what she was talking about despite my desire to avoid the subject.

"His victims have a lot of similarities to..." She paused as if she could take the thought back.

"To whom?" I said with annoyance. "To Maddie?"

She hesitated before answering, "Yes."

"I don't see what she has to do with anything," I retorted coldly.

"There wasn't a part of you that thought they would identify her as one of his victims?"

"No," I said, although deep down I knew that it couldn't be further from the truth.

"So his victims don't remind you of her?"

"No," I answered. "If that was the case, then wouldn't I want to see him get the punishment he deserves? Why am I trying to protect him?"

"Maybe you did—*before* you started working with him. But now you see him for more than just his crimes. You see the man inside the monster. And you can't deny that you have a savior complex. Ever since Maddie ran away, you've been like that. Don't get me wrong, it's part of the reason you're so good at your job. But we all have a boon that is also bane."

"So what are you saying then?"

"Don't let it cause countertransference," she said.

I scoffed. "That is not what is going on here."

"Are you sure?"

"Positive." Trying to dodge the topic, I quickly added, "Now, are you going to help me or not?"

She didn't respond for several moments, and I wondered if she had hung up on me.

"You still there?"

"Yes..."

I could tell by her tone that she was pissed at me though.

"Look, I'm sorry," I said, hoping that a superficial apology would convince her to help. "This case is pushing me more than I ever imagined it would, and I just want to make sure I get it right. For Blackford's sake and for my own sake. I can't afford to screw this one up."

"I know you're under a lot of pressure, and from the sounds of it, this prosecuting attorney isn't making it any easier. You're a professional. People will trust your judgment."

"I hope you're right," I said, although I had my doubts. "So what do you say? Will you help?"

After some more prodding and groveling, I eventually convinced Wendy to help me out. As always, she told me to be careful, sounding even more worried than usual.

My conversation with Wendy only made me doubt my speculation about Kevin's condition more, not to mention it cast a gigantic spotlight on the part of my subconscious that I desperately wanted to ignore: my estranged daughter, Maddie.

She started getting into trouble when she was in junior high school. The prison was absorbing every ounce of energy that I could muster during that time, and my parenting suffered as a result. There's only one thing more dangerous than idle hands, and that's a teenager left to her own devices in a rural community. She got caught up with a bad crowd, and by the time she was sixteen, she was addicted to every drug she could get her hands on. Given the population I have worked with my entire life, I took the tough love approach with her every step of the way. It did nothing but drive her further away from me and closer to her problems. She started to go missing the way a feral cat does. I would be sick with worry for days on end, only to have her show back up looking like she had survived fifteen rounds with a wild animal. Beat to hell. Exhausted. But alive.

It went on this way for over a year, her disappearances becoming longer and longer until one day she just never came back. I thought for sure she had overdosed and was left in an irrigation ditch to rot. I filed a missing person's report and searched every flophouse and drug hangout that I knew of, but I never found her. The people she partied with said that they hadn't seen her in weeks. A handful of them said that she had skipped town. One said she went north to Denver. Another south to Santa Fe. A third west for Los Angeles.

I didn't know what to believe or where she would have gone. Her father was never a part of her life, and aside from a whacked-out aunt on my mother's side, we had no family that she could have gone to.

I knew that one day I would receive a call that she had been found dead somewhere. The fear was a phantom that perpetually haunted my subconscious thoughts, so I distracted myself the only way I knew how: I buried myself in my work. I poured my soul into my patients as if rehabilitating them would somehow bring Maddie back home.

It never did.

When the Blue River Strangler cases started making national news, I had to fight the angst that she would be identified as one of his victims. She wouldn't have gone all the way up to Wyoming, I told myself. She wouldn't have traded one podunk town for another. But the fact was that she was a transient drug addict like many of the Strangler victims. The murders could have occurred on Mars and I still would have feared that one of them was Maddie.

What I feel toward Kevin has little to do with countertransference though. I don't see Maddie when I look into Kevin's eyes, nor do I feel her pain when I empathize with him.

Maybe Wendy was right about me hoping that she would be identified as one of his victims. As if Maddie herself was on death row without me knowing what her execution date was.

SIXTEEN

I struggled to get anything useful out of Kevin over the course of the following days. In three separate sessions, I spoke to Kevin and Jackie. As was typical, all of these personas were oblivious to the other ones. Jackie was the least helpful, but Kevin wasn't much better either. As far as I could tell, Kevin's different identities were products of his repression of whatever traumas he had experienced as a child and adolescent. Jackie was his childlike self, the innocent perspective that had yet to make sense of his mother's indifference toward him. Robbie was probably the most complex identity and, ironically enough, the most in touch with reality. It was the part of Kevin that could actually acknowledge what had happened to him as a child. The problem was that the Robbie persona was wrathful and potentially violent, at least toward his abusers. What made him so interesting, though, was his affection for Brenda. She was the only one whom he spoke fondly of. I just found it impossible to imagine that he had murdered her. Especially in the way that he had done it. It made me wonder what happened between them. It made me wonder if *that* wasn't the first of the dominoes to fall and destroy the rest.

What I also couldn't figure out was the Russell persona, or more specifically, the imaginary friend of whom Russell was so weary. Edward. His name signed to each of the Strangler letters in some variation. I knew there had to be some connection, but I didn't know what. It made me wonder if Edward or Eddie wasn't just another persona that I hadn't yet met. Maybe even the one responsible for the murders.

The problem was that the appearance of the personas seemed to be completely involuntary, and I had yet to discover the triggers for particular identities to appear. I was at the mercy of their randomness, and unless I just happened to be there when Russell was present, I feared I would run out of time before my questions about the Eddie persona were answered.

When Georg flew into Casper the following morning, I picked him up at the airport myself. I was anxious to see what Georg's opinion was. There was a large part of me that hoped that he would see exactly what I had seen in Kevin from the beginning. A deeply afflicted young man tormented into insanity by the traumas of his past. Driven to a condition that few read about, and even fewer delved into personally.

But another part of me hoped he wouldn't. Another part of me hoped that Georg could expose Kevin as nothing more than a deceitful sociopath. Someone who not only earned the death penalty, but also deserved it.

Georg looked like the quintessential Austrian despite the fact that he was a generation removed from his European roots. Blond hair, blue eyes, and the physique and acumen of a man half his age. Peak County was a four-hour drive away, and as much as I didn't want to lose a full day of observing Kevin, I knew that the drive would be a good time for me to update Georg on the case and what I had suspected about Kevin's condition.

Georg was quiet as I spoke, making notes for himself in a

small notebook. I told him everything I had observed about each of the supposed identities, and more importantly, the details that each supposedly knew. I hoped that he would be able to either catch inconsistencies with whichever personas he spoke to or confirm the legitimacy of the condition itself.

"What do others have to say about his behavior?" Georg finally asked me. "The guards are around him all day, right? Any of them confirm these identities?"

"One of the guards did a few days ago," I said, "but they don't recall anything more out of the ordinary than him throwing tantrums and beating the shit out of himself."

"What about other people who've had interactions with him recently? The prosecuting attorney or the investigators?"

I scoffed at the mention of the prosecuting attorney. "Please. She wouldn't recognize it if it hit her in the face. She's adamant about getting the death penalty. As for the investigators, I haven't spoken directly to them, but I have watched the interrogation tapes. Blackford never mentions different names, but his demeanor varies dramatically from one session to the next. In one, he's incredibly subdued. Then in the next, he's defiant. Almost belligerent. What's most suspicious is how authentic each of his different personality states seems to be."

"Have you tried speaking to anyone he knew prior to his arrest?" asked Georg. "Maybe his boss or a coworker at the community college? A roommate?"

"Not yet," I said. "I've been so caught up in trying to break him that I haven't had the time to seek them out."

"It may be something to look into. I don't expect my evaluation is going to be quick by any means."

"Yeah, you're probably right."

"How are *you* holding up anyways?" he asked. "You look like hell."

"I'm tired," I said. "I can't get any sleep even if I try to. I just keep mulling over details trying to find points of weakness." I paused briefly before adding, "Wendy thinks I'm experiencing countertransference... You believe that?"

Georg shrugged. "It happens to the best of us," he said. "Almost let it get a hold of me myself a few years ago. It's hard to recognize when you're in the midst of it."

"Do you think that's what's going on with me?" I asked.

"It's not my position to say. Especially having not evaluated the guy myself. That being said, you have to acknowledge it if you feel like that's what's happening."

"I know Kevin is guilty. But if he's mentally ill, he belongs in a psychiatric facility, not on death row. We all took an oath as physicians. *First do no harm. Apply all necessary measures for the benefit of the sick.* How am I upholding that oath if I don't do my due diligence?"

"I'm not saying I disagree with you. If this guy's condition is legitimate, then he absolutely needs to be in a psychiatric facility. But if he's faking it? Jesus... we have more of a duty to the greater good than to him."

"And what if we're wrong?" I asked. "Is it worse to wrongfully commit a sociopath or to execute a lunatic?"

Georg shook his head ruminatively. "I wish I knew the answer to that," he said. "It certainly would make our jobs a hell of a lot easier if I did."

SEVENTEEN

While Georg was at the prison evaluating Kevin, I went over to the community college across town to see if I could speak with Kevin's former boss.

I was mildly familiar with Peak County Community College already from what I had read in the Strangler case file. Not only was it Kevin's employer for twelve years, but the sixth victim, Tracy Malvar, had been a student there.

Tracy was one of four victims found in various locations along the Blue River in the summer of 1990. Two bodies had been washed into flooded meadows outside the town of Carbon, another was found lodged against a railroad bridge pylon, and Tracy's was discovered amongst the boulders of Peak Ridge Canyon by a rafting party. All four victims exhibited similar causes of death and bodily trauma as the first two Strangler victims: strangulation without the use of a ligature and wounds incurred post-mortem by the raging currents of the Blue River.

Despite being the sixth confirmed Strangler victim, Tracy was the first who was not a transient. She was a local girl, having lived in Park City her whole life. She worked at Summit Tavern in Park City all throughout high school and was still working there to pay for college until she finished her spring semester. With her associate's degree completed and ready to move on to the University of Montana to study Veterinary Medicine in the fall, she left Park City for a two-week long summer road trip. Her body was discovered three weeks after she left.

The community was devastated by her death. Up until that point, the Strangler had been targeting the homeless population, women who lived on the fringe of society. Their deaths, while tragic, were attributed to being a by-product of a risky lifestyle.

Tracy, on the other hand, was a good kid. She stayed out of trouble. Did well in school. Volunteered at her church. She was somebody whom most of the locals recognized, liked, and respected. Her folks were known well around town too. Her father was a contractor and her mother helped him keep the books. They weren't affluent by any means, but they got by just fine.

When Tracy was murdered, though, the Strangler hadn't just killed a random, nameless person. He had killed someone's daughter. Someone's sister. Someone's friend. A cherished member of the community.

I think more than anything, Tracy's murder brought the gravity of the situation to the community's doorstep. It forced people to acknowledge the terror that was circling their once-sheltered and otherwise safe community. It was the point at which malevolence toward the Strangler really began to grow in the heart of Peak County.

As if the rapid increase in victims that summer wasn't alarming enough, a letter was received by the editor of the *Peak Courier* that August:

Dear Editor,

I wish you had given me a more creative name than the Blue

River Strangler, but I guess beggars can't be choosers. I would like to tell you where you can find my next victim. I left her in a willow thicket on the north bank of the Blue River just upstream of the confluence of Badger Creek. She told me her name was Mandy, but you never can tell when people give their real names, can you?

Best wishes,
Edward, 86911

I imagined that investigators hoped they wouldn't find anything when they went out to the location named in the letter. That the letter was from some lunatic who knew nothing about the murders and simply wanted to toy with law enforcement in his own weird, twisted way.

But the body of Amanda Hatcher was found exactly where the letter had stated it would be. Completely naked, her body was posed in the fetal position amongst the willows.

Mandy gave the Peak County Sheriff's Department hope, however. Her body had not been tarnished by the water of the Blue River, so there was a chance that the killer's DNA was on her somewhere.

Skin cells were recovered from under Mandy's fingernails. When investigators sent the samples to the lab, they were convinced that the DNA would match someone in the database and they would finally know the identity of the Strangler.

There was no match though. Either the killer was an offender who managed to never have his DNA logged in the system, or the killer had never committed a violent crime before and therefore was unregistered.

The five-digit number next to the Strangler's signature continued to baffle investigators as well. They explored any possibility they could think of. Coordinates of a geographic location. An identification number of some kind, or an enigmatic code that contained the Strangler's true identity. Nothing meaningful came back, and all the investigators were really left with was unmatched DNA, seven victims, and the promise of many more.

When I arrived at Peak County Community College, the campus was even smaller than I had anticipated. There was a main administrative building at the center with single-story academic wings branching off each side.

Students were bustling about the campus. A sign that the spring semester was in full swing. The weather was decent and students were taking advantage of it. One group was throwing a frisbee about, while others were lounging on the grass in the quad. It was as if they had all forgotten about the terror that the Blue River Strangler had inflicted upon them for so long. *Amongst* them, practically. If only those students and professors had known at the time that the man mopping the hallway floors was one of the worst serial killers in American history. It made me wonder if any of them even knew Kevin existed. Before his infamy, of course. After Kevin was arrested, everybody seemed to remember who he was. The creepy janitor who lurked in the shadows of the hallways. The guy who would slip into the convenience store to get his cup of coffee without so much as a word to anyone. The type of guy that everyone knew something just wasn't quite right about him.

Hindsight bias, of course. People tricked themselves into thinking they remembered him because it helped hide the lethal vulnerability they had felt for ten decades. The only thing more terrifying than knowing the bogeyman is amongst you is having no clue which one of you he actually is.

When I entered the main office of the administration building, I didn't know who I was looking for, so I asked the front desk assistant where I could find the facilities manager.

"Is he expecting you?" she asked.

"No," I told her. "I'm working with the prosecutor's office on the Kevin Blackford case."

"Oh," she said, intrigued. "How are you involved?"

"I can't say," I replied.

"I see," she said with disappointment. "His office is down the east wing. I can show you, if you'd like?"

I smiled. "I should be able to find it. Thank you."

Classes must have been in session because the hallways were empty and quiet. The hum of professors' voices came through the gaps in the classroom doors. As I walked, I tried to imagine Kevin pushing a mop through that very hallway. Entering the classrooms after hours to clean chalkboards and empty trash bins. A living ghost of sorts. An invisible monster.

I found the office of the facilities manager in the center of the hallway. The door was cracked open.

"Excuse me?" I said, knocking lightly on the door a few times.

"Yeah?" a voice answered from within.

I poked my head into the office. "Do you know where I can find the facilities manager?"

There was an older man sitting at a small desk. "That'd be me," he said. "Somebody puke somewheres?" He had a plug of tobacco wedged in his cheek and he spat into a plastic cup on his desk.

"Oh no, nothing like that," I said.

"Thank Christ," he said. "What can I do ya for then?"

"Well... I was hoping I could talk to you about something. Some*one*, actually."

"Lemme guess," he said. "Kevin Blackford?"

I nodded.

He leaned back in his chair and gave me the once-over. "You press?" he asked.

"No," I said, shaking my head.

"Cop?"

"No, sir."

He glared at me, then grinned. "I work for a living, so you sure as hell don't gotta call me 'sir'." He sat upright in his chair, adding, "Now if you ain't a cop and you ain't press, why on earth would you want to talk to me about Kevin Blackford?"

"I'm working for the prosecuting team," I said. "Trying to piece some things together before the competency hearing in a few weeks. I'm Dr. Sharon Stevenson."

"I see. Well, Dr. Stevenson, I've already talked to the cops and told them everything I know. Blackford was an average employee. Did what was asked of him, nothing more and nothing less. Never saw him near the Malvar girl, or any student for that matter. Sometimes I wondered if he wasn't mute or retarded, he was so damn quiet. Kinda surprised me they thought he did it considering the Strangler was so damn smart and he's so... stupid."

"What do you mean?" I asked, ignoring his casually offensive manner of speaking.

"For starters, he had the memory of a goddamn chipmunk. Only real complaint I ever had about him as a worker. I'd tell him to go do something, then an hour later when I'd ask him about it, he'd look at me like I was out of my mind. I always had to remind him to do shit three, four times. Got real annoying."

"Why'd you keep him? He worked for you, what? Twelve years? Seems like a long time to keep a mediocre employee around."

"I kinda felt bad for the guy," he said with a shrug. "Not a whole lotta jobs for guys like him in this town, and it wasn't like he didn't try hard. Much rather have a dumbshit who works hard than some lazy smart-ass, if you know what I mean."

"Yeah," I said with a smirk. "I do."

"Plus, if he didn't have this job, he probably would've gotten mixed up with the wrong people. Between the homeless and the drugs, whole lotta ways for a young man to get hisself into trouble. 'Course, lotta good that did... Still can't believe he did them things to all those women."

"Yes, it's a tragedy for sure," I said, briefly considering how easily trouble found Maddie. I repressed the thought as quickly as it entered my mind and added, "Did he ever get confused when you called him by name, or did he ever ask to go by a nickname?"

"Nuh-uh," he answered. "To be honest, I hardly never called him by name even."

"Did he ever mention names of people to you? Family or friends? A girlfriend maybe?"

"Girlfriend? Shit, I didn't think that boy had ever seen a tit before." He chuckled and spat into the plastic cup. "Although he sure as hell proved that wrong too."

"How about friends or family? Anybody he ever talk about?"

"Blackford wasn't much for talking. He showed up, did his work, and left. Best part about him actually. Lot of guys sit around playing grab-ass, but not him. He'd throw earphones on his head and mop for hours on end."

"Did he ever miss shifts or disappear for a few days?" I asked.

"He wouldn't have lasted twelve years if he had."

"How about vacations? Did he ever go anywhere, or take off from work for extended periods of time?"

"Nuh-uh. Far as I know, he never left Park City."

"How about when you first hired him? Remember anything from then?"

"Not really."

"What about recommendations or reference contacts? Anybody vouch for him?"

He snickered. "This wasn't no teaching job. You don't need

references when you're scrubbing toilets and chalkboards. Especially not in Park City."

Something unintelligible came over the man's radio and interrupted us.

"Be there in a sec," he said into the microphone. "Duty calls," he added to me.

"Can I give you my hotel phone number?" I asked. "In case you think of something else?"

"Sure, what the hell," he said, grabbing a rolling mop bucket from the corner of the office. "You can just leave it on the desk."

"Thank you, Mr...?"

"Lennerson," he said as he walked past me through the door. "Wayne Lennerson."

"I appreciate your time," I said.

"You bet," he said over his shoulder, strolling down the hallway toward whatever mess needed to be cleaned up.

I was perplexed by the conversation to say the least. On the one hand, it was suspicious that Wayne hadn't noticed the different identities or his erratic behavior, but at the same time, Kevin's pattern of absent-mindedness was consistent with the temporary bouts of amnesia I had observed. The fact that he was a semi-responsible employee increased my confidence in ruling out other disorders like borderline personality disorder, bipolar disorder, and schizophrenia. But something about his supposed relationship with Brenda Wexler didn't add up. It just seemed odd that a guy who was as much in love as Robbie claimed to be would never mention it to anyone. Even something as simple as, "Pissed my girlfriend off this morning." That was another thing that didn't make a whole lot of sense: how could someone work with a guy for twelve years like Wayne had and not learn a single personal thing about him? I mean, there were people at the Supermax who I only saw a few times a year and I still knew more about them than Wayne knew about Kevin.

Wayne's demeanor made me suspicious too. If I had been in his shoes, I would've been freaked out to discover that the guy I had been working with was potentially responsible for twenty-eight murders. Wayne, however, seemed relatively unfazed by it. I don't imagine that's something you just get over in a few days. If anything, that's the type of experience that takes years to cope with. Maybe even a lifetime.

EIGHTEEN

Georg and I went to the Summit Tavern for dinner that evening. I must admit, being in that restaurant made me a little uncomfortable. Almost as if I was standing in the heart of the Park City Cemetery in front of Tracy Malvar's grave. It didn't help that our waitress wasn't much younger than Tracy when she had been murdered, or Maddie when she disappeared. Every time the waitress came over to our table, I saw their faces superimposed onto hers. It made me sick to my stomach to think of something so heinous happening to someone so young and carefree.

Throughout dinner, I suspected that Georg hadn't come to any definitive conclusions regarding Kevin. He avoided the subject, waiting until after we ate to get into any specifics. Meanwhile, I was chomping at the bit to get him to talk. I told him the little bit that Kevin's boss had said, but that was more or less to fill the void of silence between us.

Only after our waitress had cleared our plates from the table did Georg remove his notebook from his pocket.

"Well," I said. "What do you think?"

"He is fascinating," Georg began, hesitant, "but I can tell

you already that a few hours of observing him isn't going to be enough. Hell, you've been interviewing him... how long now? A week?"

I nodded.

"I'll tell you one thing... If this guy's faking it, he's the best I've ever seen."

"Do you honestly think he's lying?" I asked.

Georg shook his head slowly. "I can't say. Not yet at least."

"Shit."

"Let me tell you what I noticed and maybe you can piece some things together from what you've seen..." He flipped a couple of pages in his notebook. "When I started interviewing him, he responded when I called him 'Kevin'. His demeanor matched what you've described to me. Docile. Compliant. Confused. He wanted to know why I was there and where you were."

"What'd you tell him?"

"That I didn't know who you were. That his attorney had sent me to evaluate him as part of their defense. Basically try to make him feel like I was supposed to be in his corner."

"What'd he say to that?" I asked.

"That he didn't trust me and he didn't want to talk to me."

"I'm not terribly surprised by that. All of his personas appear to be very cautious."

"Right. So I started asking him about you. How he knew you, what he thought of you. Things like that. He said he couldn't remember when exactly he had met you, but that it was sometime recently. He said that you've been kind to him for the most part, although there are times when you get frustrated with him because he doesn't remember things, particularly things revolving around the murders. But when he gets upset, you don't leave him. You protect him when the guards get angry with him. He trusts you."

I tried to read Georg's expression, but his face remained flat and reserved.

"I tried to ask him about the whole transient global amnesia thing," he added, "but he told me that you didn't think he had it. He said you thought he might have what he called 'some identity personality thing'. Although you most recently told him that he didn't have it and that you were going to sign off that he was competent on his evaluation."

"I did say that to the Kevin persona the last time I spoke with him. A feeble attempt to try to bluff him into doing something stupid. Did *he* mention anything about having DID? Anything about having different personalities?"

"That's where it gets strange. I flat out asked him, 'Do *you* think you have this condition Dr. Stevenson mentioned?' Practically opening myself up to his lie, right? Well, he said, 'No'. All he knows about these other personas is what you've told him. Nothing else. Actually, he thinks *you* might be a little crazy..." Georg grinned at this.

"*Me?*" I said, laughing. "Jesus."

"Yeah. He thinks you've made up dissociative identity disorder. Not to try to trick him, but as a way to make him feel better about not remembering anything. To try to explain why these things have happened to him."

"Well, that's certainly a theory, I guess."

"Here's the thing: if he's lying about his condition, he is taking an enormous risk by being as subtle as he is. It means he's been counting on someone to probe the way you have. I just can't imagine someone taking that kind of gamble with his life on the line like it is."

"So what are you saying?" I asked. "You think this is legitimate?"

"Well..." he shrugged. "I don't know. The chance that he is weaving this masterful web of lies is incredibly small. That being said, we can't forget that he toyed with the FBI for the better half of a decade, and the only reason he was caught was because *he* turned himself in. *He* wanted to be captured. That's another thing I can't wrap my head around. Why would he do that?"

"I've been asking myself that same question. Maybe he really is crazy? Or maybe one of the personas recognized what was happening and wanted to finally stop it? I don't know..."

Georg nodded. "That's a possibility... My other thought was: did he just get bored? He said it in his letter to the newspaper, didn't he? *Your incompetence bores me.* Maybe murdering those women and eluding the police stopped being enough. Maybe it isn't murder at all that gives him the thrills he seeks."

"What then?" I asked.

"You remember those *Looney Tunes* cartoons with Wile E. Coyote and the Road Runner, right?"

"Sure..." I said, although I wasn't terribly clear on where he was going with the reference.

"The Road Runner knew exactly what Wile E. Coyote was trying to do. Every time Wile E. Coyote set up a trap, the Road Runner knew about it. Every time. Yet the Road Runner never took a different route to avoid the trap. Why?"

"It's a cartoon," I said, snidely.

"I'm serious," he replied. "Why did the Road Runner go through the trap even though he knew about it?"

"Because it was a silly kid's show?"

He rolled his eyes at me. "No. It was the thrill of the chase. The Road Runner wanted Wile E. Coyote to chase him because he knew he could screw with him and get away with it. The Road Runner wasn't just in control of the situation; he was in total control of Wile E. Coyote himself."

"So what are you saying?" I asked. "You think that Kevin's the Road Runner and I'm Wile E. Coyote?"

"No, that's not what I'm saying. I'm merely speculating here. I think the chances that Kevin is some brilliant mastermind is even less likely than him having dissociative identity disorder."

"I hate it when you're cryptic. Just tell me straight what you're trying to say."

"I'm telling you to be careful. As a colleague and a friend. Make sure *you're* in control of the situation and not him. Because if he *is* screwing with you, you won't be Wile E. Coyote; you'll be the anvil that crashes into the earth."

"I won't let that happen," I said, but on the inside I couldn't help but wonder if Georg wasn't right. Was I letting Kevin lead me by the nose?

"How much time do you have before the prosecuting attorney gets someone else to do the evaluation?" Georg asked.

"Three days."

"I want another day with Kevin," he said. "I'm curious to speak with one of these personas and see how authentic they really are. Maybe then I'll be more certain about a diagnosis."

"At this point, I'm open to anything," I said.

"Good. Has Wendy found anything out yet?"

"Last I checked, no. She's made a bunch of phone calls, but she's waiting on people to dig through files and get back to her."

"Maybe it wouldn't hurt to reach out to those people yourself tomorrow. See if you can speed the process up."

"Yeah, that's a good idea. I was also thinking about talking to Kevin's boss again."

"I thought you said he didn't give you much?"

"He didn't, and that's the part that's nagging me. I mean, how do you work with a guy for twelve years and not learn *anything* about him?"

Georg nodded. "Yeah. You don't think he's complicit somehow, do you?"

"No. Just not being completely honest about what he knows."

Georg thought for a moment and asked, "You think it's

possible he's trying to screw Blackford over? Do what he can to make sure he gets the death penalty?"

"I guess it's possible. Certainly not the first person in this town to want that. Although I don't know what would motivate him beyond that."

"Maybe he's connected to one of the victims somehow?"

"I suppose. The guy was pretty cavalier talking about the murders though. Kevin's involvement too. This is going to sound stupid, but it was almost like he was proud of him or something... I don't know. It could just be that his demeanor rubbed me the wrong way. Kind of a typical small-town hick, if you know what I mean."

Georg glared at me ironically. "We both work at prisons in the middle of nowhere. *Of course* I know what you mean."

NINETEEN

I dropped Georg off at the prison that following morning and headed straight to the community college. My hope was to catch Wayne before students had filled the halls and classes began. I had a feeling our conversation wasn't going to be as cordial as the day prior and I hoped to avoid making a scene.

When I arrived, there were only a handful of cars in the parking lot. I entered the main admissions building behind an older woman who I assumed was a professor. She held the door for me, but I could tell she didn't really see me. One of those polite habits of rural folks.

I wondered if she had taught Tracy Malvar when she was alive. If her murder had a personal impact on the woman in front of me.

In towns as small as Park City, everyone knows everyone. I mean, I've spent the majority of my adult life living in small towns throughout the western half of the country, and *that* is the universal characteristic of them all. A lot of people work together in some capacity. In the case of the towns I've lived in, most work at the prisons. And in a town of only a couple thousand, if one person knows your business, then everyone knows your business.

Thinking of this made me wonder how Kevin was able to fly under the radar the way he did. Was he the type of person whom people recognized and knew by name? Was he someone whom people mocked behind his back for his unusual behavior? Or was he someone so insignificant, so seemingly harmless and bland, that people didn't even bother thinking about him at all? Maybe people just saw right through him.

I skipped the main office and headed straight for Wayne's office down the hallway. His door was cracked open, a small traffic cone propping it steady.

I braced myself for a contentious discussion.

I knocked on the door and said, "Mr. Lennerson?" I poked my head into the office.

"Morning, ma'am," a younger man said to me. He was prepping the rolling mop bucket for the day's work. "Wayne's not here today," he added. "Something I can do for you?"

The young man spoke with a speech impediment, so every word with an "s" or an "r" became a Rubik's Cube for his tongue to solve.

"No," I said warmly, "just an old friend of his. Hoping to catch up over a cup of coffee."

The young man returned to his work, saying, "Yeah, sorry about that. Called me last night and said he wouldn't be able to come in. Asked if I would cover for him."

"That's too bad," I said. "Hopefully he's not sick or anything."

"Yeah..." he said, putting a hose into the bucket and filling the plastic basin with water. "He sounded a little shaken up. Little drunk too, if you ask me." He turned the water off to the hose and glanced at me. "You said you're a friend of his?"

"Yeah."

"Have you spoken to him lately?" he asked.

"No."

"You should. This Blue River Strangler business has got him *real* messed up."

"Did he know one of the victims?" I asked, trying not to sound too nosy.

"Nuh-uh," he said, shaking his head. "Far as I know, at least. But ever since we found out it was Blackford, Wayne's been a goddamn mess. Shit, freaks me out too thinking about it. Somebody doing what he did without any of us knowing about it? Could've been one of *us* next..."

"Yeah, that's..." I paused, unsure what to say so that I didn't expose my real intention for being there, "...terrifying."

"Got that right."

The young man dropped the mop into the rolling bucket and pushed it through the obstacle course of the office.

"Well, sorry that you missed Wayne," he said, scooting past me with the bucket. "Seriously though, you should talk to him... Man needs someone to talk to."

The young man began pushing the bucket and mop down the empty hallway.

"Excuse me," I called down to him. "Hold up a minute..."

He stopped. "What's up?" he asked.

"I apologize for this," I said, "but I was wondering if I could talk to you about Blackford."

The young man looked at me skeptically. "So you're not a friend of Wayne's?"

"Not exactly..." I said. "My name's Dr. Sharon Stevenson. I'm working with the prosecution team on the Blue River Strangler trial."

"I *really* need to get to work, ma'am," he said hesitantly. "I don't know much about Blackford anyways. Only worked with him the last six months or so."

"It won't take long, I promise. I'll even mop with you so I don't get you in trouble."

"I dunno... Like I told the other police, I didn't know nothing about what he did. Honest."

"I know," I said. "I'm not here to talk about that. I just want to talk about what you knew about him as a person. How he acted. How he spoke. Things like that."

The young man's eyes searched the hallway as he thought about it.

"Alright," he said. "Just a few minutes though. There's another mop in the office. Door should still be open."

"Thank you," I said.

I hurried down the hallway, grabbed the mop, and followed him to the other wing of the academic building. The young man told me his name was Patrick Hawkins, but most folks just called him "Hawk".

We got to work and scrubbed the linoleum a few times before I asked, "So you said you worked with Blackford for about six months?"

"Yeah... Worked *near* him really. Dude never talked. Certainly not to me."

"Never?" I said. "Not even about the weather or anything?"

"Nuh-uh. Wayne would tell him what to do and the dude just went off and did it."

"Was he good at his job?"

He shrugged. "Good *enough*. It's not hard to be good at mopping floors and shit, you know? But he wasn't *bad* at his job."

"Was he forgetful?"

"All the time," he said, grinning. "Wayne'd get so pissed at him too. 'How did you forget to replace the shit paper again, dumbass? I just reminded you ten minutes ago.' Between you and me, I think Blackford was retar— handicapped. You know... mentally."

"Yes, I know what you mean," I said. "So that happened a lot? Blackford forgetting things?"

"At least a few times per shift."

"Why do you think Wayne kept him around? I mean, that had to have gotten on Wayne's nerves."

"There's not exactly a line of dudes outside waiting to grab a bucket and scrub a toilet here. But as annoyed as Wayne would get with Blackford, I'm surprised he kept him around too."

"Any idea as to why he did?"

"Wayne always liked him," he said. "Maybe *liked* isn't the right word... Wayne always *looked out* for him. Made sure he was doing okay. Taking care of himself. Shit like that. Things that you wouldn't expect a boss to care about. He sure as hell never asks *me* about them things. Grouchy bastard. To be honest, I think Wayne felt bad for the guy. I think he knew that something wasn't right with Kevin and so he wanted to help him out. Keep an eye on him."

"You mean, like a surrogate father?"

"Yeah, that's it... a surr-o-gate father." He stumbled over the word and looked away from me, embarrassed.

I ignored it though. "What did you notice about Kevin in your interactions with him? What was his demeanor usually like? Energetic? Irritated? Calm?"

"Nuh-uh. Never said a word and just kinda *drifted* through things. Even when Wayne got pissed at him, he hardly even reacted to it. He just nodded his head and did what he was told."

"What about when he was working?" I asked. "Did he ever do anything that struck you as odd?"

"Odd? Sure, I guess. He always had his headset on. Dude loved music. Weird, heavy metal shit, you know?"

"Did he ever talk to himself? Want you to call him a nickname?"

"No... I guess he sang along with his music. Not loud or

nothing. I wasn't next to him when he did it, but from where I was it seemed like he was just humming along."

"What about nicknames?"

"Nuh-uh... There were a lot of times though that he'd ignore me when I called his name. I just figured his music was too loud."

"Did he ever mention anything about family, friends, a girl-friend maybe?"

The young man laughed at this. "A girlfriend? Blackford? Nah. Blackford *never* mentioned nothing about nobody. I wasn't even sure he *liked* girls..." He stopped laughing, thinking about the irony of what he had said. "So I guess that kind of makes sense *now*, right?"

"Yes," I said. "Was he ever confused or disoriented? Like he didn't know where he was?"

"Not that I saw, but again, I didn't spend much time around him. Wayne would probably know. You should talk to him. If anyone knew personal shit about Blackford, it would be Wayne."

"Now that you mention it," I said, "what can you tell me about Wayne? Aside from the way he treated Blackford."

"Dude loves football. Broncos fan, I think. He's been doing *this* job way too damn long. Chews too much. I dunno... pretty regular guy for backwoods Wyoming."

"So you don't think he knew what was going on? With Blackford, I mean?"

"Wayne? Hell no," he said. "He looked out for the guy, but he minded his own business. Probably figured Blackford didn't do a whole lot of anything when he wasn't working." Hawk paused for a moment, then added, "You guys don't think *Wayne* was involved somehow, do you?"

"No, no," I said. "I'm just asking to try to get an idea of who might know something significant or personal about Blackford, that's all."

"Well, good luck with that," he scoffed. "That guy wasn't exactly an open book."

"What about people around town? Anyone know him or talk about him?"

He shook his head no. "I doubt people even knew who the hell Kevin Blackford was until the paper started saying he was the Blue River Strangler. That dude may as well've been a ghost before then."

"Did Blackford ever strike you as an angry guy?"

"No way. He was so chill."

"What about the students here? The girls. Did he ever show interest in any of them?"

"What, like stalking them? Hell no. He wouldn't even *look* at them when they walked by. And let me tell you, there are some good views around here when the weather gets nice." He chuckled at this, then added, "But like I said, I wasn't sure Blackford was even into women in the first place."

We mopped in silence for a short time before Hawk added, "Is it true what the papers say? That his DNA is all over the bodies?"

"Some of them, yes."

"Jesus..." he muttered, dragging the mop over the same spot on the floor as he thought. "It's just crazy. I mean, the dude was weird, but not like *that*, you know?"

"Yeah," I said. "People will surprise you with what they're capable of."

TWENTY

I stopped at a pay phone to find Wayne's address in the phone book and call Wendy to see if she was able to confirm anything that Kevin had told me about his childhood. She didn't answer, though, so I left her a message to call me at my hotel when she could.

When I located Wayne's address, the street name—Squaw Pass Road—seemed oddly familiar to me, but I was too distracted at the time to think much of it. Had I realized that I recognized it from the case file, I probably wouldn't have gone to the house at all.

Squaw Pass Road was a windy gravel road that separated the Park City limits from the Griffith's Peak Wilderness. The road was a five-mile washboard with ruts that would have bottomed out my rental car had I not crawled over them. I couldn't imagine how difficult it would've been to navigate the road in the dead of winter. Even with four-wheel drive it would've been challenging. Squaw Pass Road was remote to say the least. I encountered few driveways along the way, and those I did find were little better than well-worn ruts carving their way through the dense forest. My suspicions about

Wayne only increased the more I realized how isolated his home was.

I ended up missing the driveway for Wayne's property twice because it was so inconspicuous. The only reason I found it was because an old pick-up truck was blocking the road as I was heading back toward town.

I couldn't believe what I saw at first. It seemed like the driver door was ajar and an older man was aiming a hunting rifle through the open window up the road at me.

As soon as reality struck me, I slammed the brakes and brought my rental car to a halt.

"Get out of the car!" the man called to me.

I couldn't move. I *wouldn't* move. Despite knowing that a rifle round could tear through the windshield like tissue paper, I felt less in danger by just staying in the car.

"Get out of the car!" he yelled again.

I refused to move. I contemplated driving at him, swerving around his truck on the shoulder, but there remained a foot of half-frozen snow from the winter drifted on both sides of the road.

The man stepped around the truck door and crept forward with the rifle still aimed at me.

I rolled my window down and yelled the first thing that came to mind:

"I'm just lost, don't shoot!"

He continued to move toward me though. When he was twenty feet away, I recognized the face behind the stock of the rifle.

"Wayne?" I called out. "It's Dr. Stevenson! Remember me?"

"Who?" he called out, continuing to approach.

"Dr. Stevenson! We spoke yesterday! At the college!"

He stopped, but he kept the rifle poised at the windshield.

"What the hell you doing out here?" he asked.

"I came to see you," I said. "Can I step out of the car?"

He squinted at me briefly, then nodded, motioning with the muzzle of the rifle for me to get out.

I stepped out of the car and stumbled. My legs shook with fear, and I raised my hands above my head as if *that* was going to prevent him from putting a bullet into my chest.

"Wayne, lower your rifle," I said. "I just wanted to talk some more."

He kept the rifle aimed at my head. "About what?" he replied.

"Lower the rifle. Please. I only want to talk. That's it."

"'Bout Kevin?" he asked. "So you can get what you need to bury him?"

"No," I said. "I want to *help* him. Please. Lower the rifle."

He eyed me over the stock. Eventually, the muzzle of the rifle drifted downward, but I kept my hands raised anyways.

"How you going to help him?" he asked. He wasn't aiming the rifle at me anymore, but he kept it ready in front of him just in case.

"Can we just talk?" I said. "Please?"

"How the hell'd you know I lived out here anyways?" he asked.

"I looked you up," I said. "In the phone book..."

"Even out here can't get no goddamn privacy," he said. His arms relaxed a bit and he held the rifle more easily. "Hawk called me. Told me I might see you out here."

"I swear to God, I just want to talk. That's all. I think I can help Kevin, but I need your help to do that."

He glared at me. Uncertain.

"What can you do to help him?" he asked. "Ain't you working for that woman prosecutor?"

"I am," I said.

"Then why the hell would you want to help Kevin?"

"Because I don't think he's guilty."

Wayne snickered at this. "Don't bullshit me. The woman thinks it's a slam dunk. Said something like his DNA's on a third of the bodies. How the hell could he be innocent?"

"Not innocent," I said. "Just not guilty. I think there's something wrong with him, Wayne. Something that might explain why he did what he did and why he is the way he is."

Wayne continued to glare at me skeptically for several more moments.

"Alright," he finally said. "Follow me back to the house. Cold as shit out here."

Wayne climbed back into his truck and slammed the door shut.

As his truck rolled onto the rugged driveway, I remained stuck where I was for a second. My heart was racing and my legs were shaking uncontrollably. My better judgment told me to get back into the car and drive back to town, if for no other reason than to tell someone where I was in case something happened to me. But that nagging thought from the previous day echoed in my head; Wayne knew something about Kevin, and whatever he knew could very well be the key to confirming my suspicions about him.

My rental thumped along the driveway to Wayne's house. Icy remnants of snow clawed at the bottom of the car. The last thing I needed was to get stuck out there in the middle of nowhere with a wingnut like Wayne.

I eventually made it to the house, a timber cabin that had seen better days. The type of place that makes you wonder how some people live the way they do.

The inside accommodated a Spartan lifestyle. There was a main space at the front that served as a living room and kitchen. There were two small bedrooms in the rear with an even smaller bathroom set between them. The cabin was furnished as you might imagine it would be. An archaic wood-burning stove was the centerpiece of the main room. A wall of firewood was stacked to the side of it. A few old lawn chairs served as the living room furniture.

"Sorry 'bout the mess," Wayne said when we entered. "Don't hardly have company."

He offered me one of the lawn chairs, and grabbed a six-pack of Coors Light from the fridge for himself. He sat in the other lawn chair and took a long drink of one of the beers before speaking. "I always knew something wasn't right about that boy. What do you think he's got, anyways?"

"I can't say for sure yet, but if I'm right, it'll keep him off death row."

Wayne sipped his beer again, eyeing me over the rim skeptically. "I was wondering what you was snooping around for. Like I told you yesterday, the cops have talked to me a hundred times already, asking the same goddamn questions over and over again."

"So what you told me yesterday is true?" I asked.

"For the most part," he said, chugging half of his beer and belching.

"What do you mean, for the most part?"

Wayne looked at me firmly. "You promise you ain't trying to screw him over? You're serious about something being wrong with him that might help him with all this mess?"

"Yes," I said. "If I'm right about his diagnosis, I can make sure he's admitted to one of the best psychiatric facilities in the country and can get the help he needs."

Wayne scratched his head and sighed. Hesitant.

"Mr. Lennerson," I added, "what do you know about him? What were you not telling me yesterday?"

"As long as I've known Kevin, he's always been a little strange... Quiet. To himself. More so than me even. I mean, I live out here for a reason, you know? But Kevin? He got real anxious being around people. I figured living out here would help him."

"In Park City?" I asked, not sure what he meant by "out here".

"Not just Park City," he said. "I mean out *here*... with me."

"Wait a minute," I said, confused. "Kevin lived with you?"

Wayne nodded, drinking the remnants of his beer.

That was why your address seemed so familiar, I thought. It's the same as the one on Kevin's driver's license.

Wayne must have seen that I was perplexed because he said, "Folks don't really know that he lived out here. Shit, folks didn't really know he existed at all... until *now*, of course. I imagine folks on the other side of the country know who he is by now."

"You must've seen *something*," I muttered, absentmindedly as if my thoughts were being broadcast out of my head.

"Nuh-uh," he answered. "He actually lived in the shack that's a ways back behind the cabin, so I hardly *saw* him if we wasn't at work together. Cops swept the shack anyhow and didn't find nothing. Swept the whole property in fact. Couldn't find a damn thing. I guess they figure he did them things to those women somewheres else."

I remembered the case file mentioning that investigators had searched Kevin's "home" following his arrest, yet they had found no evidence. But I didn't trust that Wayne knew nothing about what had been going on. Even if they didn't share the same house, it still seemed that Wayne would have noticed something out of the ordinary. Kevin keeping odd hours. Unusual noises. Something.

"How did Kevin come to live with you?" I asked Wayne.

"I found out that his mama left him," he said. "Ditched him at some home for kids in Colorado when he was a boy. I didn't find out for years. So when I did finally realize, I came down and got him. Told the government I'd take care of him."

I became even more confused. "Wait... how'd you know his mother?" I asked.

"She's my sister," he said. "*Half*-sister, actually."

"Your sister?" I said, more as a reaction than a confirmation.

"That's right. Goddamn mess she is. Always has been. Shocked she ain't dead yet."

"And you said he was living somewhere in Colorado before?"

"Yeah. Some place for screwed-up kids come from screwed-up parents. Can't remember the name though..."

"The Wadsworth Center?" I asked.

"Yeah, that's it. How'd you guess that?"

"Kevin told me about it once."

"Damn shame they was able to keep that place open the way they treated him and them boys. Whole system is fucked up if you ask me."

"Do you know much about his childhood?" I asked. "When he was at Wadsworth Center, or before that when he was living with his mother?"

Wayne shook his head. "Nah, Kevin ain't never been a talker. Even if he was, I doubt he remembers much. Boy can hardly remember what he ate for breakfast, you know?"

I considered mentioning Kevin's separate personalities to Wayne, but I decided not to just yet.

Instead, I asked, "Does the name Brenda Wexler mean anything to you?"

Wayne scoffed and shook his head. "Sure does," he said. "You know, I thought that boy was full of shit when he told me he had met someone. I wasn't sure what kind of woman would want to be around a guy like him. You know, considering how quiet and slow he is and all. Then I meet her and it made perfect sense."

"How do you mean?" I asked.

"Let's just say she was a few cans short of a six-pack..." He grabbed the pack of Coors Light from the floor and dangled it in the air. He popped another out of the plastic and continued.

"'Course, so was Kevin, so I guess in *that* way they was a good match. To be honest, I was shocked as hell when they said they found her body in the forest somewheres. I figured she had high-tailed it out of town years before, then to find out she was out there the whole time? And he was the one who'd done her in? Crazy..."

This made me consider how Kevin told me that Brenda was his sister, not his girlfriend, and it just further confirmed how detached from reality Kevin actually was. If there was any fragment of his psyche that was remotely sane, it was the Robbie persona.

"How long ago did she leave him?" I asked.

"Maybe fifteen years ago? Maybe longer? Hard to remember that far back. I'd say ask Kevin hisself, but he sure as hell ain't going to remember."

"You don't remember how much time passed between her leaving and her body being found, do you?"

"Shit if I know," he said. "Four or five years at least."

"Did Kevin ever tell you what happened between the two of them? A fight or anything like that?"

"No," he said, shaking his head. "She just up and packed her shit one day and got the hell out of dodge. That's what Kevin told me at least. Never actually said what happened exactly. Just that one day she was there and the next she wasn't."

The way Wayne said this made me think of Maddie's disappearance, and I lost myself in rumination for a moment.

Finally, I asked, "How did Kevin react to that? Was he upset? Angry? Depressed?"

"He was 'bout as torn up as that boy can be 'bout something."

"Really? And he seemed genuine about it?"

"You mean was he faking it or not? Sure didn't seem like he was."

"So bizarre..." I said.

"You're telling me." He paused and took another drink. "Still don't know how the hell he kept everything a secret for as long as he did."

"I keep wondering that too. It just doesn't make sense that he was able to taunt the police the way he did despite being as simple-minded as it appears he is."

"Yeah," he said with a chuckle, "but at the same time, have you *met* our cops here? They ain't going to write no books themselves neither."

"Hmm..." I said, thinking that as true as that may have been, the FBI task force didn't consist of a bunch of half-wits and rednecks. They were men and women who were the best of the best at hunting down guys like Kevin. For him to run circles around them too? *That's* what didn't make any sense.

I spoke with Wayne for a little while longer before heading back toward Park City. My mind raced in a thousand directions on the drive back. My conversation with Wayne certainly left some questions unanswered, but the fact that he corroborated much of what Kevin had told me about his past made me more confident in his diagnosis. His mother's abandonment. Living at the Wadsworth Center. His relationship with Brenda Wexler. They all helped to confirm that Kevin, or the Robbie persona, was being truthful.

At that point, it was just a matter of seeing if Georg had observed similar symptoms during his second interview with Kevin to diagnose him with dissociative identity disorder.

Only when I drove past the Peak County courthouse did I think of Prosecuting Attorney Kim Matthews and what she had demanded of me a few days prior. Do what you need to do to find Blackford competent and sane. I refused to believe that Matthews herself was genuinely of that same mindset. She wasn't some country good ole boy looking to beef up her conviction rate. Hell, conviction wasn't even the crux of the issue; she had everything she needed to put Kevin behind bars for centuries. Young and talented, Matthews would be able to use Kevin's conviction as a major cornerstone to build her career upon. Putting him on death row seemed trivial to her ambitions. Petty even.

The pressure she was feeling from the powers-that-be had to be her motivator for seeking the death penalty as ruthlessly as she was. Well, if that was the case, I thought, then I just might be able to convince her to back off and settle for the conviction alone. Especially if Kevin's condition was as legitimate as I believed it was.

TWENTY-ONE

I stopped at one of the pay phones outside of the courthouse to see if Wendy had tried calling the hotel, but there were no messages. I believed what Wayne had corroborated, but cross-checking it with Wendy's research would fully solidify my decision about Kevin. I tried calling her, but I had to leave her another message. I told her about Wayne and what he had told me. In addition to confirming as much about Kevin's history as she could, I wanted her to see what she could find out about Wayne. Just to be sure of things, I said.

I entered the courthouse afterward and went to Matthews' office, but her assistant said that she was tied up in another meeting.

"I'll wait," I told her.

I waited a half hour or so before the door to her office opened and Matthews escorted out a middle-aged man who looked like he was from Los Angeles.

When Matthews saw me sitting in the narrow waiting area, she acknowledged me with a curt nod.

I heard her tell the man, "Thank you for coming on such short notice, Dr. Kemper."

She returned to me and said, "I wasn't expecting to see you, Dr. Stevenson. You should've called."

"I was in the area," I said. "I need to talk to you immediately. I know you're busy. Just fifteen minutes is all."

She nodded. "My next meeting isn't for another half hour. Come on in."

We went into her office and sat down across the desk from each other.

"What can I do for you?" she asked. I could tell she was trying to be pleasant enough, but she seemed distracted. Anxious even.

"It's about Kevin," I said. "I have a very strong reason to believe that he suffers from dissociative identity disorder."

She snickered. "That sounds as made up as transient global amnesia," she said. "What is dissociative identity disorder anyways?"

"We used to call it multiple personality disorder not that long ago, but the general idea is similar. Basically, a person presents at least two distinct personalities as a means of coping. Usually with a childhood trauma of some kind. So it isn't really that they have separate personalities per se; it's that they create personas as a way to dissociate from whatever has caused them pain in the past."

Matthews nodded slowly. "And how many *personalities* does it appear Blackford has?" she asked.

"Four," I said. "Possibly five."

"Possibly five?" she said. "So let me get this straight. You're telling me that Blackford is essentially the male, murderous version of Sybil? Is that right?" I could tell her tone was becoming sarcastic. Demeaning in fact.

"Yes," I answered.

Matthews started laughing. Not gut-wrenching, tear-inducing laughter. But laughter all the same.

"That's ridiculous," she said.

"I beg your pardon?" I asked.

"With all due respect, that makes absolutely no sense."

I was becoming defensive. Angry even. But I kept my wits about me. "It might not make sense," I said, "but it's the truth."

She shook her head in disbelief. "I refuse to believe that a guy who screwed with the FBI for as long as he did is a complete lunatic. A sociopath? Absolutely. But multiple personality disorder? Come on. You can't be serious."

"I am serious," I said. "As a matter of fact, I've got a colleague at the prison right now confirming it."

"A colleague? Who?"

"His name's Dr. Georg Edmund. He's a correctional psychiatrist in Oklahoma."

She was confused into silence.

"I needed a second opinion I could trust," I added. "Much like you, I couldn't believe that Kevin's condition was legitimate. It's rare to begin with, and given his apparent deceit, I had to be sure he wasn't just twisting me around."

"I can't believe this," she said. "Well... I guess now is as good a time as any to tell you that *I'm* getting a second opinion too."

"What?" I said, taken aback. "From whom?"

"From the gentleman I just met with."

"Who is he?"

"That's none of your concern," she said.

"Yes, it is," I said. "If he's going to be evaluating my patient, then I have a right to know."

"Excuse me?" she said. "*Your* patient? Please don't tell me you're referring to Blackford."

"Yes, I am."

She grinned, rolling her eyes at me. "Wow," she said. "He's got you even more wrapped up than I realized."

"I beg your pardon?"

"He's playing you, and you're letting him."

"I'm not going to let you talk to me like this," I said, rising from my seat. "Do you know how long I've been doing this? Since you were still wearing diapers, my dear. How many murderers have you tried before? Hmm? Better yet, how many *trials* have you been a part of? A couple of drunk-and-disorderlies? One involuntary manslaughter that a pre-law student could have litigated? You sit there and try to tell me that *I'm* being played here. Jesus, you got some nerve. The way I see it, you have two options. Either you take my evaluation or I take it to Kevin's defense attorney and testify against whomever you're going to put on the stand. Regardless, Kevin *is* going to be found legally insane. The only question is which side are *you* going to be on? The side that positions you as nothing more than a bureaucratic puppet, or the side that establishes you as a genuine officer of the court?"

Matthews stared daggers through me as I said all of this. I hoped that I was getting to her somehow though.

Firmly, she said, "For someone who's been doing this as long as you have, you should know by now that *nothing* is that cut and dry. You stand here talking about the ethics of law like a kindergarten teacher telling her students to play nice in the sand box. You have the gall to accuse *me* of being naive? Why, because I'm young and not as experienced? Give me a break. If anybody's being naive, it's you."

"I hope you reconsider before it's too late," I said.

"Are you really willing to put your reputation on the line like that?" she said. "You do realize if you join his defense that my team and I are going to have to discredit you in court. We're going to sift through every single trial you've testified in and every evaluation you've ever conducted. Any blemish in the record is going to be put under the microscope for everyone to see. Are you really prepared for that?"

"You know, for a while there I thought you were different from the rest of them. Lawyers, I mean. I thought you honestly wanted to uphold the integrity of the law and justice system regardless of whatever biases you carried. Clearly I was wrong. Clearly you're like all the others who just want to rack up convictions. I feel sorry for you. How it must feel to be a slave to that."

And with that, I walked out of her office.

I was beyond pissed as I exited the courthouse. I stopped in front of the statue that stood sentry before the entrance. The replica of the "End of the Trail" sculpture with its exhausted, defeated Native American slumped over with his spear hanging in such a way that his silhouette gave the impression that the spear had actually impaled him through his back.

How appropriate, I thought. The perfect sigil for the Wild West justice system I had been tossed into.

I refused to let justice be so grossly perverted, though. I first needed to get to the prison to find out what Georg had discovered that morning so that I could finalize my evaluation. Then I needed to get a hold of Kevin's defense attorney.

As I drove to the prison, I couldn't help but mull over what Matthews had said to me. About her team having to dredge up whatever they could about me to try to discredit my evaluation and testimony. Professionally, there was nothing I could recall that would mar my credibility in court, but I was worried that she would find out about Maddie and try to use her disappearance as leverage. Argue that my judgment was biased somehow.

Frankly, the fact that Kim even mentioned leverage of any kind made me sick to my stomach. I've learned that it's an unfortunate part of the legal game, but I've also learned that threats are not made arbitrarily. They are usually attacks from those who feel vulnerable themselves. It was clear to me that Matthews knew she didn't have much to stand on.

When I arrived at the prison, Georg was waiting out in front of the building for some reason.

"What are you doing out here?" I asked him.

"The goddamn guards yanked me out about fifteen minutes ago. Something about orders from the prosecuting attorney?"

"Great."

"Sharon, what the hell is going on?"

"I just came from her office. She's pulling me off the case."

"What? Why?"

"Because I told her about my evaluation, so now *she's* getting a second opinion."

"You've got to be kidding me. She realized you weren't going to bend, so now she's going to find someone who will? What a bunch of bullshit..."

"Yeah, I know. Were you able to make any progress with Kevin at least?" I asked.

"Not really," he said, shaking his head with frustration. "Maybe if I had more time, but it looks like that's not going to be a possibility anymore. What about you? Did you get anything from his boss?"

"You have no idea," I said.

I told Georg about my initial encounter with Wayne on Squaw Pass Road as well as the information he had provided regarding his connection to Kevin and his past history.

"Jesus..." Georg said afterward. "Not that this probably matters in the grand scheme of things, but how did *he* not realize something was going on?"

"I asked him that very thing. He said Kevin must have been killing the women elsewhere."

"*That* seems suspicious."

"I agree to an extent, but think about past serial killers. Gacy tortured and murdered his victims in his own house. I mean, doesn't it seem odd that the neighbors didn't see or suspect anything? *Smell* anything when they walked by his home? *Hear* something at odd hours of the night? Or Dahmer—the guy killed some of those boys in his grandmother's own house, for Christ's sake. She might've suspected something because she eventually kicked him out, but I doubt she thought he was murdering those guys. Certainly didn't realize he was *dismembering* them down the hallway from her own bedroom. And Kevin's uncle isn't exactly a Rhodes Scholar either. Is it *likely* that he didn't notice anything unusual? Probably not. But is it *possible*? Absolutely."

"Fair point..." He paused for a moment and sighed. "Well, what do we do now?"

"Find Kevin's lawyer," I said. "Tell him what we suspect. Urge him to let us testify on Kevin's behalf at the competency hearing and during the trial for the insanity plea."

"*Us?*" Georg replied, hesitant. "Listen, I had no problem coming up here and giving you a second opinion, but I can't follow you down this rabbit hole."

His response surprised me to say the least.

"What do you mean?" I asked. "You know as well as I do that what Matthews is doing is bullshit."

"That, I agree with. Her not hearing you out and trusting your opinion *is* bullshit..."

"Yeah?" I probed. "Then what's the rabbit hole?"

"This isn't my evaluation. It's yours. *You* have talked to this guy for weeks, not me. *You* know this guy backwards and forwards, not me. I've barely had a day and a half with him. Do I *suspect* something is wrong with him? Absolutely. But am I confident in signing off on an evaluation? No. A diagnosis? Definitely not. And certainly not a diagnosis of one of the most rare and questionable conditions in the book. That I cannot do."

"Evaluate him with me," I said. "Help me confirm this. If we're right, think of what we can do. Think of what we can accomplish. A condition so rare is one thing, but one in a high-profile serial killer like him? Freud would raise himself from the dead for that opportunity."

Georg's expression changed and he glared at me with suspicion.

"What are you talking about?" he said. "'Freud would raise himself from the dead for this'?"

"Jesus," I said, "I'm just trying to make a point."

"Yeah, and you made it loud and clear," he said. "I know you know this already, but I'm going to say it anyway. I value your friendship. I respect you as a professional. I trust your judgment. You're one of the best psychiatrists I know. One of the most *successful* that I know. But the road you're about to go down is a dangerous one."

"And what road might that be?" I asked.

"This road of distinction. This road of... discovery. I can see it in your eyes. You're intrigued by this guy. His psychosis is what you've been seeking your entire career. Not DID specifically, but something like it. And knowing you as well as I do, it has little to do with some bullshit award like the Hofheimer Prize. It's more intrinsic than that. It's that curiosity we all have to dive into the minds of the insane and the diabolical. To understand what drives them to do the disturbing things that they do. The problem is that *your* cravings are insatiable. Granted, that quality has been your greatest asset for the majority of your career. It's what has driven you to sacrifice so much of your personal life for the sake of your career. But at what point does craving become addiction? At what point do you say 'good is good enough'?"

"I don't believe this," I responded. "I have Wendy thinking that I'm being jaded by a convoluted countertransference, and I have you thinking I'm being overly ambitious. Which is it?"

"Don't take it personally," he tried to say. "We're just trying to—"

"Help?" I interjected. "Look out for me? I don't need that from either of you."

"That's not what I meant."

"Then what is it? Christ, you make it sound like I'm obsessed with this guy."

143

"*Are* you?" Georg said, giving me a look of serious doubt.

I shook my head and scoffed, "Of course not."

He said nothing in response; he just continued to eye me with skepticism.

"Come on," I said, filtering the offense that I had taken from his comments. "Work with me on this."

"Not this time," he said with finality. "I want no part of it."

TWENTY-TWO

I dropped Georg off at the airport in Casper early that following day. I hadn't remained angry with him for very long after our argument, though. I knew he was just looking out for me. Trying to keep me out of hot water. He and Wendy both.

I finally spoke with Wendy the previous evening. She was able to confirm that Kevin had indeed lived at the Wadsworth Center for most of his adolescence. But because of privacy laws, she could not confirm if the state had signed custody of Kevin over to Wayne. In fact, Wendy couldn't even confirm if Wayne Lennerson was his actual uncle.

"Please be careful," she said to me at the end of the call.

"You and Georg," I joked. "You're like my guardian angels. I'm *fine*. Really."

"I'm serious," she said. "Don't stick your neck out too far for this guy."

"Yes, Mother," I said, laughing.

"You're a pain. Georg must be sick of you by now."

"He definitely is," I told her.

I knew I had subconscious, deeply personal reasons for why I was obsessed with my work, but neither my intrigue with

Kevin nor my desire to help him was solely rooted in that. As I had said to Georg one of those nights, it was my professional and moral duty to advocate for those who could not advocate for themselves. Nobody fit that description more than Kevin.

After dropping Georg off at the airport, I headed for Wind River in Keystone County where Kevin's public defender, Arlo Braddock, worked.

It probably seems a little ridiculous that a public defender would live in one county while serving a neighboring one, but it's quite common for rural areas to have two, three, sometimes four counties assigned to one public defenders' office. Arlo was one of only three public defenders assigned to Peak County. It's a matter of needs and available resources really. And in the world of public defense, the needs grossly outweigh the available resources.

The problem this creates is that it eats up a significant amount of time for the lawyer to even meet with their clients, no less to prepare an adequate defense. And with three hours separating Kevin from Arlo, I wouldn't have been surprised if they had only met a handful of times up until that point.

Wind River is a forsaken little town in southwestern Wyoming. Smack in the middle of desolate, high plains. Not an ounce of water or vegetation in sight. A startling contrast to Park City or anywhere in Peak County for that matter.

The Wind River Public Defenders' Office was even less impressive. Little more than a couple of used double-wides pushed together.

I had called Arlo earlier to let him know I would be dropping by, but he wasn't in the office when I arrived. The office assistant said he got held up in a meeting with a client in Sweetwater, but she didn't expect he would be too late.

I waited for nearly an hour.

When Arlo rushed into the office, he was out of breath as if he had run all the way from Sweetwater.

"Please tell me she didn't leave," he said to the office assistant.

She pointed over at me.

Arlo was hardly what I expected from southwest Wyoming. I had pictured a stout man with a bushy mustache and dusty cowboy boots. Maybe a plug of chewing tobacco wedged in his cheek for good measure. Arlo could not have been more opposite of that image. Picture the quintessential Anthropology professor at Berkeley. Tall and wiry with a heavy beard and hair standing in every direction as if he'd just been electrocuted. He wore what looked like a second-hand suit that was a few sizes too short accompanied by a neon-green bow tie.

"Geez," he said, coming over to me and extending his hand, "I am *so* sorry to keep you waiting, Dr. Stevenson."

"It's quite alright," I said.

"Can I get you anything? Water? Coffee?" Arlo spoke a mile a minute. Almost to the point where it was hard to distinguish one word from the next.

"No, I'm fine, thank you."

"Let's have a seat in the conference room and you can get me up to speed."

He showed me to a room that was better suited as a utility closet than a conference room, but there was a table with a few chairs to sit in at least.

"Let me just grab Blackford's files from my desk," he said. "I'll be right back."

I soon heard folders falling and their contents spilling out onto the floor. Arlo grumbled something and the assistant told him she would clean it up. He returned with a legal box that had paper spilling out of the top of it like an overflowing recycling bin.

"Here we are," he said, lugging the box onto the table.

I was baffled to say the least. I had imagined that Arlo, like any public defender, was overloaded with work, but his obvious lack of organization was cause for major concern.

"Alright," he added, finally taking a seat with a messy legal pad on the table in front of him. "Where should we begin?"

"Umm..." I said, trying to overcome my own surprise.

"You'll have to excuse the mess," he said, motioning to the file box. "Believe it or not, I *do* have a system. It's not the prettiest, but it works."

"Arlo," I managed to say, "you mind if I ask you how long you've been practicing law?"

"Close to ten years now. All as a public defender."

"I see. And how many accused murderers have you defended?"

"Oh... four or five maybe? Can't hardly keep track, to be honest."

"Any of them high-profile cases like Kevin's?"

"Nope," he said rather casually. "This'll be my first."

"Does that... worry you at all?"

"No, not really. Got to start somewhere, right?" He cracked a less-than-confident grin. To make me or himself feel better, I couldn't really tell.

"I guess..." I said.

"I know you're probably hesitant about me, but if what you said about Blackford is true, then this will hopefully be more straightforward than we thought."

"Straightforward?" I said. "Nothing about this case is going to be straightforward. Nothing about Kevin is straightforward either."

"Yeah, I know. I could hardly get a word out of him when I first met him. All he kept saying was that he didn't remember anything. That's why I threw the transient global amnesia out there. More to buy us some time than anything, but hey, now you're here with something *way more* promising. What was it you think he has again?"

"Dissociative identity disorder."

"*That's* right. The multiple personality thing."

"Correct..."

"Good stuff," he said, scribbling the name of the disorder onto his notepad. "And you said you'd be willing to present your evaluation in court?"

"I *did*... but..."

"But what?" Arlo looked at me expectantly, his body fidgeting with unease.

"I've got to be honest with you, you're not exactly instilling confidence in me, if you know what I mean."

"I know I'm a little disorganized," he said, "but I *do* have a system. I promise."

"What exactly was your defense strategy?" I asked. "Before I called you and told you about his condition?"

"Well..." His face contorted with embarrassment. "I hadn't actually gotten that far. You see, my client in Sweetwater—"

"Hold on," I interjected. "Is your client in Sweetwater charged with twenty-eight counts of first-degree murder and facing the death penalty? This man's *life* is practically in your hands and you haven't gotten around to figuring out how you're going to defend him yet? How is that possible, Arlo? How?"

For the first time in our interaction, Arlo didn't have an immediate response. He just stared at me. Speechless.

"You're right..." he finally said. "I haven't come up with a strategy because I have no idea how I can actually defend him. I mean, the evidence so clearly implicates him. The transient global amnesia was a Hail Mary that I pulled out of my ass because it was the only thing I could think of. An insanity defense. Put the ball in the prosecuting attorney's court and force her to disprove it. But look what happened as a result... *You* evaluated him. *You* were able to pinpoint what I could only speculate. *Now*, we have a defense strategy..."

As I looked at him, I felt terrible about belittling him the way I did. I mean, it was obvious he was in way over his head, and probably by design, I imagined. The higher authority that was lighting the fire under Kim Matthews' chair was likely the same higher authority responsible for assigning Arlo Braddock to Kevin's case. What better way to guarantee that Kevin got the death penalty than to assign him an inexperienced and incompetent public defender? It made me pity Kevin and it made me pity Arlo. Most of all, though, it made me hate the corrupt system that had brought them together.

"The problem..." added Arlo, "is that Kevin can't afford to pay a forensic psychiatrist to evaluate him. Especially not one with a reputation like yours."

"Don't worry about that," I said. "I'm doing this pro bono."

"Are you sure?" he asked. "Lord knows we could use your help, but I feel like I can't ask you to do that."

"You don't have to ask," I said.

"Don't take this as me being ungrateful..." he said, "but *why* would you do that? As far as I can tell, you have nothing to gain from this."

"Exactly," I said. "That makes me unbiased and difficult for the prosecution to discredit."

TWENTY-THREE

I called my boss to let him know that I would be staying in Wyoming for a while longer. He wasn't happy, to say the least.

"What about your duties here?" he asked.

"I can't come back yet," I said. "This case is far beyond what I imagined it would be."

"What do you mean?"

"You know I can't tell you that. Just trust me. All I can tell you is that I need more time to evaluate this guy before the competency hearing."

"Fine," he said. "I'll give you until the competency hearing. After that, I need you back here."

"Sure," I said, ignoring the fact that I would probably need to stay in Wyoming long after the competency hearing. I figured I would cross that bridge when I reached it.

I had approximately two weeks to finalize my diagnosis of Kevin and to prepare my evaluation for the competency hearing. In all likelihood, the jury was going to deem him competent because his condition didn't really prohibit his ability to understand the charges against him. He didn't remember committing the acts, but that really wasn't relevant because competency strictly referred to his present understanding of the charges and proceedings.

Where the diagnosis was going to be relevant was at the onset of the trial itself when Arlo submitted Kevin's insanity plea. Kevin would essentially admit guilt to all charges, but because of his mental illness, he was incapable of understanding the wrongfulness of his actions. This, of course, all depended on whether or not the jury believed my evaluation and testimony in the first place.

Up until that point, only six people had been given the death penalty in Wyoming over the last thirty years. None of them had committed crimes as heinous as Kevin allegedly had, so it was a toss-up as to how a jury would sentence him. Based on the attitudes of Kim Matthews and the citizens of Park City alone though, the death sentence seemed likely.

Arlo and Matthews agreed that her psychiatrist would get the mornings and I would get the afternoons to evaluate Kevin. Given that it had been several days since I last spoke to Kevin, I wasn't sure what mental state he was going to be in when I arrived at the prison.

"He's been a mess," the guard told me as he took me back to Kevin's cell because he refused to come out.

"Has he been saying anything?" I asked.

"Just that he wants to see you."

"Does anything prompt him or set him off?"

"Nothing in particular. I will say, he hates that other guy that Matthews keeps sending."

"Dr. Kemper?" I asked.

"I think so," the guard said. "Speaking of which, what's the deal with that anyways? I thought *you* were working for her."

"I can't really get into that," I said.

"I heard you're working for his defense now?" he asked, eyeing me eagerly.

"Again," I said, "I can't really get into that."

"Well, I really hope you're not working with him," he said, leading me back to the holding area. "Hate to see you get caught up with that sick bastard."

I nodded, ignoring the comment.

When I reached Kevin's cell, Kevin was sitting on the floor with his back resting against the edge of the bed. Motionless and staring at the opposite wall. "How's it going, Kevin?" I asked.

He didn't respond.

"Kevin?"

No response again.

"Robbie?" I added, thinking another persona had taken over for the time being.

"Don't call me that," he grumbled, his eyes still fixed on the wall.

"What do you want me to call you then?"

"I don't want you calling me anything," he said. "Just go away."

"Why?" I asked. "Didn't Arlo tell you that I'm going to be working more with you?"

"I don't care," he said. "Just go away."

I took a seat on the folding chair. "You know I can't do that. If I'm going to help you, you got to talk to me."

"I don't need help."

"No?"

He shook his head.

"Then why are you in this situation if you don't need help?" I asked.

"Maybe I *want* to be here."

"You want to be in prison?" I asked, wondering where he was going with that.

He finally turned his head and glowered at me. "You know what I mean," he said.

"I don't actually. What do you mean you *want* to be here?"

"That other doctor seems to think I do."

"What other doctor?" I said. "The one who met with you earlier today? Dr. Kemper?"

"Yeah. He said that because I turned myself in that I must want to be here. What's he even talking about, me turning myself in?"

"He's referring to the last letter that was sent to the newspaper. The package with the cup and your driver's license, which led the police right to you."

"Yeah, well, I don't remember that..." he said, shaking his head slowly.

"I know you don't," I said. "Why don't we talk about something else?"

Kevin only shrugged in response.

"The guard told me you don't like Dr. Kemper very much," I added.

"No," he said. "Guy's an asshole."

"What do you mean?"

"I dunno..." he mumbled.

"Sure you do. You don't just call someone an asshole for no reason, do you?"

"No. It's just hard to explain, is all."

"I understand," I said. "Why don't you try to, at least?"

"Doc, I don't want to," he said with more finality.

"Alright," I said. "Then why don't you tell me about Wayne? How come you didn't mention him before?"

He shrugged. "You never asked."

"It seems like your uncle is somebody you would've mentioned. Especially to me."

"Yeah, I guess. I dunno."

"Well, do you like your uncle?"

"Sure."

"How long have you lived with him?"

"As long as I can remember," he said.

"How long would you say that is? Five years? Ten years?"

"I honestly dunno..."

"Well," I added, "how was it working for him?"

"Fine, I guess."

"Just fine?"

"Yeah."

"Why just fine?"

"I dunno... he'd yell at me sometimes."

"Because you couldn't remember things he asked you to do?" I asked.

"Sometimes..."

"What do you mean sometimes? Like sometimes he would yell at you and sometimes not?"

"No."

"What then?"

He didn't respond.

"Can you please answer my question?" I added.

"What question?" he said, his tone becoming firmer.

"The question I just asked you."

"I don't know what the hell you're talking about." He paused and glared at me. A look I hadn't seen from him before. "What the fuck do you want anyways?"

"Excuse me?" I said, stunned by the response.

"No, *Doc*, I won't excuse you," he said, rising from the floor and approaching the bars of the cell.

I looked at him in confusion. "Kevin," I said, "what in the world are you talking about?"

He leaned against the bars and grinned. His face reminded me of Jack Nicholson's poking through the busted bathroom door in *The Shining*.

"Oh, I get it," he said, his tone livelier. "It's *Kevin* you're wanting to speak to, is it? I'm sorry to inform you that Kevin's not here right now."

He stared intently at me, and for the first time since working with him, made me extremely uncomfortable.

"Then who *am* I talking to?" I asked. "Russell? Robbie?"

"No, no, no, Doc..." he said, shaking his head slowly back and forth. "Think about it... *Who. Am. I?*" He eyed me fiercely, his pupils narrowing to minute pinpricks.

"I really don't know," I said. "We've never met, so how would I know?"

But I did know. At least, I had an idea of who it might be.

"We *have* met," he said, "in a... manner of speaking of course."

"I don't understand," I said.

"I've *always* been here," he said. "Waiting. Watching. I can see *you*, but you can't see *me*. I could probably touch you and you wouldn't even feel me." He reached his hand out through the bars slowly, holding it in the air between us when he couldn't reach any further. "Go ahead," he added. "Try it."

"I'll pass," I said, not shrinking away from him but certainly not moving near him either. "Why won't you tell me your name? You had no problem telling the papers what your name was, right? Why so cryptic now?"

Kevin pulled his hand back through the bars. Grinning.

"I knew you were smarter than those other dumbshits," he said. "And do you know why, Doc?"

"No," I said. "Please enlighten me."

"You *listen*," he said. 'You *really* listen. Those other jerk-offs just talk. They love the sound of their own voices, so I just oblige them. Let them ramble while I, Kevin really, nod my head to make them think I'm there. Even that doctor *you* sent. Dr. Edmund? Yeah, I met him too. *Watched* him really. Nobody actually meets *me*. If only they shut their mouths for three seconds, they might hear what they want to hear, but they just can't do that, can they? But *you* can. That's why *you* are still here and *they* are not. That's why *you* are going to get what you want, and *they* will not."

I leaned back in my chair, trying to make sense of what was happening. "And what is it that I want?" I replied.

"*Me*," he said, standing tall and spreading his arms out. "You don't want those other pussies and morons. Kevin. Jackie. Russell. You want *me*."

"Why would I even care about you?" I asked, intentionally trying to challenge him. "What have you done that would be meaningful in any way to me?"

He grinned again. "You know," he said.

"Nope. I don't."

Kevin snickered.

"What's so funny?" I asked. "*You* got caught, remember? *You* are on trial for first-degree murder."

"Twenty-eight murders," he corrected, "but who's really counting? One or twenty-eight, it's all the same to that bitch prosecutor, isn't it? And *I* am not on trial. *Kevin* is."

"You *are* Kevin," I said.

He scoffed at this. "No. *I* am not Kevin. Kevin doesn't even know I exist. Kevin is a vacuous non-entity. A puppet really. A blundering, simple-minded puppet. But he makes for a wonderful smoke screen, don't you think? My beautifully ignorant scapegoat."

"What do you mean, your scapegoat?" I asked.

"Now, you're just being dense on purpose, Doc. I know you're smarter than that."

"Am I?"

"Of course," he said. "After all, you found me."

"So *you* killed all of those women, Edward?"

"Technically?" he said, making a shrugging motion with his shoulders and hands, "No. Kevin killed them. That is to say, *his* hands broke their necks. *His* arms carried them into the woods and left them to rot. I was just... borrowing the car. Taking it for a joy ride, you could say." He took a seat on the edge of the bed, never breaking his gaze from me. "That's the beauty of our justice system, isn't it? Someone commits a crime and someone else gets fucked for it. Especially now with DNA and forensic science. You'd think it would be harder to frame someone, but it's actually easier. All it takes is a single hair or a drop of saliva and you've got them. A little trail of breadcrumbs that leads investigators where you want them to go. And the beauty of it is that I didn't have to worry about covering my own tracks because I do not even exist. At least, not in the sense that people can see. I share an existence with that mindless fool, so any physical trace of me is a trace of him. We're like Siamese twins, he and I."

"Then why stop yourself?" I asked. "Why allow yourself to be caught?"

"What did my package say, Doc?"

"Your incompetence bores me," I recited.

He nodded, grinning.

"I don't buy that," I said. "I think that's what you want everybody to think, but I don't believe that's really why you did it."

"Well, it's the truth," he said. "It got to the point where it was like fishing with dynamite. Sure, it's fun to see all those fish rise to the surface, but after a while it stops being enough. You need more to *really* get your dick hard, you know? So I upped the ante."

"With your life?"

"Yes. *His* life, actually. But I guess it's all the same to you people, isn't it?"

"So then, what's next in this master plan of yours?" I asked. "He goes on trial and pleads insanity? What do *you* get out of that? Even if the jury believes that, you still get locked up for the rest of your life. It makes no difference whether that's in a cement cage or a padded room."

He grinned. "So narrow-minded, Doc... You are not going to let that happen."

"What the hell are you talking about?"

His eyes narrowed as he stared at me.

"Edward?" I probed. "What are you talking about?"

"Huh?" he said.

"Edward?"

His brow furrowed and he looked at me quizzically. "*Edward*?" he said. "Why are you calling me that?"

"Kevin?"

"Yeah..." he answered, baffled once again. "What is going on?"

I shook my head with disbelief, saying, "You wouldn't believe me if I told you. I'm not even sure *I* believe it."

TWENTY-FOUR

"Are you telling me that he remembers committing these crimes?" Arlo asked me when I called him from my hotel room later that evening and told him what had happened at the prison earlier.

"In a way?" I answered. "Possibly."

"What do you mean *in a way*? This is the most bizarre thing I've ever heard of. And let me tell you. In *this* job, I've heard just about every bizarre thing you can imagine."

"I believe it's part of his condition," I said. "The dissociation. Anything that happens to him that he finds traumatic or troubling becomes compartmentalized into one of these alternate personas that he's created. It's sort of his way of cleaning up and organizing all this shit that's floating around in his memory. He can't consciously deal with it, so he dissociates himself from it and hides it behind a fictional identity so that he never has to actually acknowledge it or confront it."

"You mean like hoarders tucking shit away in their basements and attics?"

"Kind of, yeah. He doesn't know what to do with all of this mental garbage, so he hides it and pretends it isn't there."

"Meanwhile it's festering away?" Arlo added. "Making the whole place stink to high hell?"

"Exactly."

"So bizarre..." he said. "When do you think this even occurred?"

"Your guess is as good as mine," I said. "It could've started when he was a child, honestly. Almost the way kids create imaginary friends, except in Kevin's case, the imaginary friends took on a life of their own and became so dominant that he doesn't know which ones are real and which ones are imaginary."

"So what of this Edward persona? You said you've never talked to this one before?"

"No, never. The Russell persona mentioned Eddie once, but that's all. I imagine Kevin subconsciously tries to bury the Edward persona the deepest into his psyche because it's where he's compartmentalized his violent tendencies."

"Goddamn..." Arlo breathed. "Have you ever seen anything like this before?"

"Never," I said. "I've seen some pretty extreme cases of schizophrenia and bipolar disorder, but nothing like what I've seen with Kevin. He is a rarity, to say the least."

Arlo sighed and silence fell over the phone for a moment.

"Where do we even go from here?" he finally asked.

"If anything, this only confirms Kevin's defense that much more. I mean, I had my doubts for a while there, but now? It'll be difficult for Matthews' psychiatrist to disprove it."

"Don't forget where we are. This state loves its retributive justice."

"Yeah, well, thank God you and I stumbled onto this case. I'm not saying it will be easy, but at least he has a better chance than he did a few weeks ago."

"I hope so," he said, although he sounded unsure. "Maybe," he added, "I could talk to Matthews and see if we can work out a plea deal. Get the death penalty off the table if nothing else. You know, try to leverage her with the diagnosis?"

"And send him to Wyoming State Pen or some other maximum-security prison? He'll end up dead in no time. Bludgeoned to death like Dahmer. Or worse. You wouldn't believe what goes on in some of those institutions. And despite the fact that Kevin has done some heinous things, his core personality is a fragile simpleton. He won't last six months in one of those places."

"What if I can get her to agree to put him into a maximum-security psychiatric facility? He'll end up in one if the insanity plea goes through anyway, so why not see if we can skip the trial outright?"

I scoffed as I was losing my patience. "This is a woman who a week ago instructed me to basically forge my evaluation to keep the death penalty in play. Do you honestly think she's going to agree to put him into a psych facility for the rest of his life?"

"No, but it's worth trying, isn't it? I mean, what do we have to lose?"

"Competitive advantage. Revealing every aspect of Kevin's diagnosis to her is only going to give her and her psychiatrist more time to fabricate rebuttals and strengthen their own strategy. Right now, competitive advantage is about the only thing we've got."

"I dunno..." he said, hesitant. "I hate the idea of leaving it up to a jury to decide. That's a huge leap of faith to rely on the decision-making power of twelve people who know him only as the Blue River Strangler. They aren't going to care that he's mentally ill. All they're going to remember is that he murdered twenty-eight women in the most intimate, barbaric way. Period. The media has been a circus since he was taken into custody. His face has been on every news network every single night practically. I don't care what kind of spin we try to put on it; *that* is all a jury is going to remember. Mentally ill or not."

"Then it's our job to make them change that perception of him," I said abruptly. "Show them that his psychotic mind has essentially hijacked his body and that he cannot *legally* be held responsible."

"And how do you suggest we do that exactly? Put *him* on the stand and hope this Edward persona appears in the middle of cross-examination? You've had to chisel away at him every day for weeks just to get to where you've gotten with him. I'm telling you, if we can just come to a reasonable agreement with Matthews—"

"Will you stop thinking like a personal injury lawyer already? This isn't some bullshit insurance claim that can be settled outside of court. What's with you? Are you that terrified of being a trial lawyer?"

"Don't insult me," he retorted, his tone becoming more assertive than I had ever heard from him. "I mean, disagree with me if you want, but don't insult me. You wanna know how many active cases I've got going right now? Settling outside of court is one of the only ways I can stay sane while doing the most good for my clients as a whole. Could I do better if I litigated the shit out of some of my cases? Absolutely. But time is a luxury I don't have."

"I'm sorry," I said. "I'm just frustrated by the situation more than anything."

"I understand. Trust me, I am too."

"You know what I think you should do?" I said. "See if you can scrounge up some people who would be willing to testify to Kevin's bizarre behavior or confirm the presence of these personas. Start with the uncle, Wayne. I still have a feeling he knows more about Kevin than he's letting on. Call him, though. Or catch him at the community college. Don't go out to the house unannounced. The guy's a little..."

163

"Off?" said Arlo.

"That's putting it nicely," I said. "Also see if we can get a background on him. I had a friend of mine trying to look into him, but she won't be able to get as far as the state defense office will be able to. See if you can confirm that Wayne became his legal guardian or anything. Maybe throw Brenda Wexler's name in there too."

"I thought you confirmed everything about her?"

"Kind of, but I'm still wondering what happened between her and Kevin. She's not as big of a concern in my opinion as Wayne is, but learning more about where she was from or who knew her might help me figure out what happened. I'm convinced she was his first victim and I doubt he killed her for no reason. If we can figure out what that was, the better I can understand every side of him. In the meantime, I'm going to continue to evaluate Kevin and see if I can get as clear of a picture as possible about his condition. I need as much detail as I can get if we're going to convince a jury he has DID. I might lean on my buddy, Georg, again to stand as an expert witness when the trial starts. The more credibility we can have behind the diagnosis, the better."

"Got it," he said before hanging up the phone.

After my conversation with Arlo, I made notes of everything from my encounter with Kevin that afternoon. Speaking to the Edward persona made me feel like I was getting a grasp of what made up Kevin's psyche, at last. I had finally accessed seemingly everything I needed in order to understand him; it was just a matter of diving into each of his past and present selves to piece the entire riddle together.

A case such as his intrigued me beyond description. The complexity of the psyche in general is miraculous when you think about it. Especially in the context of the anatomy and physiology of the human brain. At its most basic level, the brain really is nothing more than single neurons connecting and firing electrical impulses amongst each other to coordinate the release and uptake of just a handful of neurotransmitters. These, in turn, control every function of a human being from something as simple as making the heart pump blood to something as inexplicable as formulating abstract thought. Eighty-six billion cells coming together to form a nanoscopic rat's nest that is constantly rewiring and adapting itself.

The perfect machine when it runs properly. And in Kevin's case, the most lethal machine when it runs amuck.

That's the beauty of psychiatry, in my opinion; it's the perfect combination of psychology and neurology. The abstract fused with the measurable and observable. Yet, even so, there is so much of the abstract that the measurable and observable cannot explain. Sure, the ventricles of a schizophrenic brain are larger than those of an unaffected brain, but these things don't *explain* why schizophrenics see what they see, hear what they hear, and feel what they feel. And what good does that information do us anyway? You can't just shrink the ventricles and cure the condition. All you really can do at a neurological level is intervene with psychoactive drugs.

Band-Aids.

Masquerades.

We're not *fixing* the problem; we're merely *hiding* it.

But that's the best we can do, I suppose.

I thought of Kevin's condition. We couldn't just slide him into an MRI machine and snap a photo of his diagnosis. His brain, in all likelihood, didn't look that different from anyone else's. But somewhere in that nanoscopic rat's nest of his, connections between neurons were formed that were never meant to be formed. Or maybe the neurons themselves went haywire.

Tiny insurgents whose warfare could take the lives of twenty-eight young women. Whose work could terrorize a community for a decade. Whose malice ultimately destroyed its host.

Yet they themselves were undetectable.

For all intents and purposes, Kevin Blackford was their Trojan horse.

TWENTY-FIVE

Three days passed before I heard from Arlo again. I wasn't terribly concerned because I figured he was busy tracking down Wayne and preparing for the competency hearing. I myself was interviewing Kevin as much as I could, although making little progress in the process. I spoke to Robbie several times, who was unhelpful in addressing the questions I wanted answered. Namely, the matter of Wayne's involvement. But any time I tried to probe Kevin about his relationship with his uncle, he or whatever given persona I spoke with provided nothing.

Kevin himself was becoming more withdrawn. The dejected, confused nature I had encountered when I first met him was only becoming magnified, and I worried that he was on the verge of slipping into a severely depressed state.

That's when Arlo finally called me.

"Have you found anything on the uncle yet?" I asked, hoping he had made better progress than I had with Kevin.

"Nothing so far," he said.

"Were you able to speak to him directly at least?"

"No," he said. "He won't return my calls and the few times I dropped into the community college he wasn't there. What about you? You get any further with Kevin?"

"No," I said. "The personas are so hit or miss; I never know which one I'm going to get. I wish I could just call upon the ones I wanted to speak to, but his condition doesn't work that way."

"Yeah, I know..." His tone wasn't fiery and clipped the way it usually was. He was hesitant.

"You alright?" I asked.

"Yeah. Just tired is all."

I could tell he wasn't alright though.

"We'll chisel away at this," I reassured him. "It's going to take time, but we'll get there."

"Mmm..." he said, trailing off. After a few moments, he asked, "Do you trust that I'm working in Kevin's best interest?"

"Of course I do," I said, the question catching me a little by surprise. "You're about the only other one who actually believes he's mentally ill."

"Yeah, but do you trust my judgment? You know, to act on his behalf and do what I feel like is legally best for him?"

"Sure," I said, pausing as I wondered why he was even bringing this up. "I feel like there's something you're wanting to say to me. Don't build up the suspense. Just tell me."

"Fine," he said with a sigh. "I met with Kim Matthews today."

I was surprised, particularly considering our conversation a few days prior.

"At her request or your own?" I asked.

"Mine," he said. "I know you told me not to, but I wanted to discuss a potential plea deal."

"Jesus. What did I tell you?"

"I know, I know," he said. "Just hear me out, alright? Hear me out." I could hear him rifling through papers, and I could only imagine the disarray that his desk was in. "Okay, so I told her about your findings and his diagnosis. I didn't give her any specifics though. Just that you were certain about his condition. I told her Kevin would be willing to plead guilty to all charges if she took the death penalty off the table and if she could get him into a psychiatric facility instead of Wyoming State Penitentiary."

"And?" I said, annoyed that he had done the very thing I had told him not to do.

"Well, she shot it down. She said her psychiatrist hasn't found any evidence of mental illness. Certainly not dissociative identity disorder."

"That figures," I said. "Fine then. We go to trial and put my evaluation up against his. Let a jury decide who's more credible."

Arlo hesitated. That's when I knew he had done more than just talk to Kim Matthews.

"They've tested his IQ," he added ominously.

"So what? So have I," I said. "It's come back in the mid-seventies every time. He's right on the edge of being intellectually disabled. That only *proves* our case more."

"Not according to Matthews' psychiatrist," he replied. "Supposedly her guy tested Kevin at one twenty two."

"*One twenty two?*" I said, stunned. "Are you kidding me?"

"No."

"That can't be right."

"I have a copy of the test right in front of me. One twenty two. Superior intelligence."

"Which test did he use?"

"The Wechsler."

"There's got to be a mistake," I retorted. "He scored 76 when I gave him the Wechsler a few weeks ago."

"I agree that the man you and I have gotten to know does not appear to be that intelligent. Certainly not above average or superior intelligence. But..." He hesitated.

"But what?" I said.

"The test isn't going to lie, Sharon. Not a score that high. I suppose it could just be luck or a coincidence, but—"

"I gave him the Wechsler *and* the Stanford-Binet, and I had to practically read the questions to him. The guy has the reading ability and the vocabulary of a fifth-grader."

"Does he?" asked Arlo. "Or is that what he *wants* us to think?"

I didn't say anything for a moment, considering what Arlo was implying. "What are you getting at?" I said. "You think he's lying to us?"

Arlo didn't respond and a dull white noise filled the silence over the telephone.

"Matthews' psychiatrist must've coached Kevin through the test," I added. "Told him the answers or something. Hell, he might've taken the test for him for all we know."

"Really?" asked Arlo skeptically. "With all due respect, do you realize how far-fetched that sounds?"

"More far-fetched than the two of us being blatantly manipulated by a guy who can't remember what he ate for breakfast? Give me a break. If anyone's trying to play us, it's Matthews and this shrink she's got colluding with her."

"I don't know..."

"What do you mean, you don't know? You're not telling me you believe them, are you? What happened to all that crap about having Kevin's best interest in mind?"

"I *do* have his best interest in mind," he said.

"Then why are you trying to screw him over?"

"I'm not trying to screw him over, Sharon; I'm trying to keep him off death row. And honestly, right now, our defense is nothing but your opinion against that of Matthews' psychiatrist. Couple that with these grossly conflicting IQ tests? Who knows how a jury's going to rule."

I deflected Arlo's concerns, adding, "I say we take our chances."

Arlo hesitated.

"I can't do that," he finally said. "It's too much of a risk. I have to do what I feel is best for my client."

"What are you saying?" I replied, despite having a good idea of what he meant.

Arlo sighed. "I already made the deal. Just got off the phone with Matthews as a matter of fact. It's done."

"What do you mean, it's done?" I said, a void inflating in my gut. "What deal?"

"The plea bargain," he said. "A full confession in exchange for a life sentence instead of the death penalty."

"What? You can't do that without his consent."

"He already agreed. I spoke with him earlier today."

"Bullshit. He never would have agreed to that."

"Well, he did," he said.

"Does he even understand what that all means for him?" I countered.

"As a matter of fact, he seemed very pleased about it. Almost as if that's what he's been wanting all along."

"Goddammit, I..." But I stopped, speechless with frustration.

"With all due respect, Sharon, this wasn't either of our calls to make in the first place. It was *his*. I simply put the opportunity in front of him, but it was ultimately his decision to make."

"Which persona were you speaking to?" I said. "The psychopath, Edward?"

"No," he said. "It was Kevin alright. And he was... *relieved*. If that can even be a way to describe it. He actually smiled. I don't think I've *ever* seen him smile."

"Son of a bitch..." I breathed, still angered. "So what's going to happen to him then?"

"He pleads guilty to all charges at the plea hearing next

week and the judge sentences him to life at Wyoming State Penitentiary. Then it's done. Case closed."

I can't explain exactly why I was so frustrated by the decision. It's something I've had many years to think about and I've never come to any solid conclusion. Initially, I thought it was because I believed the justice system had taken advantage of him, that it had done nothing to protect someone like him who, given his condition, legally should not have been deemed culpable for his crimes.

But then I wondered if what I had perceived as a perversion of justice wasn't simply me rationalizing my own frustrations about the wasted time and energy I had spent fighting for him when it was all for naught. Along with that was Kevin's IQ score. The one that Matthews' psychiatrist had gotten out of him. One twenty two. That type of score placed him in the superior category. It's impossible for a man with below average intelligence to manipulate the test to get a higher score, but it *is* possible for a man with superior intelligence to get a below average score.

So then the question in my mind became: was Kevin actually that intelligent, and if so, why intentionally score poorly on the tests I had given him earlier?

As infuriating as it was, the only logical conclusion I could draw was that, just as Arlo had said, Kevin *wanted* us to think he was a moron when in fact he wasn't. He *wanted* us to believe he wasn't culpable when in fact he probably was. Maybe he even *wanted* us to believe he was mentally ill when in fact he really wasn't.

I was starting to wonder if I had been wrong the whole time. Had I allowed myself to be played by a brilliant sociopath?

TWENTY-SIX

I've had some pretty terrible nights of sleep throughout my career, but that night was one of the worst ever.

At first, I was angry at Arlo for making the deal when I told him not to. I felt like he was terrified to set foot in the courtroom and defend a man who had done the horrific things that Kevin did. I thought Arlo was being an incompetent public defender, taking the easiest road for himself even if it wasn't in the best interest of his client.

But as I tried to fall asleep, I wondered if Kevin had been playing us—playing *me*—the entire time just to get the death penalty off the table. It seemed impossible that he could have faked a rare condition that he appeared to know nothing about, but the more I thought about it, the more I wondered if it wasn't true. I didn't want to admit it though, to admit that I had allowed him to get into my head and manipulate me.

I figured with the plea bargain settled that Matthews' psychiatrist would no longer be evaluating Kevin, so I went over to the prison first thing the following morning. Even though it was probably going to get me nowhere, I needed to confront him about the IQ tests and the plea bargain. I don't know what I was hoping for exactly. No scenario was good. If the IQ scores were legitimate and he did in fact have superior intelligence, then I had allowed myself to become his pawn. If his condition was real, then an insane and vulnerable man was going to be thrown into the abyss that is the general population of a state penitentiary. For the latter, I figured he had a few months before someone beat him to death in the shower.

These thoughts became a dissipating fog, though, as I waited in the interview room. Before the guard opened the door and escorted Kevin into the room, Kevin was doing something I'd never heard him do before.

Whistling.

Kevin was whistling what sounded like the jingle from the old Oscar Mayer Wiener commercials.

He was smiling too. A broad, shit-eating grin that seemingly told me everything I needed to know about what he had done to me over the last few weeks.

Despite the anger that boiled within me, I remained calm on the outside. Even when he sat in the chair across from me and his pinprick eyes, shining victoriously, locked with mine, I remained calm.

"Man, I got to hand it to you, Doc," he said, chuckling. "You must've had that bitch prosecutor spiraling for her to hand over that plea deal like she did. How'd you do it anyways? I thought for sure she wasn't going to back off. I mean, I figured she'd want to give me the needle herself."

I stared back at him, but I didn't say anything. I hid my anger, keeping my expression indifferent.

"You're not mad, are you?" he asked. "Don't take it personally. Really. I've actually come to think of you as a friend."

"Is that what friends do?" I responded. "Lie to each other and manipulate each other?"

He grinned. "Now, *that* isn't very fair, is it? You're telling me that you weren't trying to manipulate *me* that whole time?

Like I told you before, I saw and heard everything even when you didn't think I was there."

"What the hell are you talking about, Kevin?" I said. "*Even when I didn't think you were there?*"

His grin widened and his eyes lit up. "Oh, shit..." he said, "you haven't talked to him yet, have you?" He started laughing.

"What?" I asked, my confusion growing by the second. "What do you mean, I haven't talked to *him* yet?"

"Kevin," he said, still laughing. "Does he even know yet?"

I glared at him for a moment before saying, "You don't have to jerk my chain anymore, Kevin. You got what you wanted. You won. Is that what you want to hear? You played me and you played Arlo and you got exactly what you wanted."

He smiled mockingly, but he said nothing.

"So give up the act already," I added. "Even if I went back to Arlo or Matthews and told them you were playing me the whole time, they wouldn't believe me. My word doesn't mean a goddamn thing anymore."

Kevin continued to smile. "You think that dumbshit is capable of playing you?" he said. "The guy couldn't manipulate his own dick to take a piss, no less manipulate you or anybody else. Christ, he can hardly dress himself in the morning. *I'm* in control of Kevin. Ever since he created me, I have been. Hell, the moron doesn't even realize I exist."

I eyed Kevin quizzically. His gaze and tone were exactly as they had been when he faked the Edward persona with me before.

"I'll admit it," I said, "you were very convincing, Kevin. *Obviously.* But why keep it going? Don't you want to gloat? That *is* what you do, isn't it? You do these things you do and then you gloat about it, right? That's why you wrote the *Courier* all those times, isn't it? To brag about your murders. To rub them in people's faces because you thought you were invincible."

"Just when I start thinking you're smart..." he said, trailing off briefly. "*Invincible*? Really, Doc? That's why you think I did it?" Kevin scoffed, shaking his head. "Do you know how goddamn aggravating it is to have your work credited to someone else? Take this whole dissociative identity disorder thing that you've uncovered, for example. What if that dullard that's working for Matthews took credit for it instead of you? Better yet, what if people gave the credit to him even if he didn't want it? Didn't *believe* in it? You'd be pissed, right? It was *your* effort. Your work. Your discovery. To not get credit would drive you fucking crazy, I would imagine."

Kevin sighed, adding, "*That's* how I've started to feel, Doc. When the cops and the papers started crediting my glorious work to that goddamn imbecile, I just couldn't stand for it. Quite frankly, it was embarrassing. Pathetic, really. I mean, Kevin, of all people? How can they believe that he's the Blue River Strangler? How? Kevin can hardly remember to mop the floor when he's told. It's bullshit really. Fucking bullshit..."

I watched him with disbelief as this rant spilled from his mouth. It seemed ridiculous that he was still trying to maintain the different personas in light of not needing to play me any longer. I honestly did not know what to believe.

"Why are you looking at me like that?" he added.

"Sorry..." I said, shaking the surprise out of my brain and refocusing. "So let me make sure I'm understanding all of this. Kevin does in fact have dissociative identity disorder, and *you* committed the murders and *you* taunted the police without his knowledge?"

He smiled. "*Yes*. Why is this so difficult for you to understand?"

"And the reason why Kevin scored so poorly on the tests he took for me and so well on the tests he took for the prosecutor's psychiatrist?"

"*I* took the test for the other guy," he said. "*Kevin* took the tests for you."

"Why?" I said. "Why didn't you just take all of them?"

The question seemed to offend him almost. "You think I *like* watching Kevin bumble his way through everything? You think I *enjoy* him making us look like fucking morons? If it was up to me, *I* would be the primary one and Kevin would be the one stuffed so far down that he'd never see the light of day."

"So why don't you?" I challenged him. "If you're as strong as you claim you are, why not just snub him out?"

"You think I haven't tried?" he said. "Just when I *really* start taking control of things, that piece of shit Russell intervenes and shuts me out. He was getting pretty good at it for a while there too. Sometimes months would pass before I could slip out of confinement again. I'd have all this energy pent up and I just couldn't help myself, you know? Fuck, those were some good times. Then *you* came along? Holy Christ. You may as well have built a brick wall in front of my cell door. The more Kevin became aware of things because of you, the harder it was for me to get out and take over."

"Why turn yourself in then?" I asked. "You had a good thing going, it seems. Did you get bored? Did you need more of a challenge?"

"Please," he said, waving his hand in disregard, "I was living my best goddamn life. I mean, I was *really* getting into my work, you know? I could've gone on for another ten years at least. But like I said, that piece of shit Russell made it his life's goal to fuck me over anyway he could."

"What are you saying?" I asked. "Russell turned you in?"

Kevin nodded. "He pretended to be me and ruined the whole thing. Pretended to be *us* actually, but it's all the same, isn't it? I'm telling you, he's a real piece of shit, that one. That's alright though. *I'm* going to get him back, just you wait and see."

"What do you mean?" I said. "How so?"

"Sorry, Doc. Just because I like you, sure doesn't mean I trust you. You'll rat me out to the others and we *definitely* cannot have that. But he'll get his time, sure enough. Don't you worry."

"Does it have anything to do with ending up in Wyoming State Penitentiary?"

Kevin grinned. "I've said too much already, Doc. You're smart, so you might figure it out before it's too late..."

"Tell me what you're planning, Edward."

"Sorry," he said, his grin growing wider.

"Goddammit, what are you planning?"

Kevin's face contorted and his gaze softened. "Planning?" he said. "Doc, what are you talking about?"

"Edward?"

"Edward?" he said, confusion overcoming him. "Who's Edward?"

"Who's Edward? Who are *you*?"

"Doc, it's Robbie."

I stared at Kevin firmly, trying to see through his facade. Like always, though, his bewilderment seemed genuine.

"Robbie?" I said.

"Yeah. Why were you calling me Edward?"

TWENTY-SEVEN

As soon as I had finished talking to Kevin, I called Arlo on the pay phone outside the prison. He sounded exhausted when he answered.

"I just spoke with Kevin again," I said. "You have to convince him to reconsider this plea deal."

"Jesus," he grumbled, "you know I can't do that. He's made his decision and everything's been finalized with Matthews already. The deal is done. It's just a matter of the judge signing off on it at the plea hearing in a few days. Besides, *this is what he wants.*"

"Who did you speak to when he agreed to it?"

"What?" he said.

"Which persona were you speaking to when he agreed to the plea bargain?"

"Kevin, of course, but I thought you said he was faking—"

"You're sure?" I interjected. "You're certain that it was Kevin and not Edward or Russell or one of the others?"

"Sharon, what are you talking about? Didn't we decide yesterday that he's been faking this whole dissociative identity thing all along?"

"I had considered it, yes. But after speaking to him this morning, I really do think it's legitimate."

"How do you explain the IQ test result that Matthews' psychiatrist got then?"

"Edward was taking the test at that time," I said.

"Edward? What you believe is his homicidal mastermind personality?"

"Yes."

"Do you realize how absurd that sounds? I mean, even if that *is* true, how the hell am I supposed to convince a judge or a jury of that?"

"What do you mean, *if* it's true?" I said. "You do realize how long I've been doing this, right? You think I would just make this up?"

"Of course I don't think you're making this up. I trust that *you* honestly believe he has this condition. But just because *you* believe it, does not mean that anyone else is going to believe it. Especially with Matthews' psychiatrist disputing your argument."

I scoffed at this. "I have no problem putting my expertise and reputation up against his," I said.

"Well, *I* do," Arlo interjected. "The thing we have to consider in all of this is the believability of your diagnosis. As far as I can tell, it isn't something that we can conclusively prove with a particular test or diagnostic tool. It's *your* opinion based solely on *your* observations of him. That's it. And like it or not, this Jekyll-and-Hyde theory of yours does not make a whole lot of logical sense. I'm not saying I don't believe it, but even you have to admit that it's a hard sell. Especially to a jury of his peers. And *that's* who we ultimately have to convince. A jury of his peers. I don't know if you've noticed, but we're in Peak County, Wyoming. A county that is as conservative as it is white. Not exactly the mecca of bleeding hearts and abolitionists, if you know what I mean. If I'm going to convince a jury to not only pass on the death penalty, but also deem Kevin legally insane so he can live out his life in the comfort of a mental hospital, I'm going to need something more than your observations alone."

"*Please*," I scoffed, "that's a cop-out and you know it."

"Cop-out or not, it's reality," he said. "It's not my job to entertain fantasies and delusions for him. It's my job as his lawyer to present his options to him and let him decide what he wants to do. If he wanted me to take this to trial and plead insanity, then I would. But even *he* recognizes that the odds are grossly stacked against him. *He* realizes that his chances of getting convicted and sentenced to death are much greater than his chances of pleading insanity. It's his choice, Sharon. *His*."

"What if *I* can convince him then?" I said. "What if I can prove that the personality that agreed to this plea deal was not him, and that in fact he, Kevin, does not agree to this deal?"

"You're more than welcome to," he said. "But you've got two days until the plea hearing. In two days, we have to move forward with it, alright?"

"Fine," I said.

"Before I forget," Arlo added, "I got the background check on the uncle. You want me to try to fax it to the prison or just give you the highlights over the phone?"

"Highlights are fine," I told him, still distracted by everything.

To be honest, I had completely forgotten about asking for the background check in the first place. Wayne's involvement had quickly dropped on my list of priorities, but I was curious all the same.

"Alright," Arlo said, shuffling through some papers. "The background check doesn't give any family information so I can't confirm if he is in fact his uncle. What *is* interesting is the guy's got a rap sheet a mile long. From the time he was a teenager, he was racking up assault and battery charges every couple of years. Drug possession a few times. Shit, the guy was even on the hook for a homicide until the charges were dropped."

"Are you serious?"

"Yeah. Looks like he got his act cleaned up about twenty years ago though. Not a single charge since 1981. Maybe he found Christ or something." Arlo chuckled.

All I could remember was my second meeting with Wayne when he pointed the muzzle of his hunting rifle at me.

"He hardly seems like the churchgoing type," I said. "I find it hard to believe that a guy with that kind of a record could just turn over a new leaf like that."

"Yeah," he said. "People will surprise you, though."

"I guess. What about the girlfriend? Brenda Wexler? You find anything on her?"

"Yeah..." he said. The shuffling of additional papers came over the phone. "That girl was a real mess, let me tell you. Runaway as a sixteen-year-old. A few minor stints for solicitation and drug possession throughout the Rocky Mountain region. One stint in Colorado. Another in Utah. And one in Wyoming. Nothing major though. Just a homeless drug addict, it seems. You said this was Kevin's girlfriend, right?"

I didn't respond for a moment, the phrase *homeless drug addict* lingering in my mind and all I can think about is Maddie. How she could have just as easily ended up the way Brenda Wexler did.

"You there?" Arlo added, interrupting my rumination.

"Yeah," I replied. "The Robbie persona at least believes that Brenda was his girlfriend. Kevin thinks she's his sister."

"Well, I would doubt they were related," he said. "She grew up somewhere in northern Nevada. Does any of this help us even?"

"Not particularly," I said. "If anything, it hurts Kevin's credibility because the Robbie persona appears to be more in touch with reality than him."

"Is that common in DID?" Arlo asked.

"It's not uncommon," I said. "After all, dissociation is the root of the condition."

I heard Arlo sigh over the line. "I feel like we're pissing into the wind on this," he muttered.

"I know, but we have to at least try," I said.

"Maybe... I feel like it would take us years to unravel all this. And the fact still remains that he killed all those girls. Maybe he wasn't of sound mind when he killed them, but he killed them all the same. At the end of the day, *that's* what people are going to focus on."

"Yeah," I said. "And *that* is the very problem."

"What do you mean?" he asked.

"People don't care about what causes these things to happen or why someone like Kevin does what he does. All this country wants to do is blame someone and get revenge on them. An eye for an eye. They don't care at all about *preventing* the crimes. They won't address the poverty or the childhood neglect or the mental illness that is often the root of criminality. We only consider something a problem when it becomes *our* problem. Take Peak County, for example. Nobody gave a damn about homelessness and the causes of it, even after several transients were found strangled to death. Only when local girls started disappearing did they suddenly give a shit. With that kind of approach, justice will never really exist in this country, and these types of crimes will only continue."

"I hear you," Arlo said. "That was why I became a public defender in the first place. But we can only do so much, you know? We can't fix everything and we can't save everybody."

"No, we can't..." I said, ignoring the irony of my own refusal to accept such a fact as it related to Maddie. "But it's worth trying anyways."

Over the course of the next two days, I spent as much time as I could with Kevin, trying to convince him to reconsider the plea deal. Most of the time, though, I didn't speak with *him*, and the other personalities, with the exception of Edward, didn't have a clue what I was talking about. I tried to delve into these various personalities too, but that proved to be fruitless. Edward retreated into the depths of Kevin's psyche the more I poked and prodded him, and the others were becoming more and more withdrawn as time passed.

When the day of the plea hearing finally arrived, I hadn't made any more progress with him.

I attended the plea hearing amongst the family members of the victims and the swarm of reporters from news outlets across the country. At the time, the only other newsworthy story was President Clinton's sex scandal, so a trial for a serial killer was a hot commodity. But to their disappointment, a plea deal was an anticlimactic end to what could have been a sensational spectacle. Especially a deal that took the death penalty out of play. The media wanted a circus sideshow like the O.J. Simpson trial a few years prior, but what they got was nothing more than a run-of-the-mill daytime court show.

People didn't really know who I was at that point yet, so the media left me alone when I entered the standing-room-only courthouse.

The hearing itself was sterilized by legal procedure, so aside from the revulsion that the judge showed for Kevin during his sentencing remarks, there wasn't much for the media to report except that the Blue River Strangler's reign of terror was finally over and that justice had been served. Partially, at least. The death sentence would have been the coup de grâce in the public's opinion, but twenty-eight consecutive life sentences served at Wyoming State Penitentiary would suffice.

As for Kevin, he was trapped in a fugue for the majority of the hearing. Staring blankly at the judge as if zoned out in front of the television, hardly realizing he was attending his own sentencing. Unaware that he would be spending the rest of his life in a six-by-eight cell. Who knows which personality was present in those moments? Jackie? Robbie? Russell? In the grand scheme of things, it didn't matter anyways. Who everybody saw was Kevin Blackford. Kevin Blackford the serial killer. Kevin Blackford the Blue River Strangler.

When the guards led Kevin out of the courtroom, he scanned the crowd casually. I didn't realize he was looking for me until his gaze locked with mine. For a split second, Edward must have taken control, because as he looked at me with pinpoint pupils, he smiled and winked.

It didn't take long for the media to discover that I was the recipient of Kevin's friendly gesture, and you better believe the media pounced on that little morsel. Despite the fact that I refused to answer their questions outside of the courthouse, Kim Matthews had no problem filling in the gaps for them during her press conference after the hearing.

She told them I was the psychiatric evaluator for the defense team. That I had been prepared to diagnose him with dissociative identity disorder to solidify his insanity plea. That Blackford's lawyer had used that and my credibility as leverage to negotiate the plea bargain. That I was responsible for Kevin Blackford "skirting justice". Her words, not mine.

Once the media knew who I was and my involvement in the case, it was over. They weren't going to leave me alone until they had redirected all of their frustration with the outcome of the case onto me.

That press conference was the tipping point for everything.

TWENTY-EIGHT

After the plea hearing, I tried to meet with Kevin before they moved him to the state penitentiary in Rawlins, but the guards refused to let any visitors see him. The only way Arlo could even speak with him was by telephone.

I wanted to stay in Wyoming so I could continue to work with Kevin, but they transferred him within a few days of the plea hearing. I sent my evaluations and case notes to the lead psychiatrist there, Dr. Carla Moneta, but my work with Kevin appeared to be finished.

Despite the fact that we had successfully kept Kevin off death row, I knew it was only a matter of time before something terrible happened to him in prison. With the exception of Edward, Kevin's personas were just too meek for him to survive within the general prison population. There's this inexplicable honor code within a prison, and crimes against women and children tend to fall beyond the confines of that code. The penal justice system is not operated by the guards or the warden; it is operated by the prisoners. A sort of Hammurabian retribution. Considering the nature of Kevin's crimes, it was only a matter of time before that law of retaliation struck Kevin.

If he got lucky, the warden would put him into solitary confinement, but that had its own set of problems. It's hard to imagine what that kind of isolation can do to a man, but it'll drive even the sanest inmates batshit crazy. Put a guy like Kevin into that situation? He'd hang himself with a rope fashioned out of his own t-shirts before the month was out.

I returned to Colorado exhausted and altogether defeated. I felt like I had somehow failed Kevin. Not only had I not fulfilled my duty to advocate for him and protect him, but it also felt like I had let Maddie down yet again. The motherly instinct that, as hard as I tried to stifle it, I couldn't fully repress.

On top of all of that, my boss and I had an unpleasant conversation when I finally returned to work. Not only had he lost his patience for my extended absence, but he was also furious that the case had drawn so much negative attention toward me and, by default, the Supermax.

"We do everything we can to fly under the radar as much as possible," Allen said, "and then this shit comes down on us?"

"I know, I know," I said. "But you know how the media is. Just give them a few weeks. The next scandal will rise and Kevin Blackford will become old news."

"If *only* we were that lucky," he said. "Just promise me you're going to keep your distance from this guy from now on. He's Wyoming's problem now, not yours."

"He should be *here*," I said, "so I can continue to work with him."

"Christ..." he muttered, rolling his eyes.

"What? It's true. This place was made for guys like him."

Allen sighed. "Take my advice and let this go. If for nobody's sake but your own."

"How am I supposed to do that?"

"Look where you are. We've got four hundred of the most violent men in America here. You've got more than enough fucked-up minds to keep you busy."

"Do you know how much I've got invested in him? Not just my time and effort, but now my credibility. My reputation. All of it is being scrutinized. It's not just about him anymore."

"Who gives a shit what the media says? Like you said, they'll move on to the next scandal soon enough."

"Yeah, but once the media runs you through the mud, there's no way of undoing that."

"You'll at least have something left to salvage if you drop this now though. Accept your losses and move on; doubling down on a shitty hand is only going to make it worse."

"I can't do that," I said, my mind distracted. "I can't just let it go..."

Silence fell between us briefly before he added, "Can I be frank here?"

I nodded, but I really didn't want to hear what he had to say.

"This Blackford business has nothing to do with your ego," he said, "or what you perceive as a failure to fulfill your professional duty."

"No?" I said, wondering where he was going with this because he did not know about Maddie as far as I knew.

"I think you have this need to know beyond a shadow of a doubt that his condition is legitimate," he answered. "That he hasn't been jerking your chain this whole time."

"Are you kidding me?" I scoffed. "If I wasn't positive about it, I wouldn't have gone to work for his defense in the first place, and I sure as hell wouldn't have exposed myself to the scrutiny I'm getting now."

"If you're so certain about it, then why keep pursuing it? Why do you need to keep working with him if not to confirm that he has this disorder?"

"Honestly?" I said. "I have never seen a condition like his in my career before. Ever. Not even with Worden or Gullmar. Imagine an archaeologist who's found a bone of what she believes to be a creature she's only heard about. She's not going to stop digging until she has every single bone recovered and the entire skeleton reconstructed. Even if that takes years to do. Only when she's unearthed the entire thing does she stop digging. *That's* the compulsion I feel with Kevin."

Allen shook his head. "I sure as hell don't get it. Seems like a gigantic waste of time to me."

"Well, that's why you do what you do, and I do what I do."

"Fine," he said. "Just take my advice. Let this go. Take a day or two to clear your head if you need to, but walk away from this. Before you get so far down the rabbit hole that you can't get yourself out."

"Sure," I said, wanting only to end the conversation.

Trying to explain my fascination with Kevin to a guy like Allen Kranick was as pointless as trying to explain quantum mechanics to a child. In many ways, there was no logical explanation in the traditional sense. Kevin's mind was like some Russian stacking doll that the more I uncovered, the more I wanted to see what was hidden in the next one. Unstacking and discovering. Unstacking and discovering. It seemed endless, yet I knew eventually I would reach the epicenter where there was nothing left to unstack except the driving force of his psychosis.

Of course, as far as everybody else was concerned, Kevin's condition was a hoax entirely. A ploy enacted by a sociopathic mind to avoid the death penalty.

But I refused to believe that.

Maybe that was my own selfish pride because I didn't want to accept that he had played me.

Or maybe that was my own ambition because I wanted to be the one who uncovered a condition as rare as his.

But I didn't believe either of those things. I believed he was a deeply afflicted young man then, and to this very day, I still do.

TWENTY-NINE

I hadn't been back in Colorado for more than a week when the breaking news began to flood the media outlets.

"We have just confirmed," the reporters said, "that another body has been discovered along the banks of the Blue River near Carbon, Wyoming. Investigators have not yet revealed any information except that the victim is female and that the cause of death is likely strangulation."

Footage of the investigation could be seen on every news channel. Aerial coverage of crime scene analysts combing the grassy banks of the Blue River as if they might discover five more bodies hidden within the undergrowth. Little yellow nylon flags sticking out of the ground like fresh dandelions, marking a potential piece of evidence.

"The Peak County Coroner has not confirmed how long the victim has been dead, but given the M.O. and the placement of the body, investigators are confident that she is the twenty-ninth Blue River Strangler victim."

They aired footage of Kevin in his prison jumpsuit looking as maniacal as he was capable of looking. Footage of Kevin smiling and winking at me in the courtroom on the day of his hearing.

Every channel regurgitated information as if they were the ones with the exclusive story.

"Blackford strikes again," they said.

"Twenty-nine so far. How many more lie undiscovered in Peak County?"

"Although unconfirmed by the coroner, investigators speculate that Blackford strangled the victim to death approximately three to six months ago. Perhaps weeks or days before he was apprehended by police for the murders of twenty-eight other young women."

There were headshots of the other victims. School photos of Amanda Hatcher and Tracy Malvar. Family album portraits from those whose families still gave a damn about them.

Then there was the footage of Park City and the Blue River cutting its way through town. Then interviews with random citizens.

"We should've given him the death penalty when we had the chance," many said.

"A monster like Kevin Blackford doesn't deserve to live out the rest of his life at the taxpayers' expense."

"How long must we wait for justice to be served?"

Then Kim Matthews began making her appearances.

"If there was any way to reverse the decision for the first twenty-eight victims, we would," she said. "But we can't. Blackford's deceit may have worked the first time, but as my father used to say, 'Fool me once, shame on you. Fool me twice, shame on me.' I can assure you, my office intends to charge Kevin Blackford again, only this time there won't be a plea bargain. Kevin Blackford will not fool us twice."

That's when the media's muzzle pointed toward me.

"You might remember," reporters said, "that much of Blackford's original plea bargain was heavily influenced by the psychiatric evaluation of Dr. Sharon Stevenson, lead psychiatrist at the Supermax Prison in Florence, Colorado. Stevenson believed that Blackford potentially suffered from dissociative identity disorder, the rare and controversial condition that was once known as multiple personality disorder."

There was an interview with Kim Matthews' evaluating psychiatrist, Dr. Brandon Kemper:

"There is no condition in the *Diagnostic and Statistical Manual of Mental Disorders* that is disputed more than dissociative identity disorder," he said. "It was hoaky in the days when we called it multiple personality disorder, and despite the new name, most psychiatrists believe it's still a farce today."

"But what of Dr. Stevenson's evaluation?" an anonymous reporter asked. "She's performed dozens of these psychiatric evaluations throughout her career, hasn't she?"

"That is true," he said, "and I don't doubt Dr. Stevenson's experience or her expertise. I think it just confirms the power of Blackford's sociopathy and his ability to deceive and manipulate even the most highly trained individuals. I personally evaluated Blackford several times, and while I can't provide specifics, I believe he is highly intelligent and highly dangerous. And it wouldn't be the first time that a serial killer has faked a mental illness. Kenneth Bianchi, one of the Hillside Stranglers, faked multiple personality disorder as part of his own insanity defense in the late seventies. He didn't fool just one psychiatrist; he fooled several."

"Did you ever observe these *personalities* that Dr. Stevenson reported to have interacted with, though? Did you see any indication of this condition whatsoever?"

"No," he said, stifling a grin.

"Then why the discrepancy?" they asked. "Isn't it really just your word against hers?"

"I don't want to stomp on a woman's reputation," he answered, "particularly someone as highly regarded as Dr.

Sharon Stevenson, but sometimes clinicians can subconsciously allow their work with former patients to cloud their judgment. In my personal opinion, I believe Dr. Stevenson unintentionally fell under this spell."

I was paralyzed by the television as the stories flooded in. As my work was questioned and my name was sullied as a result as the updates on the twenty-ninth victim unfolded before the nation's eyes. "Stunning developments," according to reporters.

"Investigators have just confirmed that hair follicles were found on the victim and are at the crime lab as we speak to hopefully confirm the identity of the killer. You'll remember that DNA was left almost intentionally on several of Blackford's victims, yet matches could never be made because he wasn't in the DNA registry. The DNA traces became a ghoulish calling card of his; however, it could be the very thing that earns him the death penalty for his latest murder."

Reporters added, "The conviction could prove to be monumental for Wyoming, which reinstated capital punishment in 1976. In that time, only one prisoner has been executed; Mark Hopkinson was executed by lethal injection six years ago for the murders of the Vehar family and Jeffrey Green."

More interviews of random citizens in Peak County.

All were asked the same question: "Should Blackford get the death penalty?"

"Absolutely."

"Without a doubt."

These were people who would make up the jury of his peers.

"No question."

"Hell yeah!"

THIRTY

I called Arlo shortly after the news broke. I told him I needed to speak to Kevin immediately. Preferably in person, but over the phone would be fine too.

"Are you crazy?" he answered. "I'm up to my neck in this shit right now. And have you seen the news lately? Your name is mentioned just as much as his. The last thing you need to do is be more involved in the case."

"The media can kiss my ass," I said. "This is about him, not me."

"This is a ticking time bomb," he said. "This latest victim couldn't have been a better opportunity for the prosecution. Not only do they get another shot at him, but now they can completely taint the jury pool *and* discredit our defense. I mean, Kim Matthews is on the news every chance she gets saying whatever the hell she wants."

"Trust me, I've seen it. What do they actually know about the victim?"

"Come on," he said, "I can't tell you that."

"Let me help you. There's no way you can do this on your own."

"No way," he said. "The obvious reasons aside, why do you even *want* to be involved? If I were you, I'd get as far away from this thing as I could."

"Because it's the right thing to do. Because he's mentally ill and should be sent to a psychiatric facility, not the goddamn execution chamber."

Arlo scoffed. "Don't give me that holier-than-thou shit. What are *you* getting out of this?"

"My reputation," I said. "What took me decades to build up, they've torn down in a week. The only way I'm getting that back is by proving once and for all that Kevin has DID. In the end, we both win. I keep my credibility and my career, and Kevin keeps his life."

"You're insane," he said. "I'm serious, you need to let this go while you still can. Before you lose everything."

"That's not going to happen. If anybody can prove his condition, I can."

"If he even *has* this condition," grumbled Arlo.

"What the hell are you talking about? Of course he has it."

He sighed. "I'm not so sure. I mean, I don't doubt these things you've told me about him, but in all the times I've spoken to him, I've *only* talked to him. Kevin. No Robbie. No Russell. Certainly no Edward. Just Kevin. The man who claims he remembers nothing about these crimes, yet his DNA was found on the victims."

"What if I can convince other psychiatrists to evaluate him and back up the diagnosis?" I asked.

"Everybody's watching what's happening to you right now. With all due respect, who's going to want to stand next to you in front of the firing squad?"

"I'll find someone," I said. "Trust me."

"If you say so..."

"In the meantime, you have to let me speak with Kevin."

There was a long pause as Arlo thought about it.

"Fine," he finally said, "but under two conditions: *I'm* in the room with you and we videotape the conversation. I want to be able to show a judge and jury exactly what you're seeing."

I wasn't wild about the idea, but I knew there was no other way.

"Are they even looking into other suspects or are they just hoping it's him?" I asked.

"As far as I know, he's the only suspect."

"*That* is bullshit. What happened to his presumption of innocence?"

"It vanished when he turned himself in," Arlo said bluntly.

"*Edward* turned him in," I corrected.

Arlo said nothing.

THIRTY-ONE

Arlo picked me up at the airport in Casper and drove us two hours south to Rawlins. As majestic as the western edge of Wyoming is, the rest of the state is comparatively miserable. Just as Florence is an appropriate location for the Supermax, so also is Rawlins the appropriate home to the Wyoming State Penitentiary. Only rolling scrubland and drought-infested plains are visible from Interstate 80. There's no real evidence of human life, no less the home of Wyoming's most dangerous criminals.

Rawlins' only real claim to fame is the Wyoming Frontier Prison, which was opened in 1901 and used as the state prison for eighty years before being moved to the southern outskirts of town.

Entering the prison and walking through its concrete labyrinth, I was struck by the stark contrast it had to the Peak County Jail. By comparison, the Peak County Prison was as authoritative as a folding chair outside of a principal's office. Yet to me, the Peak County Prison seemed to be a more appropriate home for a guy like Kevin. I would never forget the crimes he had committed—or was *accused* of committing—but housing someone of his temperament in a high-security state prison just seemed excessive and ridiculous.

The guards were silent as they led us back to an interview room, me armed with Kevin's case file and Arlo with a camcorder.

Arlo set the camcorder up on the table as I organized my notes and gathered my thoughts. I was nervous. Uncertain how Kevin was going to behave with Arlo present and the camera watching him.

The door to the interview room opened hollowly and the guards escorted Kevin into the room. He looked like he hadn't bathed in weeks and he had a full beard. Chains that could have contained a gorilla were wrapped around his waist and connected to his wrists and ankles.

When he saw me though, his eyes brightened a little.

"Doc?" he said. "What are you doing here?"

"I'm here to visit you," I answered, smiling.

"Boy, I didn't think I was going to ever see you again," he said.

As the guards prepared to sit him in the chair, I asked, "You guys mind removing his shackles?"

They glowered at me before saying, "The shackles have to stay. Policy of the prison."

"Fine," I said, not wanting to get into a confrontation with them. "You can leave now."

They hesitated, but left soon enough.

"I'm so sorry about what's happened," added Kevin. "You know... the stuff from the hearing and all."

"I've been meaning to ask you about that, Kevin—"

"Before we get into anything," Arlo interjected, "do you mind if we record our conversation, Kevin?"

Kevin eyed the camera warily. "Record? Why?"

"In case one of your other personalities sprouts up again, we can show the video during the trial so the jury can better understand your condition."

"My condition?" he asked. "What condition?"

"The dissociative identity disorder," I said. "You know, what I was going to diagnose you with before you agreed to the plea deal?"

"Oh, *that*..." he said, glancing uneasily between us. "Yeah, I guess you can record it."

Arlo positioned the camera and gave me a nod when he hit the record button.

"Alright, Kevin," I said, "tell me more about what happened after the trial."

"What do you mean?" he asked.

"When you winked at me, Kevin."

He shrugged. "I've seen the news so I know I did it, but I don't remember doing it."

"What *do* you remember from the hearing?"

He thought about it briefly before saying, "Not a whole lot... Some stuff that the judge said, I guess. Nothing specifically though."

"Okay," I said. "What about the plea bargain? Do you remember anything about what Arlo told you?"

"I dunno, I guess."

"What do you mean, 'I guess'?" I asked. "You either remember Arlo going over the plea bargain or you don't."

"I think so," Kevin scratched his head as he tried to remember. "I guess I remember him telling me there was a way for me to not get the death penalty."

"Anything about what you would have to do to avoid it?"

He shook his head slowly.

"Sure you do, Kevin," said Arlo. "Remember how I said you'd have to plead guilty to the charges?"

"No..."

"Why are you lying to us, Kevin?" Arlo added.

"I swear to God, I'm not."

"It's alright," I interjected, preventing Arlo from continuing to probe. "I want to talk about what's happened the last few days anyways. The stuff that's been on the news about this new victim. Do you know anything about that, Kevin?"

"Of course not," he said fervently. "I don't know nothing about that."

"So you don't have the slightest clue who that woman might be?" I asked.

"Nuh-uh."

"You're positive?" Arlo chimed in. "No idea?"

"What did I just say, dumbshit?" retorted Kevin.

"Excuse me?" Arlo asked, taken aback by Kevin's sudden change in tone.

A silence fell between the three of us. Although it was subtle, Kevin's expression became more devious.

"Edward?" I asked, eyeing him closely.

"Hey, Doc," Kevin answered with a grin. "How the hell have you been? Haven't seen *you* in a while. You miss me?"

I glanced at Arlo, who appeared to be stunned that Kevin had lashed out at him in the first place.

"Edward," I said, "what do you know about this woman they've just found?"

"Woman?" he said. "What in God's name are you talking about?"

"Don't jack with me. I know you've seen the news."

"Oh!" he said. "The twenty-ninth victim? *That* woman."

"Yes, Edward, *that* woman."

"As much as I hate to admit it," he said, "she wasn't mine."

"What do you mean, she wasn't yours?"

"I mean, she wasn't mine. Too old." He smirked at me, adding, "Sorry to disappoint you, Doc."

"Wasn't yours?" interjected Arlo. "That's impossible. Kevin's DNA was found on her. She had to be yours."

Kevin grinned. "Did you ever think that she could be Kevin's without being mine?"

"No," Arlo said. "You *are* Kevin."

Kevin scoffed, "You're too narrow-minded, Counselor. You gotta learn to think outside the box a little bit. Like Dr. Stevenson here. She gets it."

"Refocus, Edward," I interrupted. "Why do you say this victim is Kevin's but not yours?"

"Because I didn't kill her," he said.

"But Kevin did?" asked Arlo, frustrated.

Kevin glanced at me mockingly. "This guy... No wonder we ended up in this joint, right, Doc?"

"Did you kill her?" I asked.

"Seriously, both of you are either fucking deaf or stupid, I can't decide which."

"Humor us," I said. "Did you kill her? Yes or no?"

Kevin rolled his eyes. "*Like I said*, she wasn't one of mine."

"Then how do you know her?"

"I don't *know* her. I just remember seeing her. Our old friend had a thing for her..." Kevin gave us a perverse look and winked, adding, "You know what I mean."

"Old friend?" I said. "What old friend?"

"No, no, no... I have been sworn to secrecy." Kevin crossed himself like a priest before the altar.

"Quit jacking around. Who's our old friend?"

Kevin looked at me with confusion. "Doc, I don't have the slightest clue what you're talking about."

"What did you mean by our old friend, Edward?"

"Edward?" muttered Kevin. "That's the guy you were asking me about before, isn't it?"

"What in God's name is going on?" asked Arlo, glancing between me and Kevin.

"Kevin?" I asked.

He nodded slowly. "Yeah?"

"What was the last thing we asked you?"

"Umm... If I knew who this woman was?"

"Yes."

"I don't get it," he said. "How would *I* know her?"

"You've got to be kidding me," Arlo grumbled.

Kevin looked worriedly at me. "Doc, what is going on?"

I glanced at Arlo who was getting more frustrated and confused by the second.

"Kevin," I said, "your persona, Edward, said that you knew who the twenty-ninth victim was."

"Did *he* kill her?" he asked, horrified.

"No. He said 'our old friend' did. Do you have any clue what that might mean?"

He thought about it momentarily and shook his head. "I don't really have any friends," he said.

"How about people you work with?" I asked. "Patrick Hawkins, maybe?"

"Hawk?" he said. "No, Hawk hated me."

"Did you work with anyone else ever?"

"Besides Wayne?" he asked. "Not really."

Kevin mentioning Wayne reminded me of the background check that Arlo had told me about before.

"Do you think Wayne knows something about these murders?" I asked.

"*Wayne?*" He shook his head. "No way."

"You sure? We ran a background check on him and he was convicted of some pretty violent crimes when he was a younger man."

"No," Kevin said, steadfast. "Sure, Wayne is a little rough around the edges, but he wouldn't ever hurt no one."

"That's not what his background check says," retorted Arlo.

"I don't understand..."

"When we were just talking to Edward about this woman

that was recently murdered, he said that 'our old friend' had a thing for her."

"I told you," he countered. "I don't know what you're talking about."

"Did you ever notice anything odd about Wayne when you were living with him?" I asked.

"Odd?" he muttered.

"Yes, Kevin," I said. "Did you ever see anyone go over to the house that you didn't know? Or did you notice Wayne was off doing something for a long time?"

"I don't know…" he said. "Why does that stuff matter anyways?"

"Because I'm starting to wonder if Wayne had something to do with murdering this woman," I said, "and I'm wondering if he was involved in the others as well."

THIRTY-TWO

"You don't honestly believe that the uncle had something to do with this, do you?" Arlo asked me as we drove from Rawlins toward Park City. "And even if he did, what good is that going to do for Kevin?"

"I worked a case a while ago where the accused was charged with the rape and murder of a young girl from his neighborhood. When I started evaluating him, I found out that he had some pretty significant cognitive impairments. IQ somewhere in the high sixties. As I started digging, he told me about an older cousin that was in the picture. Some guy who was known in the neighborhood to be a troublemaker. I told the investigation about it and they discovered that the cousin was not only involved in the crime, but he had also coerced the accused into being an accessory. The jury gave the older cousin life without parole and knocked the younger one's sentence down to twenty years with the possibility of parole after twelve."

"Jesus..." Arlo breathed. "You're thinking a similar thing is going on with Kevin and Wayne?"

"Possibly," I said. "I mean, Wayne's record as a younger man sends up red flags automatically, then he magically stops committing crimes over the last fifteen years? I don't buy it. Violent criminals don't just stop being violent criminals overnight, so I don't imagine that Wayne stopped breaking the law; he just got better at not getting caught. And isn't it convenient that around the time he stops getting arrested, that's when Kevin enters the picture? They move up to a small town in Wyoming together where they can both have a fresh start."

"And together they become one of the most notorious serial killers in history?" Arlo added skeptically.

"I'm not saying it's likely, but it wouldn't be the first time either. Everybody thought the Hillside Strangler was one man, but they came to find out later that it was Buono and Bianchi colluding together. And my encounter with Wayne out at his place really freaked me out. Maybe he didn't kill those women himself, but I think he definitely could have something to do with it."

"I guess..." said Arlo. "But Kevin isn't some invalid. His IQ test with Matthews' psychiatrist proved that."

"Yeah, I know. I still think Edward took that test though, not Kevin."

"I still don't know what to think of these different personas," he said. "It's just so damn bizarre."

"Do you at least believe that he's got dissociative identity disorder now?"

Arlo shook his head. "I don't know what the hell to think of what I witnessed back there, but something is definitely wrong with him. What I can't figure out is if it's a legitimate mental disorder or if it's just him being a sociopath."

"That's why we need to see *if* there's a way to connect Wayne to these murders," I said. "The way that Matthews and the media are working against us, Kevin's defense is shit if we're solely relying on his diagnosis."

We continued to speculate and theorize for the remainder

205

of the three-hour drive to Park City, but we came up with nothing definitive.

Driving through the town made me feel uneasy. The discovery of the twenty-ninth victim had created a media fiasco, particularly around the courthouse. News vans lined the streets, and reporters and cameramen surrounded the "End of the Trail" statue in front of the entryway as they awaited developments with the investigation. Locals floated around the periphery of this horde, waiting for their potential thirty seconds of fame and glory on national television.

As we approached the community college, I could see a crowd of reporters milling about. Probably questioning students about the killer janitor that had been lurking in the hallways amongst them for the last ten years.

"I don't want to deal with this circus right now," I said to Arlo as he pulled into the parking lot. "They're going to know who we are as soon as we get out of the car."

"We drove all the way out here to talk to the uncle, though," he said.

"Yeah, I know..." I answered, thinking. "What if we go out to the property instead?"

Arlo scoffed at this. "That sounds like an even worse idea. The guy pulled a gun on you, for Christ's sake. And if he really is involved, what's going to keep him from killing the two of us?"

"Quit being dramatic," I said, although I had my reservations as well. "He's been flying under the radar for fifteen years," I added. "The last thing he's going to do is compromise that. Besides, he probably thinks nobody suspects him."

"I hope so," said Arlo warily.

We left the community college and I directed Arlo to Squaw Pass Road, through the labyrinth of the Griffith's Peak forest. The road was still in terrible condition, and Arlo's sedan thundered down the washboard roadway.

When we reached Wayne's driveway, Arlo was reticent

about taking his car down the ice-covered ruts leading to the cabin.

"Fine," I told him. "We'll walk in."

Before we got out, Arlo opened his glove box and removed a revolver and a box of bullets.

"I don't trust this guy," he said, loading the chambers.

We were cautious as we trudged through the melting snow that lingered from the winter. I figured at any moment that Wayne would appear with his rifle fixed upon us. When the cabin came into view, though, we had yet to see any sign of him or his old truck.

"He must still be at work," I said.

Despite our desire to speak to Wayne, we were relieved all the same. Our suspicions, although far-fetched, caused us to be more apprehensive than we probably needed to be.

We knocked on the cabin door several times, but nobody answered. I checked the doorknob and it was unlocked.

As I opened the door, Arlo said, "You're not going in there, are you?"

"Why not?" I said. "Door's open, and he probably won't be back until this evening. Maybe we'll find something."

"Alright..." he said, drawing his gun from his coat pocket.

The inside of the cabin was exactly as I had remembered it from a few months prior. The living space was in disarray and a stale odor lingered in the air.

"Well *this* is about what I expected," commented Arlo as we tiptoed through the trash that was scattered across the planked floor. "What are we looking for exactly?"

"I don't know..." I said, searching. "Anything out of the ordinary, I guess."

"This whole place is out of the ordinary," he said.

We passed through the cabin haphazardly, rifling through empty pizza boxes and crinkled beer cans. I didn't have a clue what to look for. I guess I was hoping I was going to accidentally stub my toe into something significant, but we encountered nothing but Wayne's garbage.

"This was stupid," I said after we made our way through the cabin.

We stepped out of the house and closed the door behind us.

"Maybe I'm wrong," I added. "Maybe I'm trying to uncover something that isn't even here. I don't know..."

I walked down the porch steps, but on the bottom step, I hit a patch of ice and fell straight to my rear end.

"Jesus," Arlo said, "you alright?"

"Yeah..." I groaned.

I sat there for a moment to allow the stinging sensation in my tailbone to dissipate. As I sat there, I noticed a large splinter in the post that supported the railing. Wedged into the splinter were several strands of long, brown hair.

"Arlo..." I said, leaning near the post to get a closer look. "You don't remember what color the twenty-ninth victim's hair was, do you?"

"Brown, I think?" he said. "At least, I'm pretty sure they said she was brunette. Why?"

THIRTY-THREE

Arlo nearly destroyed the suspension on his sedan as we raced down Squaw Pass Road toward town to notify the police of what we'd discovered. We would have stayed out at the cabin and called from the landline, but it must have been busted from one of the snowstorms earlier in the winter because it was dead when we tried calling.

We figured it would be a while before Wayne returned from work anyways, but the sooner we could get the cops out to investigate, the better.

When we arrived at the police station, the parking lot was bustling with law enforcement. Deputies from Peak County, Keystone County, Natrona County, and Teton County. All helping with the recent developments in the Blue River Strangler case.

Arlo didn't even bother finding a parking spot; he just left his car at the curb in front of the station. We hurried inside, hoping to avoid the attention of the media that was also milling about the area. Before we could get to the front desk to report what we'd found, though, we ran into Sheriff Averson walking alongside Kim Matthews. She in particular looked incredibly pleased about something. Smug, in fact.

Just seeing her made my stomach lurch.

"Counselor?" she said when she spotted Arlo and came over to us. "We've been trying to get a hold of you. What are you—" She cut herself short when she recognized me. "Dr. Stevenson?"

I nodded and said flatly, "Hello, Ms. Matthews."

"What are you doing here?" she said. "I thought you were back in Colorado."

"No," I said. "When this recent victim was found, I figured Arlo was going to need some help."

"I see..." she said, although I could tell I was the last person she wanted to see.

"You said you've been trying to reach me?" asked Arlo.

"Yes, can we speak in private?" she asked. "*Just* you."

"Sharon's working the case with me," he said.

"Fine," she said, glancing at me. "Let's see if we can find an empty office somewhere."

As she led us back into the police station, Arlo attempted to tell her about what we had found at Wayne's cabin.

"I'll send someone to take a look," she said distractedly, as if that was the *least* of her worries. "What were you two doing out there anyways?"

"We wanted to talk to Mr. Lennerson," answered Arlo. "See if he knew anything about the victim."

"We've already questioned him a few times and searched his property," she said. "Came up with nothing."

"But what about the hair?" I interjected. "Your guys didn't notice that?"

"Are you sure it's not animal hair, Dr. Stevenson?" She said this rather condescendingly, as if I was incapable of distinguishing squirrel hair from human hair. "A lot of wildlife out here. Could have been something using it as a scratching post for all we know."

"I saw it too—" Arlo tried to say.

"Please," she interjected, "I don't have time for this right now." She opened the door of a small interrogation room, adding, "Have a seat. This shouldn't take long."

We entered and sat down in the folding chairs. Matthews closed the door but remained standing.

"The DNA on this recent victim finally came back," she said. "Exact match to Blackford. Just like the samples found on all the other victims. The medical examiner thinks he killed her just before we caught him."

"Do you have any proof of that?" asked Arlo.

"I have the M.E.'s expert opinion," she answered.

"I want a second opinion," he said. "Before you start spouting theories off to the press."

Matthews rolled her eyes. "This is still an ongoing investigation, Counselor. We're not saying anything to the press that they don't already know. We've got the task force searching the surrounding areas as well as the wilderness where some of the other remains were discovered. Who knows how many more Blackford left out there."

"What happened to his presumption of innocence?" retorted Arlo. "Or does Peak County not acknowledge *Coffin v. United States* anymore?"

"Don't give me that bullshit. Your client pleaded guilty to twenty-eight murders that are nearly identical to this most recent one. I think it's safe to say there may be more."

"*Nearly*," he said. "We'll see if the evidence actually proves it."

"Of course it does," she said, almost laughing at the presumption that it wouldn't. "And when it does, he won't dodge justice again. He *will* get the death penalty. I'm going to see to that."

"Why are you so hell-bent on the death penalty?" I jumped in. "Have you seen the conditions at Wyoming State

Pen? Who knows if he'll even survive more than a few years there."

"Let me ask *you* something, Dr. Stevenson; why are *you* so hell-bent on helping him? Some feeble attempt to save face?"

"Don't pretend that you know anything about me or my motivation for helping Kevin," I said. "The law specifically states that the insane cannot be executed. Period."

"The *legitimately* insane," she retorted. "Not ruthless serial killers who've gotten lucky enough to fool a psychiatrist with a personal vendetta against the system."

"That's bullshit and you know it," I said. "What are the powers-that-be promising you if you pull this off anyways?"

"That's none of your business, is it?"

"But there is *something* in this for you, right? Or do you just want to watch a man fry?"

Before either of us could add anything further, Arlo interjected, "Will you two get over yourselves already, please? Another woman is dead and you're here squabbling over your goddamn egos." He rose from the chair and made his way for the door. "Can I trust you'll call me when your deputies have finished searching Lennerson's property, Ms. Matthews? I want to know whose hair that is out there and how Wayne might be involved."

She didn't respond for several moments as she eyed me with contempt.

"Ms. Matthews?"

"Yes," she finally said. "Can I trust that you won't interfere with our investigation?"

"As long as it doesn't interfere with ours," I said, rising and following Arlo out of the interrogation room.

Arlo and I hurried out of the police station, but as we opened the doors, a swarm of reporters and cameras descended upon us.

"Do you have any comment on the present investigation, Mr. Braddock?"

"What is Dr. Stevenson's current involvement with the defense?"

"Do you still think Blackford's innocent, Dr. Stevenson?"

"Are you starting to suspect that you've been manipulated by Blackford?"

I'd had enough of the media by that point, but Arlo spoke before I could say anything that I would later regret.

"We are declining all questions at this time," he said. "Our hearts go out to the families of all of the victims."

The barrage of questions continued as we hustled into Arlo's sedan and the swarm of cameras encircled the vehicle. Only after Arlo honked the horn and inched the car forward were we able to escape the mob and exit the parking lot.

"Bunch of goddamn vultures," I said.

Arlo was silent for several minutes.

"Where are we going?" I finally asked.

"The community college," he said. "We're going to talk to Wayne ourselves and see if we can't figure out what his involvement is."

"What do you mean *we are?*" I asked.

"You think the cops are going to talk to him again? We'll be lucky if they even check the cabin for the hair. One thing we're going to have to realize is that the burden of proof is on *our* shoulders, not theirs. *We* have to prove Kevin's insane, and *we* have to prove that Wayne was somehow able to coerce him because of it."

"I agree," I said, "but how do we do that exactly? Wayne isn't going to just admit it to us."

"Yeah, I know..." he said, thinking. "Maybe if he knows we suspect him though, he'll do something stupid out of haste. Incriminate himself or make a mistake somehow."

"Christ, that seems like a long shot. We'd be better off talking to Kevin and seeing what we can get out of him."

Arlo shook his head. "Then I have to put *him* on the witness stand during the trial, and he couldn't be a more unreliable witness. The volatility of his condition aside, a jury is not going to sympathize with him or trust him."

"Yeah..." I admitted. "But if the personalities show themselves in court, then that's proof of his condition."

Wayne glanced at me. "You really think we can afford that kind of risk? Even if the personalities do appear, who knows if a jury is going to believe him. Our only real hope is proving that Wayne somehow coerced him. We just have to figure out how to do that..."

THIRTY-FOUR

There were still several reporters bustling about the community college when we pulled into the parking lot of the main administration building.

"Let me do the talking with Wayne," Arlo said to me as we got out of his car. "Also, not to labor the point, but do not talk to the press if we get confronted again. 'No comment' on everything. All they really want is a sound bite to sensationalize. All talking will do is weaken our defense and strengthen the prosecution's."

"I know, I know," I said, although it was really getting to me the way they asked such provoking questions.

To my surprise, we were able to enter the administration building without incident. Classes were in full session and students filed through the packed corridors. I led Arlo down the main hallway where Wayne's office was. The door was propped open by a small traffic cone again.

Arlo knocked on the door and said, "Mr. Lennerson?"

"Yeah?" Wayne said from within.

"Arlo Braddock," he said, poking his head into the doorway.

"I was hoping I could talk to you about your nephew, Kevin? You mind if I come in?"

"Yeah, I do," I heard Wayne say gruffly. "You goddamn reporters don't know when to stop."

"Oh, I'm not with the press," Arlo said. "I'm Kevin's lawyer."

"His lawyer? Why the hell you wanna talk to me? Shouldn't you be talking to *him*?"

"Well, I was hoping we could discuss that since you're his closest living relative."

"I see..." Wayne said.

Arlo added, "I also have Kevin's psychiatrist, Dr. Stevenson, here with me. She's agreed to help with Kevin's defense."

Arlo stepped away from the door and motioned for me to show myself. When I poked my head into the office, Wayne was slouched in his chair with a wad of chewing tobacco in his lip.

"Is it okay if we go somewhere to talk?" asked Arlo.

Wayne glanced at his wrist watch and sighed. "Sure... why not?" he said, rising from his chair. "Should be an empty classroom around here somewhere. Follow me."

We followed Wayne along the hallway, and he stopped at a door a few rooms down from his office and showed us inside.

"So how you plan on getting him out of this new mess he's in?" Wayne asked, taking a seat on one of the desktops.

"To be honest with you," answered Arlo, "we were kind of hoping to get your help with that."

"*My* help?" he said. "What makes you think I can help?"

"Well, we have a theory that we want to run by you," Arlo said. Meanwhile, I kept my mouth shut because I didn't have a clue as to what theory Arlo was referring to. "You've known Kevin for... what? Fifteen years now?" he added.

"Something like that. Sure."

"With all that time that you've known him, do you think

he's capable of committing these crimes? Physically or mentally?"

"Hell, no," Wayne said. "Physically? Maybe. But mentally?" He paused and chuckled. "That boy don't know his head from his ass half the time. Been working on him to fix it, but you can't fix stupid. Stupid's forever. Can't believe that other doctor thinks he's some kind of genius. What'd he call it? Superior...?"

"Superior intelligence," I said.

"That's it!" Wayne laughed. "What a crock of shit. Ain't nothing superior about that boy."

"And he never got in trouble with the law before this, correct?" Arlo asked.

"Far as I know," Wayne said. "Maybe he got into scrapes as a kid, but as long as he's been under my wing, he's kept his shit together. Just hard to believe he was hiding it all this time."

"That's what we thought at first too," said Arlo. "Yet a guy that dumb wouldn't be able to hide it the way he did. He would've slipped up much earlier."

Wayne shrugged. "I s'pose... What are you getting at? You think he didn't do them things?"

"I don't know about *that*," Arlo said. "The DNA evidence is pretty convincing. But what I am wondering is if he had someone helping him. You know, someone to clean up everything after the fact."

Wayne shook his head. "I doubt that. Never saw him with nobody. Boy kept to hisself pretty good."

"How about the other guys on your staff?" Arlo said.

"Who? Hawk?" Wayne scoffed. "He ain't a whole lot sharper than Kevin, let me tell you."

"Are you sure about that?" I asked. "People can surprise you, can't they?"

"Not that boy," Wayne answered with a grin. "He hasn't worked with us all that long. Certainly not as long as them bodies have been showing up."

"I see," Arlo said, glancing at me. "Well, that puts a hole in that theory, I suppose."

There was a brief pause before Wayne muttered ruminatively, "Should've never taken that boy in..."

"How did Kevin come to live with you anyways?" I asked.

"Found out about him after he was put in that shithole of a home in Colorado. His mother was a goddamn mess and treated him like hell. Should've never been a mother, that one. Anyways the state somehow linked me to him and asked if I wanted to help out. Told them no for a few years. I was dealing with my own mess at the time."

"What do you mean?" Arlo asked.

"Agh..." Wayne groused. "Trouble with the law because I was young and stupid and didn't know no better. After a few stints in the can, finally figured it out. Decided to take the boy in and get my life together."

"And you haven't been to prison or arrested since then?" Arlo said.

"No, sir."

"What about—" I tried to say, but Arlo interrupted me.

"That's admirable," he said.

Wayne eyed both of us skeptically. "Not sure how admirable it is *now*," he said, "especially knowing what that boy was involved in all these years."

"And you never suspected anything?" Arlo asked.

"No," Wayne replied defensively. "Everybody keeps asking me how I didn't know what he was doing, but that bastard was quiet. Hardly knew he was living with me half the time." He shook his head with disappointment and added, "I busted my goddamn hump trying to make a man out of that boy, but clearly nothing I did worked. Always going to be worthless 'til the day he dies."

"That's pretty harsh, don't you think?" said Arlo.

"That's life, ain't it?" Wayne said. "Harsh and unfair. Just ask all them girls. 'Course, doesn't sound like many of them had much to live for anyways."

"Why do you say that?" I asked, trying not to sound too accusatory.

"I used to hang around with them types," he said. "Drug addicts and drifters and what not. They ain't got shit going for them except their next hit. Probably better off dead than alive, honestly. Horrible goddamn existence."

"What about Amanda Hatcher and Tracy Malvar?" I countered, thinking of my own daughter. "Two young college students with promising futures. Are they better off dead too?"

"Now, hold on," Arlo interjected, "I'm sure that's not what he meant."

"I'm sure them girls were nice enough," Wayne answered, unfazed by my tone. "And I ain't saying those women *deserved* what happened to them neither. What I'm saying is that *most* of them girls were trapped in a shitty way with no way out of it. Having lived that life myself, I know."

"Sure, but—" I started, but Arlo interrupted me again.

"We appreciate your time, Mr. Lennerson," he said.

I wanted to press Wayne harder, particularly on his semi-violent record as a younger man and his cold remarks about the victims, but Arlo wouldn't let me.

"What was *that* all about?" I asked as we left the community college. "Why'd you keep cutting me off?"

"Because," he said, "the last thing we need to do is make him more suspicious than he already is. Even if he confessed straight up to us, what good would that do? We'd have no way of proving it. Certainly no physical evidence to back it up. But I'll tell you one thing: that's not going to be the last time we speak to Wayne. He's involved somehow. His story about how Kevin came to live with him? That's a load of shit if I've ever heard any. We know for a fact that he knew Kevin as a child *and* that he was in contact with Kevin's mother. But that doesn't prove he coerced Kevin into committing these murders. Hell, it doesn't even prove he knew anything about them at all."

"Yeah, but how about the way he talked about the victims?" I added, the sting fresh as if he had mentioned Maddie by name. "Saying they were better off dead? And I know he meant that about Amanda and Tracy too, despite what he said."

"I don't disagree with that—"

"Then why aren't we still questioning him?" I asked.

"You think he's the first person who's said something like that about the victims? Shit, for the first year, that's all anybody was saying. Besides, being a cold, heartless prick doesn't make him an accessory to murder."

"Great..." I said. "So where do we go from here then?"

"Honestly?" Arlo said, shaking his head wearily, "I don't know."

THIRTY-FIVE

Despite my own suspicions of Wayne, the thing that gnawed at me the most was why Kevin wouldn't tell me and Arlo about Wayne's connection to the murders if there truly was a connection. Be that Kevin or Russell or any of the other personalities. Edward hinted that an old friend was involved, but it was hard to say if he was just messing with me or not.

Arlo thought we would be able to prove that by talking to Wayne again or by somehow convincing the authorities to look at him more closely, but I knew that was going to be pointless. Wayne wasn't going to explicitly implicate himself, and if someone tried to confront him about it instead, he would clam up immediately. As far as I was concerned, Kevin was the only way to prove Wayne's involvement.

I managed to convince Arlo to interview Kevin with me again, probably because Rawlins was on the way back to his office in Wind River.

"If we aren't getting anywhere, though," he said, "we got other leads we need to work."

When the guards escorted Kevin into the interview room,

he looked even worse than he did before. To be honest, I was surprised they were able to coax him out of his cell.

After the guards left the three of us alone, Arlo asked Kevin, "Is it okay that we record our conversation again?"

"Again?" Kevin mumbled with confusion.

"Yeah. Remember we recorded our last conversation with you?"

Kevin shook his head.

"Kevin?" I asked. "Russell?"

"Russell?" he said. "Geez, Doc... It's Robbie."

"Right, sorry," I said. "Well, do you mind if we record our conversation?"

He shrugged and said, "Whatever..."

Arlo set the camera up on the table and began recording.

"Robbie," I said, "what can you tell me about your uncle Wayne?"

"My uncle?" he said, surprised. "I didn't even know I *had* an uncle."

"Yeah, on your mom's side," I said. "You've never met him or heard anyone talk about him before?"

Kevin shook his head.

"Well, what about Eddie? You remember him, don't you?"

Kevin scoffed at this. "Yeah, of course I remember that asshole. Why does it matter anyways? Did he do something again?"

"Possibly..." I said, going through the case file until I found one of the photos that the coroner had taken of the most recent victim. "Do you mind if I show you a photo? It might be pretty disturbing."

"Yeah, whatever," Kevin said.

"Sharon," added Arlo, "you think that's a good idea?"

I nodded, pushing the photo toward Kevin. "Do you recognize this woman?" I said.

Kevin became visibly disturbed as he eyed the photo.

"Did the Strangler do this?" he asked.

"They believe so."

"But..." Kevin muttered as he thought about it more closely, "don't they think *I'm* the Strangler?"

I nodded slowly.

"How could that be?" he asked. "I mean, I've been here this whole time..."

At that point, Kevin's voice trailed off as he stared at the photo again. He started to cry softly, his head cast down.

"I'm really sorry, Robbie." I reached out to his shackled hand on the table and put my hand on his.

As he cried, a sound escaped his throat. At first, I thought he was whimpering, but the longer it went on, the more I realized that he was stifling laughter.

"Robbie?" I asked, pulling my hand away quickly.

Kevin lifted his head, a wide grin smothering his face with tears still fresh on his cheeks.

"Oh, Doc..." he said mockingly. "You guys are still at this, huh?"

"Edward?" I said.

"Now you're getting it," he said with a wink.

"You said last time that 'our old friend' had a thing for this latest victim. What did you mean?"

"Jesus, you two are thick. What else would it mean? He had his way with her."

"He raped her?" I asked.

Kevin grimaced and said, "More or less..."

"*More or less?* What does that mean? Either he did or he didn't. Which is it?"

"Damn, you're getting uptight these days," he said. "You need a vacation, I think. Don't you think so, Arlo?"

"Just answer the question, Edward."

"*Just answer the question, Edward,*" Kevin mocked. "I swear, you two are pathetic. Why do you care what happened to her anyways? She was just some junkie whore. You know all about those types, don't you, Doc?"

"Excuse me?" I replied, dumbfounded.

Kevin grinned, adding, "Do you see her when you see all those victims? Her once-childish glow washed out and bloated. Rotting like a mutt on the side of the road."

"I don't know what you're talking about," I retorted, my mind swirling as I wonder if he's talking about Maddie and if so how he knows about her.

"Come on, Doc. We're all friends here, after all." Kevin glanced over at Arlo and added, "Surely you've told *him* your little secret."

"He's just needling you," Arlo muttered to me. "Just trying to get under your skin."

"That's right," Kevin said. "Just like all those needles that found their way into your daughter's skin."

"I don't have a daughter," I replied apathetically, trying to remain firm under his pressure.

"Not anymore you don't, thanks to you."

"That's enough," Arlo tried to interject. He touched my arm and added, "Let's stop for now. We're not going to get anything out of him."

I was mesmerized though. By guilt or anger or sadness, I don't really know. As badly as I wanted to get away from him, I couldn't.

"Does it drive you mad that they haven't found her yet?" Kevin added. "They've been able to find all those others, but not your precious little girl. Even amongst junkie whores, nobody gives a shit."

"We're done," Arlo retorted, grabbing me by the arm and startling me out of my bewildered stupor.

Kevin laughed briefly. "Tell me something, Doc. How do

you know I haven't been fucking with you this whole time? Ever since that first day you met us?"

"I don't," I said, my agitation rising despite my efforts to control it. "And I don't really care, to be honest with you."

He eyed me mockingly. "I don't think you actually believe that. Otherwise, why else would you still be here if not to make sure that Kevin really is as crazy as you think he is?"

Attempting to side rail his taunting, I asked him, "Who's 'our old friend', Edward?"

"Now you're just being stupid," he replied. "Think about it: what people do we both know?"

"Wayne?"

"Wayne?" Kevin scoffed. "Give me a break! That old crook couldn't slap his ass with both hands no less strangle some bitch to death. Try again."

"I'm not playing this game with you," I said.

"Oh, come on... Don't get sore about it."

"I'm not," I said flatly, my sense of self-control slowly returning. "But we're not going to waste my time anymore."

"What about Kevin?" he asked. "Don't you care about him?"

"The hell with Kevin," I said, hoping I could somehow provoke him. "Or are *you* too dense to realize that I've been using you this whole time?"

"Using *me*?" he laughed. "And tell me how you've been doing that exactly."

"You know how hard it is to find a condition like yours?" I said. "You've given me a career-defining case study, Edward. A sociopath trapped in the body of an imbecile."

"How do you know the condition is legitimate?" he asked. "Maybe that's part of the game too?"

"It isn't," I said, motioning to Arlo to shut off the camera and pack it away.

"How can you be so sure?"

"Because you're out of cards to play, Edward. And because you can't stand to see that someone other than you is getting credit for all of this. *Your work* as you called it. You wanna know what everyone's going to remember about you, Edward? Nothing. Kevin will get all the credit. He'll join the ranks of the others and nobody will know anything about you."

I helped Arlo pack up the camcorder, and Kevin replied, "Just wait'll you see the trump card I got up my sleeve."

"Looking forward to it," I said, opening the door and following Arlo out into the hallway.

For several moments, we both stood in silence as we tried to process what had just happened.

"Well," I finally said, "I think it's safe to say that we're not going to get anything else out of him today."

"*Anything else?*" commented Arlo. "I didn't realize we got anything out of him in the first place."

"He's protecting Wayne," I said. "I could just see it in his face when I was talking about him. Like he was trying to provoke me while deflecting suspicion at the same time."

"Jesus..." Arlo muttered with a shake of his head. "And what was he trying to pull with that bit about your daughter?"

"Who knows," I replied. "Probably nothing more than psychotic ranting with the hope that it would somehow fluster me. Not the first time I've encountered that."

"What a lunatic..."

I nodded, although I couldn't help but wonder if Kevin actually knew about Maddie, and if so, how? He never mentioned her by name specifically, but he seemed to know about her drug addiction and transience. He even indicated that he had killed her and left her remains with the others. The thought alone overwhelmed me beyond description. It was as if every one of my worst fears had spiraled into a cyclone and torn my soul to pieces.

Of course, there was also the possibility that he knew nothing about me and was simply drawing straws to try to get under my skin. The fact that he was right about Maddie could have been nothing more than a lucky guess.

THIRTY-SIX

That evening, I sat in my hotel room in Wind River and combed through the case file and all the notes from my interviews with Kevin yet again. I just felt like there was *something* that I was missing, *something* that would give me some stroke of insight. I stumbled upon Georg's evaluation from a few months prior, but there was nothing in there that I hadn't already seen or heard.

The longer I searched, though, the more I started to wonder what I was really trying to accomplish with all of this. Was I trying to piece my shattered reputation back together? Was I trying to protect someone from being screwed by a corrupt system? Was I trying to prove to everybody as well as myself that I had not fallen victim to the mind games of a brilliant sociopath? Was I trying to redeem myself for my failures with Maddie?

Maybe it was all of those things. This convoluted entanglement of motivation that was so far gone that its individual parts could never be discerned or separated.

The only thing I was certain about was the doubt that had begun to form within me. Doubt about Kevin. Doubt about the system and everyone involved in it. Doubt about my own abilities.

My ruminations were interrupted by the abrupt ring of the telephone.

"This is Dr. Stevenson," I answered.

"Sharon, it's Arlo. I just got off the phone with Matthews."

"Matthews?" I said. "I thought you were going to call her tomorrow?"

"I was," he said, "but she called me. We've got a problem. *Several* problems, actually."

"What are you talking about?" I asked.

"The coroner found traces of bleach and acetone in the new victim's mouth. Apparently it's some type of homemade cocktail for chloroform. They're thinking Kevin used it to render her unconscious before he... did whatever he did to her."

"Have they found these on any of the other victims?" I asked.

"The bleach, yes. They figured it was just him trying to clean the bodies, but the acetone makes them think otherwise. The problem is that Kevin had access to both at the community college."

"So did Wayne and every other janitor there," I said.

"Yeah, but none of their DNA was recovered from the bodies."

I thought about this briefly, then suddenly the chloroform cocktail started to make more sense.

"Why would Kevin render the women unconscious, Arlo? He's certainly strong enough to handle them on his own. Why knock them out?"

"Any number of reasons," he said. "Power? Control? Ease of dealing with them? You name it."

"I don't think so," I said. "That doesn't fit with the Edward persona at all. He's too sadistic for that. He wouldn't want them just lying there unconscious. He would want them struggling, resisting him so that he could look them dead in the eyes as he dominated them. Feed off their terror as he slowly choked the life out of them. He would view chloroform as something that a weakling would use."

"What are you getting at?"

"I don't think Kevin did it," I said. "I think the Edward persona wants to *believe* he did it, but I don't think he actually did."

"That's ridiculous," he said. "What about the DNA?"

"Someone could have planted it on the bodies to frame him," I said. "Think about it: who better to pin a murder on than someone who's so mentally screwed up that he has no way of remembering anything or defending himself after the fact? Kevin's the *perfect* scapegoat."

"Who the hell did it then?" asked Arlo. "The rickety old uncle?"

"Yes!" I exclaimed. "He wouldn't be strong enough to strangle those women without knocking them out first. Not anymore at least. And think about his record as a younger man. Like I said before, he didn't just stop committing violent crimes. He just got better at it. And Lord knows, he could have easily gotten Kevin's hair or saliva and planted it on the bodies."

There was a brief pause on the line before Arlo said, "So let me get this straight... You think that Wayne intentionally adopted his mentally ill nephew so that he could murder young women and frame it on Kevin? *That's* what you're arguing?"

"I know it sounds a little absurd..." I said.

"What about the letters to the *Courier*?" he asked. "The handwriting was a match to Kevin. He even used the name Edward, for Christ's sake."

"Wayne could have easily coerced him into writing those. Maybe Wayne knows about the dissociative identity disorder and knew about the Edward persona. Maybe—"

Arlo interjected, "Goddammit, listen to yourself. This is insane."

"I know it's out there, but—"

"No," he said. "You've got to stop doing this."

"Doing what?"

"Trying to find something that isn't there," he said. "Listen, do I agree with you that Kevin is psychotic in some way? Absolutely. Any dumbass off the street could see that. But there's a fact that I think the two of us need to face. *Kevin is guilty of these crimes.* Not Wayne. Not Edward or any other personality that sprouts up out of his head. Kevin. All of the evidence points directly at him."

I remained silent for several moments, thinking.

Finally, I muttered, "I just don't know what the hell to think anymore."

"Neither do I," he said.

Silence fell between us again until I remembered that Arlo had mentioned *several* problems had arisen.

"What was the other problem you mentioned earlier?" I asked. "Besides the evidence of the chloroform?"

"Shit, I forgot," he said. "I asked Matthews about having the investigators interview Wayne again, and she told me that they tried to but haven't been able to locate him."

"What?" I said.

"They've tried him at his house and the community college and found no trace of him."

"That just further proves my point! He's on the run now that he knows we suspect something."

"Hold on a second," he said. "They spoke to the community college, and apparently he requested a leave of absence in light of everything. He said the harassment from the media has started to wear on him, so he's getting out of town until the trial is over."

"And they're just going to let him go?" I said. "He's clearly involved somehow!"

"They don't seem to think so," he said. "As far as they're concerned, Kevin is the Blue River Strangler. The *only* Blue River Strangler."

"What about the hair we found at the cabin though?"

"She said the investigators didn't find any when they went out there."

"*That* is bullshit," I said. "You and I both saw it there. Wayne must have cleaned it up before they got there."

"I don't know," he said, "but the fact remains that there is zero physical evidence linking Wayne to any of the murders."

"Unbelievable," I scoffed. "So they won't look at Wayne as a potential suspect or accomplice, and the media coverage has essentially tainted our insanity defense. What does that even leave us with?"

"Not a whole lot..." Arlo said dismally.

"Goddammit," I muttered, racking my brain for some other answer. After a few seconds of nothing, I added, "He's going to get the death penalty, isn't he?"

"More than likely," answered Arlo.

THIRTY-SEVEN

A week passed with little development in Kevin's case. I continued to interview Kevin, but he was slipping further into psychosis and depression with each session until he got to the point where he hardly spoke at all. The times he did speak, I only saw Robbie and Jackie.

If I had to guess, I think the reality of the situation was bearing down on him, and his only solution was to regress into his adolescent and childish selves. I worried more and more about his safety at that point. Guys who are driven to those kinds of dismal depths often end up attempting suicide in their cells in the middle of the night.

At the plea hearing for the new charge of first-degree murder, Arlo pleaded not guilty by reason of insanity, and the criminal trial was set to begin two weeks later.

Arlo and I spent every waking hour of that time trying to piece a defense together, but Wayne was nowhere to be found and I couldn't convince anybody I knew to evaluate Kevin and stand as an expert witness alongside me.

When the trial began, Arlo and I were not optimistic. Matthews and the prosecution team first presented the evidence of the crime itself, all of which was incredibly condemning. She began with the DNA evidence of the hair follicle found on the recent victim's body. She dove into the details of his mother abusing him and eventually abandoning him, as well as the sources of his motive for killing all of his victims, in Matthews' opinion. Next came the traces of bleach and acetone found in the victim's mouth, both of which Kevin had unlimited access to as a janitor at the community college. Circumstantial, Matthews admitted, but a vital piece to the whole puzzle. Then Matthews presented the cause of death and the placement of the victim near the Blue River, obvious similarities to many of the twenty-eight murders to which Kevin had pleaded guilty in his previous trial. And while Arlo tried his best to exploit inconsistencies in testimony and investigative procedure, the evidence said everything it needed to say. Kevin was guilty.

With the burden of proof clearly met by the prosecution team, it was Arlo's turn to try to convince the jury that Kevin did in fact suffer from a mental illness that could have significantly impaired his judgment during and after the crime was committed. That's when he called me to the stand to testify.

Despite standing as an expert witness a number of times before, I've never been more nervous than when I took the stand for Kevin.

The direct examination went as well as we could have expected. I spent the majority of the day walking through my initial evaluation of Kevin as well as my subsequent interviews with him over the past months. I went into great detail regarding my observations of his behavior and the presentation of his condition, even showing the footage of our most recent interviews with him so the jury could see for themselves what I was seeing. Arlo questioned me on the validity of dissociative identity disorder as a mental disorder so that we could establish that, despite its rarity, there were still a number of cases that were similar to Kevin's. By the end of the direct examination, I was a little more hopeful than when the trial first started. The jury wasn't openly averse to my testimony, so I figured as long as I could endure Matthews' cross-examination, Kevin had a decent chance.

Despite preparing exhaustively with Arlo, I still felt anxious as I took the stand for cross-examination that following morning. It was the first time in my career that I had been on the defense side of a trial, and I had seen prosecutors tear into defense witnesses before. I had to remind myself that Kim Matthews was no veteran of criminal litigation, though; she was young and inexperienced, and as long as I could stick to the facts and maintain my composure, I was confident that I could keep the defense afloat.

Matthews roasted me on everything regarding my diagnosis: the dismally low prevalence of DID; the lack of empirical diagnostics for the condition; the striking similarities of symptoms between DID and borderline personality disorder. She even dredged up an old psychiatric evaluation of mine that listed the same symptoms as Kevin's, yet I concluded the patient was not mentally ill and competent to stand trial. For every answer I had, Matthews had a counterpunch that twisted my words to contradict something else. The cross-examination could not have gone more poorly.

Arlo did his best to pick up the pieces that Matthews had left in her wake, but too much damage had been done. We needed to provide indisputable evidence that Kevin was legally insane, and the cross-examination combined with the testimony of the prosecution's psychiatrists gouged too many holes into our defense for a jury to accept it.

The jury deliberated for a day and a half before finding Kevin guilty of all charges.

Because the prosecution team was seeking the death penalty, the judge scheduled the sentencing trial for a month later, at which time a jury of Kevin's peers would have to unanimously decide to sentence him to death.

As grim as this may sound, I didn't feel as hopeless as you might expect. It wasn't like the criminal trial where we had to convince all twelve jurors that Kevin was insane. All we had to do was convince one person to have mercy on him. One person out of twelve. That alone improved our odds immensely, in my opinion.

Arlo wasn't so optimistic.

"I'm going to need you to step away from the case," he told me shortly after Kevin was found guilty. "I'm afraid that a jury is going to view your testimony as biased and moot."

As much as I wanted to argue with him about it, I knew he was right. Matthews had destroyed any credibility I had left, not to mention the media had clearly tainted the jury pool for the criminal trial because of their coverage of me. We would have been delusional if we didn't expect the same thing to happen during the sentencing trial.

"I know you've sacrificed everything for this case," Arlo added, "but there's nothing else we can do. I'm going to see if I can find another psychiatrist to confirm your diagnosis. Maybe Kevin can persuade one of the jurors when he gives his remarks. In all honesty, though, I don't know what else to do."

"What if we can prove that he was coerced or that someone else committed the crimes?" I said.

Arlo shook his head with discouragement. "How are we going to do that? Find Wayne and torture him until he confesses? Besides, the verdict is in. As far as everybody is concerned, Kevin did this. Our only chance is to convince one of the jurors that he genuinely feels remorse for what he did. Convince one person to simply have mercy on him."

THIRTY-EIGHT

There was no mercy for Kevin.

I was back in Colorado when Arlo called me about the sentencing. I already knew. Every media outlet across the country had used it as a powder keg for their ratings.

BLUE RIVER STRANGLER SENTENCED TO DEATH

People across the nation were ecstatic about the ruling. Justice had finally been served.

The media raised Kim Matthews up as some kind of heroine.

FEMALE PROSECUTOR TRIUMPHS OVER STRANGLER

was printed in headlines across the country. She even had a story about her in *Time* magazine shortly thereafter.

It amazed me how much someone could benefit from a man's death sentence.

The ruling devastated me for a million reasons, and

despite Arlo's warnings to separate myself from Kevin's case, I couldn't help it. If nothing else, I wanted to make sure he was holding up okay and to let him know that not everybody was rooting against him. That he had at least one friend on the outside.

I was relatively familiar with the lead psychiatrist at Wyoming State Penitentiary, Dr. Carla Moneta, so I called her to see how Kevin was doing.

"He's lonely," she said. "He's the only one on death row here, so he only sees me and the guards. He hasn't spoken to anyone since the sentencing."

"Can I try speaking to him?" I asked.

"I'll ask him, but I doubt he'll even give me an answer."

"Have you seen any of the other personalities?"

"It's hard to tell right now," she said. "He's an unresponsive void at this point."

"So he hasn't mentioned anything about filing for an appeal yet?"

"Goodness, no," she said. "I can hardly get him to eat, no less consider the process of appealing his sentence."

I was terrified to even ask my next question. "Has he attempted to harm himself?"

"No, not yet," she said. "I honestly think he's so far in the depths of depression that he wouldn't have the energy to do anything. But we're keeping a close eye on him, just to be sure."

"If that isn't ironic, I don't know what is..."

"What do you mean?" she asked.

"The guy is on death row, yet we can't let him take his own life. Only the State gets to have that pleasure."

"Yeah..." Carla said. "It's the nature of the field though. Not just for death row. For all of them serving life sentences. We can try to help them, but at the end of the day, they're going to rot in a cell no matter what we do."

"I hate it," I said. "Maybe I should retire. Kranick's been

hounding me about it ever since Kevin's case blew up in my face anyways."

"What would you do?"

"I don't know. Learn how to paint."

"No offense, but I can't picture you painting, Sharon."

"Neither can I," I said dejectedly.

Carla and I reminisced for a few minutes before I hung up the phone and went to the living room to stare mindlessly at the television. My better judgment told me to avoid the news, but as I flicked through the channels, I couldn't help myself.

The news feed at the bottom of the screen turned my blood cold:

BODY FOUND IN ENCHANTED CIRCLE WILDERNESS

"Investigators have yet to release the identity of the victim," the reporter said. "However, they did confirm that the victim is female, approximately twenty to thirty years of age."

They showed aerial footage of a mountainous terrain that looked uncomfortably similar to the area near Park City.

The reporter added, "A group of fishermen stumbled upon the body about fifteen miles east of Del Norte, New Mexico, a popular skiing destination in the winter."

"We were hiking the Tarryall Creek Trail to fish the beaver ponds," said one of the fishermen in an earlier interview. "My buddy Dale was the first one to notice something jammed up against one of the dams."

"How far from the trailhead did you find the victim?" asked the reporter.

"Only a half mile or so," he said. "Maybe not even that far."

A separate reporter added, "Although the coroner has not confirmed the cause of death, investigators believe the victim might have been strangled to death."

"It's just unfortunate," a local said in an interview. "Del Norte is a peaceful little town. I mean, we hardly have any crime that I can think of, so to have something like this worries me."

"Do the circumstances of this murder seem similar to those of the Blue River Strangler murders in Wyoming?" asked the reporter.

"Gosh, I don't know..." the local said. "Sure hope that this is the only victim."

Another reporter added, "Although the Blue River Strangler, Kevin Blackford, is safely locked away on death row at the Wyoming State Penitentiary, it wouldn't be the first time someone tried to copy the murders of a serial killer. Veronica Compton tried to mimic the Hillside Stranglers in 1981 by attempting to strangle a cocktail waitress she had lured to a motel. Investigators have not yet said that they believe this murder was committed by a Blackford copycat; however, the potential cause of death and the way in which the body was disposed of both bear an odd resemblance to the Blue River Strangler murders."

The more I watched the news feeds, I couldn't help but wonder if Wayne wasn't involved in this most recent murder somehow. It just seemed too coincidental that this victim was found only a month or so after he had left Wyoming. However, speculation was only speculation until the coroner confirmed the cause of death and if they recovered any physical evidence from the body. What I really hoped was that Wayne's DNA was found, but if nothing else, there were traces of the home-made chloroform cocktail used to incapacitate the twenty-ninth victim. If either was uncovered, then that might be the evidence Kevin needed to appeal his sentence and maybe even his convictions.

Three days later, the Copycat Strangler became the buzz of every news station in the country. Not only had the coroner confirmed strangulation as the cause of death, but trace amounts of bleach and acetone were found on the victim's tongue. If that wasn't enough to send the media into a frenzy, a second body was found along an old forestry service road near the base of Carol Peak. Eight miles away from the location of the first body.

As soon as I saw the news, I called the tip hotline for the Taos County Sheriff's Department.

"I believe I know who the killer is," I told the man who answered the phone.

"Okay," he said, his tone more indifferent than I would have expected. "Do you have a name or a description, ma'am?"

"Both," I said. "The name is Wayne Lennerson. He's in his late fifties, about five-nine, graying hair."

"Okay... And what makes you suspect that he's the killer?"

I told the man who I was and immediately his tone changed.

"Dr. Stevenson," he asked, "do you mind holding for a minute?"

Another man soon picked up the line. "Dr. Stevenson? This is Detective Luna. I understand you might know who our suspect is?"

"Yes," I said.

"A Mr. Wayne Lennerson?"

"Yes."

"And why do you suspect Mr. Lennerson?"

"Mr. Lennerson was a person of interest in the Blue River Strangler case," I said. "Mr. Lennerson is Kevin Blackford's uncle, and at the time, we suspected that he had some type of involvement in the murders. Peak County didn't investigate him enough, though and he ended up leaving the state about a month ago."

"I see. Do you know if Mr. Lennerson is in New Mexico at this time?"

"No, I don't," I said.

"Well," said the detective, his voice losing some of the enthusiasm it had when he first answered the phone, "we'll definitely look into Mr. Lennerson's whereabouts."

"That's all?" I said.

"For the time being, yes. We have hundreds of potential leads to sift through and we have to give all of them our attention."

"Can you notify me when you *do* find out if Mr. Lennerson has been seen down there?"

"I'm sorry, but I won't be able to discuss details of the investigation with you. You understand, I'm sure. Thank you for your help."

And before I could say anything else, Detective Luna hung up.

THIRTY-NINE

Del Norte, New Mexico was only a four-hour drive away from Florence, so I decided I would drive down there myself and see if I could convince the investigators to find Wayne before another body showed up.

I reached out to Arlo to see if he would join me since he had been just as suspicious of Wayne as I was.

"Hello?" Arlo answered, his voice exhausted.

"Arlo, it's Sharon."

"Sharon?" he said. "I'm sorry, but I don't have the time or energy to get into Kevin's sentencing right now."

"I'm not calling about Kevin's sentencing."

"You're not?" he said. "I figured you'd be dying to give me a piece of your mind about it."

"Maybe some other time, but not today," I said. "I'm calling about what's going on in New Mexico."

"New Mexico?"

"Yeah," I said. "Have you not seen the news?"

"No..."

"They found two bodies somewhere near Del Norte," I

said. "Young women strangled to death and dumped in the Wheeler National Forest."

"Jesus," he breathed. "That's terrible."

"Yeah, and doesn't it sound an awful lot like a Blue River Strangler murder to you?"

Arlo sighed. "Sharon... please don't say what I think you're going to say."

"What do you mean?" I asked.

"You think someone else is involved somehow, don't you?"

"It certainly seems like a possibility," I said. "Don't you find it convenient that only a month after Wayne Lennerson leaves Wyoming, a body is found in northern New Mexico? Similar circumstances and everything?"

"Similar circumstances? For all we know it's a copycat. I mean, as much national attention from the press as Kevin's case got, I'm honestly shocked there wasn't a copycat murder sooner than this."

"You're wrong," I said. "This is no copycat. This is the Blue River Strangler. The *real* Blue River Strangler."

"Why are you even calling me about this?" he asked, his tone agitated. "There's nothing I can do about a murder in another state."

"Come down to Del Norte with me," I said. "Help me convince the investigators to look into Wayne."

"*Come down with you?*" he scoffed. "Why don't you just call them?"

"I already have and they basically hung up on me."

"Can you blame them?" he said. "Aside from your theory being completely absurd, you're not exactly a reliable source of information these days. Not in the public's opinion at least."

"Go to hell, Arlo," I retorted.

"You know that's the truth," he said. "And while we're being honest with each other, I think you've let the situation with Kevin significantly cloud your judgment here. You need to let this go once and for all before you do more than destroy your reputa—"

I hung up the phone on him. I wasn't about to be lectured by him, especially when he had no clue what was truly motivating me.

In my frustration, I considered calling Wendy and asking her to help me, but part of me knew she was going to give me as hard of a time about it as Arlo had. Plus, she wouldn't even set foot in a prison, no less track down a serial killer; nor would I *want* her to in all honesty. It was a ridiculous idea that I quickly tossed out.

That's when I called Georg.

"Hello?" Georg's wife, Theresa, answered the phone.

"Theresa, it's Sharon," I said.

"Hi, Sharon," she replied pleasantly.

"Is Georg there, by chance? I really need to speak with him."

"I'm sorry, he isn't," she said. "Ever since his mom fell a month ago, her health has really declined, so he's been out in Taos trying to take care of her."

"Oh, I'm sorry to hear that," I said. "He never told me."

"He's pretty shaken up by it, but you know him: he'll do anything to keep people from seeing it. He wouldn't even let me go out there with him."

"Yeah, that sounds like Georg."

Theresa laughed briefly. "Yes. Always the stubborn Austrian."

Only then did the location of Georg's mother's house dawn on me.

"Wait a minute: did you say he's in *Taos*?" I asked. "Taos, New Mexico?"

"Yeah," she said. "Why?"

I didn't answer for a moment, pondering the fact that Taos

was the largest town within the Enchanted Circle. No more than an hour's drive away from Del Norte.

Theresa must've sensed something in my silence because she asked, "Is everything alright?"

"Yeah," I said. "Sorry... Do you know where I can reach him?" I asked, my mind still chewing on the coincidence.

Theresa gave me the phone number to his mother's house. "Are you sure everything is alright?" she added, her voice hesitant.

"Yeah," I said. "I'm just a little strung out from the trial still."

"You should go on vacation for a while," she said. "Get away from work and relax."

"Yeah," I answered, "I might just do that."

As soon as I ended the call with Theresa, I called the number she had given to me.

"Georg, it's Sharon," I said when he answered.

"*Sharon?*" he asked as if I was the last person he expected to hear from. "How'd you know to call me here?"

"I spoke to Theresa and she said you were helping your mother down there."

"Yeah..." he said hesitantly. "I had to move her to a hospice a few days ago."

"I'm sorry to hear that. I didn't know she had fallen or else I would have reached out sooner."

"Don't worry about it. I've been pretty distant as it is." He paused for a moment before adding, "So what's up? I'm sure you didn't call just to hear about my mother."

"Well..." I said, feeling uncomfortable, "I'm sure you've seen the news about those two bodies they found in Del Norte?"

"Yes?"

"Don't the circumstances seem a little... *similar* to the Blue River Strangler murders?"

"Geez, Sharon," he sighed. "Don't go there. For Christ's sake, don't go there."

"What do you mean?" I countered. "I just have a theory is all."

"And what theory is that? That Blackford is innocent and the real Blue River Strangler is down here now?"

"Not exactly," I said. "But I *do* think someone else was helping him. Maybe even coercing him."

"*Coercing* him?" he scoffed. "That's just as ridiculous as him being innocent. Who would have coerced him anyways?"

"His uncle," I said. "Wayne Lennerson."

Georg was silent for a moment before saying, "Have you talked to the authorities about any of this?"

"I've tried to," I said, "but they won't hear any of it. I'm planning on driving down there today to try to convince them in person."

"You're going to do *what?*" he retorted. "How is *that* going to convince them?"

"I'm bringing the Strangler case file with me to show them all of the evidence linking Wayne to the murders."

"*What* evidence? And what happens when they shut you down?"

"I don't know," I said. "I'll find Wayne myself, I guess."

Georg replied, "*You're* going to find him? How do you even know he's there?"

"I don't, but if he is—"

"Even if he *is*, Sharon, what are you going to be able to do? Apprehend him yourself? A citizen's arrest with nothing to go on but wild hunches?"

"Well, no..." I said.

"Then what?" he added.

"I don't know exactly..."

"Jesus," he said with a sigh. "You have to let this shit go already. You're driving yourself nuts."

"Don't go there," I said. "I'm not going crazy."

"Could've fooled me," he said.

"Of all the people who should understand, *you* should."

"I don't understand though," he said. "Look at what you're doing to yourself. Look at what you've done to your career. For what? Take my advice. Stay home. Let the police deal with this before you get yourself into trouble."

"Trouble?" I said. "I'm trying to *help* them."

"Not to them you aren't. To them, you're interfering with an investigation."

My anger left me speechless, and an awkward silence fell between us.

"I need to get going," Georg eventually said. "Stay in Colorado, Sharon."

And before I could say anything else, he hung up.

FORTY

I threw an overnight bag together, made a hotel reservation in Del Norte, and gathered everything I had from the Blue River Strangler case file before heading out of Florence toward New Mexico.

Despite the fact that most of southern Colorado and northern New Mexico are desolate wastelands, Taos County and the surrounding Wheeler National Forest was spectacular, with the majestic Walker Peak standing at the center. Four towns along the circular highway provided the best skiing and snowboarding across the southwest part of the United States. Dozens of creeks ran down all sides of the peak to form the Gila River to the east and the Questa River to the west.

As was the case with the Blue River Strangler murders, the breathtaking beauty of the Enchanted Circle made the copycat murders that much more heinous. What unnerved and angered me the most was that the two most recent murders could have been prevented had Matthews and the Peak County investigators actually heeded our warnings about Wayne. It only made me that much more determined to convince the Taos County Sheriff's Office to listen to me.

As soon as I had checked into my hotel in Del Norte, I drove to the sheriff's office. I told the deputy at the front desk who I was and that I had urgent information about the Copycat Strangler.

Detective Luna soon came out from the back of the station. He was a wiry man who had an old-school air to him. Quiet and cerebral, yet abrupt when he did speak.

"Dr. Stevenson," he said when he greeted me. "You're awfully far from Colorado, aren't you?"

"I felt like a phone call didn't do justice to my concerns," I said, "so I figured I'd go for a drive and talk to you in person."

"That's quite a drive," he said. "You really didn't have to do that."

"Trust me," I said, holding the Blue River Strangler case file up for him to see. "You'll be happy I did."

"Okay," he said with a nod. "Follow me."

He led me into the back of the station where his cubicle was.

"I brought the entire Strangler case file for you," I said after we sat down at his desk. "Everything you need to understand Wayne is all there."

"Thanks," he said, taking the file and placing it off to the side on his desk.

"Have you been able to locate Wayne Lennerson yet?" I asked.

"We haven't," he said. "We haven't even had time to look into him, actually."

"What do you mean?" I said. "Why not?"

"Frankly, we have more promising leads. Descriptions of people of interest that don't fit your description of this Lennerson guy."

"What descriptions?" I asked.

"For one," he said, "this Wayne Lennerson is way too old to be our killer. We're looking for someone at least fifteen years younger. Forties maybe. Another thing is that we believe our suspect has blond hair, not graying hair as you described Wayne."

"Well, they're wrong," I said. "I'm telling you, Lennerson is your guy."

"And I don't doubt that you believe that," he said, "but I called up to the Peak County Sheriff's Office about you after you and I spoke on the phone. Folks up there seem to think Blackford's using you to go on some vigilante witch hunt to exonerate him."

"That's ridiculous," I said. "I'm down here to try to prevent more young women from being murdered, which is more than anyone else can say. As for Kevin using me, whoever you talked to up there hasn't seen him recently. Kevin hasn't uttered a word in months."

"Look, Dr. Stevenson, I'm going to level with you: the fact that you drove all the way down here from Colorado worries the shit out of me. Regardless of your reason for coming down here, I think you're too personally invested and trying to connect dots that aren't meant to be connected. We have a strong reason to believe the person responsible for our two murders had nothing to do with the Blue River Strangler murders."

"And what reason is that?" I scoffed.

"I can't get into those details with you," he said. "The sheriff will release those to the press when we feel it's appropriate to do so."

"I can't believe this," I said. "I'm handing you the suspect and you're just going to blow me off?"

"I don't doubt your belief in that, ma'am, but I think you're too emotionally connected to Blackford to see beyond that. Trust me, the Blue River Strangler had nothing to do with these two murders."

"Fine," I said, rising from my chair. "I'll show myself out."

"Don't forget the case file," he said.

"Why don't you hold onto it. You know... so you have it on the off chance you need it."

"Please," he said to my back as I walked out. "Go home and let us do our jobs."

I had no intention of going back to Colorado. If they refused to look for Wayne, then I was going to find him myself.

I stopped by my hotel to see if Georg had tried calling, but no new messages awaited me. I headed east on Highway 38 toward the general location that the second body was discovered, then due south toward the town of Sugarloaf.

What had been so deceptive about the Blue River Strangler case was that most of the bodies were not found in the order in which the victims were killed, so in the midst of the investigation, the placement of the bodies seemed completely random. After the fact however, we figured out that the placement wasn't random at all; the Strangler left the bodies in a circular pattern with the newest victims forming the periphery. With the second New Mexico victim found east of Del Norte, it seemed that Wayne was working in a clockwise fashion along the Enchanted Circle. Sugarloaf was the next populated area before Buffalo Creek on the southeast rim of the circle and then Taos on the opposite side of the Palo Flechado Pass.

My plan was to stop in Sugarloaf and see if anybody in town had noticed a man matching Wayne's description. Sugarloaf's downtown area was only a few square blocks in size, so I figured it wouldn't take me more than a few hours to question shop owners and tourists milling about.

Based on the volume of people in Sugarloaf alone, you never would have known that a serial killer was on the loose. The streets were packed with tourists, none of whom seemed alarmed by the two bodies dumped in the wilderness only fifteen miles away.

When I asked shop workers if they had seen a man fitting Wayne's description, they either said, "That describes half the men I see on a daily basis here," or "You know how many people cycle through here? I'm not gonna remember if I saw one particular person."

Needless to say, if Wayne was in Sugarloaf, he had gone completely unnoticed by the general public.

An hour passed before I decided to head back to Del Norte and get a fresh start the following morning. When I was making my way down Main Street to go back to my car though, I could have sworn I saw Wayne walking in the opposite direction of me on the other side of the street. His hair was longer, but the slightly hitched gait was unmistakable.

Not wanting to spook him, I went in the direction he was going on my side of Main Street, keeping my eyes fixed upon him so as not to lose him in the horde of tourists. Despite his rickety movements, he cut through the crowd faster than expected, so I was having to dodge pedestrians on my side while trying to keep my eyes on him across the street.

That's when he disappeared into an outdoor apparel shop and I almost ran into the person in front of me.

"Watch it," the guy said to me, but I was too fixated on the storefront to pay him much attention.

As I watched for Wayne to come back out of the store, my mind raced as I considered what I was going to do when I confronted him. Flashbacks of my encounter with him on his driveway in Park City appeared, and for all I knew, he was carrying a pistol now. I wondered if I shouldn't have stopped at the sporting goods store and purchased a gun myself before coming down here. Not that holding him up at gunpoint in the middle of a tourist town was the wisest thing to do.

I decided that approaching him directly wasn't safe for anybody. I needed to confirm without a doubt that it was him and call Detective Luna. If Luna refused to listen, then I would call 911 and falsely report a crime. Anything to get Wayne in custody.

My contemplation disappeared when I saw the man whom I thought was Wayne emerge from the store and continue down Main Street. I followed from a distance, my eyes never leaving him. He wove his way through the crowds of tourists for another block, then stopped at the corner to cross to the other side of Main Street. As he waited for the traffic light to change, I tried to get a better look at him to confirm it was him, but he was still too far away for me to tell. I needed him to get closer, but I worried if he got too close that he might recognize me.

When the traffic light changed, he walked with the other pedestrians across the intersection. I figured catching a passing glance at him was the safest move, so I inched my way through the crowded sidewalk toward the intersection. He stepped onto the curb and started walking with the flow of foot traffic in my direction. Through the throng of pedestrians, though, I struggled to make out the details of his face. Only when we were twenty feet from each other did I finally get a good enough look at him.

The hair color and hitched gait were close matches, but his face was completely foreign to me.

I immediately stopped where I was and watched the man shuffle past me with the rest of the pedestrians.

The man I was following was definitely not Wayne Lennerson.

I'm losing my goddamn mind, I thought, practically saying it out loud. I remained motionless for several seconds, the flow of foot traffic rolling around me, unfazed by my obstruction.

Despite the fact that I had wrongfully followed someone, I was still convinced that Wayne was involved in the two most recent murders; he just wasn't in Sugarloaf. Maybe Buffalo Creek or even Taos by this point.

When I decided to return to my car and continue west toward the next town, I thought I heard someone calling my name.

I turned abruptly, and a woman walking behind me nearly ran into me. She skirted me and scowled as she passed.

I *am* losing my goddamn mind, I thought, turning to continue down the walkway.

As sure as I was about Wayne's involvement, Georg's warnings lurked in the back of my brain when I got to my car. The fact that I had followed someone who was not actually Wayne made me wonder if a part of what he said wasn't accurate. Maybe the stress of Kevin's trial really had worn me down to a breaking point.

FORTY-ONE

I drove back to Del Norte that evening and went straight to my hotel. I really needed to rethink what I was trying to do down there, and my lack of sleep was not helping things either.

But when I walked into the foyer of the hotel, I saw Detective Luna sitting in an easy chair in the lobby. He rose from the chair abruptly when he saw me.

"Detective Luna?" I said. "What are you doing here?"

"I've been thinking about our conversation from earlier, Dr. Stevenson, and I was wondering if we could talk more?"

"More? Why?" I asked indignantly. "You didn't seem all that interested in what I had to say before."

"We've had some developments since we last spoke," he said. "Would you mind coming down to the station with me?"

"Can't we just talk here?" I asked. "We can go to my room if we need to speak in private."

His eyes narrowed and his face hardened. "Down at the station would be better," he said firmly.

I looked at him skeptically, saying, "Have *I* done something, Detective?"

"Not that we know of," he said.

"What does *that* mean exactly?"

"It means that it's incredibly unusual that you've come all the way down here to assist with the investigation. It's not uncommon for killers to snoop around their own investigations to deflect suspicion."

"*Suspicion?*" I asked, shocked. "You're saying *I'm a* suspect now? How could I possibly be involved? I just got here."

"So you say," he said, stepping toward me. "If you ask me, I think you're obsessed with Blackford and his crimes. Maybe you wanted to see what it was like for yourself?"

"That's ridiculous," I scoffed.

"Prove it then. Give us a DNA sample so we can compare it to the trace amounts found on the first victim."

"Why don't you run what you found against Kevin's?" I said, reeling from the accusations. "You'll probably get a partial match because of his relation to Wayne."

"We did that already," he said. "We got nothing. None of Blackford's relatives could have done this, including this uncle you keep bringing up."

"What?" I muttered, baffled. "There's got to be some kind of mistake..."

"Please," Luna said. "Just come with me?"

"Do you seriously think *I'm* capable of abducting and strangling those women?"

"Nobody suspected Dorothea Puente either," he said.

"The Death House Landlady?" I replied, my outrage growing. "She was poisoning her elderly renters, not strangling young women!"

He disregarded my outburst, saying, "Please, Dr. Stevenson. Come to the station with me."

I was so flustered by that point I didn't know what to think or do. There was no sense in causing more of a scene, so I gave in and followed Luna. I knew I had nothing to hide.

When we arrived at the sheriff's office, they immediately

took me back to an interrogation room and a technician took saliva and hair samples from me. Because I was innocent, I knew I had nothing to worry about, but the process alone made me anxious all the same.

Once the technician was finished, Luna took a seat across from me.

"You're wasting your time," I told him. "I've got nothing to do with any of this."

"When did you say you arrived in New Mexico?" asked Luna, ignoring my protest.

"Earlier today," I said.

"And where have you been for the past week?"

"In Colorado," I said. "Where else would I be?"

"So you haven't made other trips to New Mexico in that time?"

"*What?* No."

Luna looked at me firmly. "You sure about that?"

"For Christ's sake, yes!"

"You got anybody who can vouch for that?" he asked. "A husband? A friend? A barista at your local coffee shop?"

"I don't know," I said. "I live alone and haven't gotten out of the house much in the last month."

"So no alibis of any kind?" he probed.

"I'm sorry, but do I need a lawyer?" I asked.

"I don't know," he said. "You tell me."

"I haven't done anything!" I retorted.

"That's not what I hear."

"I beg your pardon?" I said. "What exactly have you heard?"

"That since your dealings with Blackford, you've become..." he paused, searching for a word, "...*unpredictable.*"

"Unpredictable?" I said. "What does that mean and who the hell told you that? Kim Matthews?"

"No," he said.

"Who then?"

Luna removed a steno pad from his pocket and flipped to the first page. "Dr. Georg Edmund," he read.

The shock took my breath away and I stammered like a fool for a moment.

"That must be a mistake," I finally managed to say. "Dr. Edmund is a close friend of mine. Has been for a long time. He even helped me evaluate Kevin at one point."

"Yes..." Luna said, scanning the notes of the steno pad. "He told us all about that."

"So he must have told you about Wayne then," I said.

"He mentioned the name, but he didn't have much to say about him. He *did* however have a great deal to say about you."

"*Me?*" I asked, confused.

"Yes. He said you've become obsessed with the Blue River Strangler case. Blackford specifically. Said that Blackford's gotten so far into your head that you don't know whether to shit or go blind. Dr. Edmund is concerned that you've had some type of psychotic breakdown or something. That maybe even *you* committed these two murders to try to exonerate Blackford somehow."

"*What?*" I retorted. "That's insane. I know Georg; there's no way he would say any of that."

"Maybe you don't know him as well as you think you do," said Luna.

"Clearly," I said. "Regardless, I'm done talking to you. I want a lawyer. *Now.*"

"Fine," Luna said, rising from the chair.

"Am I under arrest, or am I free to go?" I asked indignantly.

"For the time being, you're free to go," he said. "Don't leave Del Norte until you hear from me about the DNA results though."

Luna escorted me out of the station and had one of the Taos County deputies drive me back to my hotel.

Despite being exhausted, I could not calm myself down after the interview. Not only was I pissed about Luna considering me as a suspect, but I also could not believe what Georg had told them about me. I tried calling him several times, but each time the phone rang out to his mother's voicemail.

In the grand scheme of things, confronting Georg was low on the list of priorities. Despite my innocence, I was in a world of trouble. I needed legal counsel first and foremost. The problem was that there was only one attorney I could think of calling, and considering my last conversation with him, I was not looking forward to the conversation.

Arlo's phone nearly went to voicemail before he picked it up on the last ring.

Before he could even say hello, I said, "Arlo, it's Sharon. For God's sake don't hang up."

"Sharon..." he said with a sigh. "I really don't have time for this."

"I've got a problem and I could really use your help," I said.

"What kind of help?" he asked.

I told him about everything that had happened that day and how I had managed to make myself a suspect in the copycat murders.

"Jesus..." he said when I was finished. "Did I not tell you to keep yourself distanced from that shit?"

"Well, it's a little late for that lecture," I said. "So what the hell can I do now?"

"Well, you surrendered your DNA to them, so at least you showed your willingness to cooperate. Of course, if you had consulted me prior, I would've told you to wait for them to get a warrant for fluid sampling. But, here we are..."

"So what should I do?" I asked, frantic.

"Stay in your hotel and hope to God the DNA doesn't match."

I didn't respond for a moment, expecting he was going to add something more meaningful than that.

When he didn't break the silence though, I said, "Wait and hope? *That's* your brilliant legal advice? Are you kidding me?"

"There's not much else you can do, Sharon. Until the DNA results come back or the copycat strikes again, you're stuck in limbo."

"Wonderful," I grumbled.

"I hate to ask you this," said Arlo after a pause, "but if I'm going to represent you, I have to know... *Are* you involved somehow with these murders?"

"*What?* Of course not."

"Sharon?"

"I swear to God, I have nothing to do with this. You believe me, don't you?"

Arlo hesitated before saying, "Yes, I do."

FORTY-TWO

Thunderous knocking on my hotel room door woke me up early that following morning.

"Open the door, Dr. Stevenson," a voice called from the hallway. "It's Detective Luna."

My heart jumped into my throat, and despite the fact that I knew I had no connection to the copycat murders, I was still terrified that a false positive had come back on the DNA results.

I threw the latch on the door jamb and opened the door, expecting a SWAT team to barrel into the room and tackle me to the ground.

To my surprise, there was only Detective Luna waiting in the hallway.

"What is it?" I said, my mind reeling as I tried to figure out why else he would be there.

"Can I come in?" he asked. "I need to speak with you." His tone was disconsolate, as if whatever we needed to talk about was grim.

"Not without a lawyer," I said coldly.

"It's not like that," he replied. "We cleared you as a suspect. Your DNA didn't match the killer's."

"Then what else do you need to talk to me about?" I asked, hiding the intense relief that washed over me when I heard I was no longer a suspect.

"Really," he urged. "Let's speak inside."

"No. What is going on?"

He hesitated briefly before answering. "Your DNA wasn't a match to the killer's, but it was a partial match to the victim."

"I beg your pardon?" I replied, my worst fears rising before me.

He continued hesitantly. "Partial matches result from either incomplete samples or familial connections. I have to ask... do you have any blood relatives that are female, aged twenty to thirty?"

My stomach leaped into my throat and choked my airway.

"A niece, maybe?" he added. "Or a..." He couldn't bring himself to say the word, and his voice trailed off into the silence of the hallway.

"Daughter?" I muttered in disbelief, slowly realizing what he had come to my hotel to tell me. "I have a daughter. Her name's Maddie."

"I see," he replied, his shoulders sinking as if he had been hoping that the partial match was the result of a laboratory error.

I stared at him for I don't know how long. I felt the air catch in my lungs and my chest tighten.

A sense of terror and dejection rose within me that I never imagined was possible.

All I could manage to say was, "Is it her?"

"I don't know for sure," he said. "But it's a strong possibility."

My legs went weak as if I had finally reached my breaking point beneath a monumental load. I stepped back from the door as I tried to maintain some semblance of balance. I felt no control over my body, though, and I knew at any second that I would fall to the ground.

Luna was quick to grab me, guiding me to the side of the bed before I fainted.

My mind struggled to make sense of the stark reality before me. Seemingly every memory of Maddie that I had tucked away in my psyche suddenly burst into my mind's eye. A flood of images and emotions from as early as the day she was born until this very moment. The elation I felt when I brought her into this world, the innocence and joy she exuded as a child, the angst and frustration of her adolescence, the desolation she left in her wake when she ran away, and the emptiness of knowing for certain that she was never coming home.

I didn't cry. As badly as I may have wanted to curl up on that bed and howl with sobs, I couldn't. I learned early in my profession that any sign of emotion was weakness, and weakness inside a maximum-security prison was a liability. I learned to internalize everything instead. Rather than the bomb exploding outward, scattering millions of shards around it, it imploded upon itself. No collateral damage. No external casualties. Just a crumpled piece of steel that was too damaged even for scrap.

One of the many occupational hazards of my profession.

Luna added, "I hate to ask, but can you come to the coroner's office to identify her?"

"Sure," I said, dazed. "Just give me a minute to get dressed and we can go."

"I'm so sorry," Luna replied.

"It's okay," I said. My voice was hollow as if someone else was speaking for me. "As awful as it is to say, I've been expecting this for almost ten years. She ran away when she was a teenager and, ever since then, I've been waiting for this day despite hoping it never would come."

Luna said nothing in reply because there was nothing to say. Maddie was gone. Nothing was going to change that.

It felt like some external force took over me because I don't remember getting ready or the drive down the mountainside to the county coroner's office. I was quietly absorbing the reality and letting the numbness overcome me. I didn't feel pain or anguish; I simply felt emptiness.

The coroner guided us to an examination room where there was a form covered by a sheet on a table. He pulled the sheet away from the victim's face slowly, and I don't know if it was because I was in shock or because so much time had passed since I last saw Maddie, but I barely recognized the dead young woman as my daughter. Her face looked so gaunt and her complexion so pockmarked, I had to look at her for several moments before I could tell them for sure that it was her.

"Was she raped?" I asked the coroner.

The coroner glanced uneasily at Luna, seeking his guidance on how to answer. Luna nodded as if to tell him that I could handle the truth.

"Yes," he responded. "She fought back though. Several of the bones in her hand were broken."

I suppose the comment was intended as a consolation, but it didn't soften my reaction. Of all the things to feel in that moment, I felt anger rising within me. Anger and hatred toward whoever was responsible.

"I'm going to find this bastard," Luna told me, as if there was certainty he could deliver on such a promise.

"Let me work with you," I said. "I know this isn't the work of some copycat. This is the Strangler. The *real* Blue River Strangler."

"Absolutely not," he replied. "As if you weren't emotionally connected to this case enough, now this? No way."

"All the more reason—"

"No," he retorted. "Go back to Colorado and let me do my job. I won't rest until I've found him. You have my word."

I wasn't so confident, but I wasn't in the mood to argue with Luna either.

I acquiesced and had a deputy drive me back to my hotel in Del Norte.

Despite being on my own since Maddie ran away, I've never felt as lonely as I did in that hotel room. Even clinging to the microscopic possibility that she was still alive out there somewhere was enough to make me feel like I hadn't lost my entire family. She was the final strand. Without her, it was just me.

I didn't want to be alone, but the only person I knew within a hundred miles of me was Georg. I was still angry with him for suggesting me as a potential suspect though, and I debated calling him until my loneliness got the best of me. Maybe I *was* too emotionally involved, I told myself. I wasn't listening to his warnings, so he did the only thing he could do to keep me out of harm's way. That's how I rationalized calling him at least.

He sounded annoyed when he first answered, as if he was dreading having to talk me out of another spiral.

"They found Maddie," I told him.

"What?" he replied, shocked. "Where?"

"Near Del Norte," I said. "She was..." My throat tightened and I couldn't bring myself to finish the sentence.

"Holy shit," he muttered. "Sharon, I-I don't know what to say..."

"I know. I'm still trying to sort it out myself."

"Where are you?"

"My hotel."

"I can be there in thirty minutes," he said.

"You don't have to do that."

"It wasn't a question," he retorted. "I have something I need to do for my mother in Buffalo Creek, so I was going to drive through anyways."

"Okay," I said, relieved that he wouldn't allow my stubbornness to deter him.

When he hung up, the deadness of the line trapped me in a fugue for several moments. It felt like the silence of the room was encasing me. Suffocating me, in fact. I couldn't help but imagine what Maddie's final moments must have been like and my throat tightened as if I myself was locked in the Strangler's grasp.

Then the memory of my last interaction with Maddie surfaced. The anger I felt toward her for doing everything she could to destroy her own life. The hatred she felt toward me for trying to stand in her way. And, of course, the last thing I ever said to her: *Don't come back.*

FORTY-THREE

Seeing Georg's face made me feel a little bit better. It was familiar and, at that point, familiar was what I desperately needed.

"I still can't believe it was her," Georg said, just as dumbfounded by the news as I was.

I nodded in agreement. "I don't know what's more shocking for me: the fact that she's gone or the fact that it was the Strangler who did it."

"I know..." he muttered, his voice trailing off contemplatively.

I glanced around the hotel room and the silence morphed into a high-pitched ringing that only I could hear. The walls seemed to close in around us, and immediately I felt anxious.

"I need to get out of here," I said. "I can't keep staring at these damn walls."

"Where do you want to go?"

"Just out. Anywhere but here."

"You want to go to Buffalo Creek with me? It's nothing special, but it's a nice drive at least."

"Sure," I said, not caring where I went as long as I wasn't in that hotel room for another second.

Georg rolled the windows of his car down, and the cool alpine air washed over me as we drove.

I watched the landscape. The steep, rocky cliffs. The sprawling forests. The lush meadows that wove their way in between all of it. I tried to forget about what had happened. To ignore my sorrow and my grief. It's the exact opposite of what you're supposed to do when you mourn, but I didn't care. Do as I say, not as I do.

"What do you need to do for your mom?" I asked as we neared Buffalo Creek.

"She has a little cabin out here that I need to check on," he said. "My father's, actually. She hasn't been out here since he passed. I just need to make sure that the roof hasn't caved in or that squatters haven't taken it over."

"How is your mother?" I asked.

"Comfortable," he answered, obviously not wanting to discuss it.

Given my own circumstances, it was easy to understand that desire.

Buffalo Creek was a wrinkle of a town. The type of place that had a gas station, post office and grocery store crammed into a single building. But it was quiet and peaceful, and if Georg's father was anything like he was, I could see why a cabin out there was so appealing.

Georg turned the car off the main highway and guided us along a series of dirt roads that ambled deep into the surrounding forest.

"This was an old mining camp at the turn of the century," Georg told me. "When it went bust, the mine owner parceled it out as vacation lots. Mostly Texans looking to escape the humidity. And my father, of course. Looking for a place to escape the rest of humanity."

"It's nice," I said, savoring the clean air and the solitude.

We passed through a narrow valley before climbing up the slope on the opposite side. Pine trees as dense as molasses surrounded us. Not even the breeze could sneak its way through the branches to disturb the air below.

When we finally reached the cabin, it was as if someone dropped us into the remote Alaskan wilderness. The air smelled earthy and damp from the peat moss that covered much of the forest floor. Not another cabin in sight nor any other sign of human presence.

"Roof seems to be okay," I said as I got out of the car.

Georg approached the cabin, reaching into the back of his waistband and removing what looked to be a pistol.

"Jesus, Georg, what the hell is that for?"

"I wasn't kidding about squatters," he said nonchalantly. "I've heard stories about people driving all the way here from Dallas only to find their cabin's been overrun by a bunch of bums." He glanced back and saw the nervousness on my face. "Don't worry," he added with a smile. "The gun's just a precaution. Like they say: better to be prepared for the worst than hope for the best."

"I don't think that's how the expression goes," I replied, following him to the front door of the cabin.

The pine bark siding looked like the original lumber that Georg's father had nailed in fifty years before, and dead pine needles were heaped in piles along the foundation from decades of neglect.

"Mother has been wanting to sell this thing for years," Georg said as he jostled the door open, "but even if we had an interested buyer, none of this shit is up to code. The whole thing would have to come down."

The inside of the cabin smelled musty and stale, and I wondered if racoons or squirrels hadn't gotten inside and taken up residence.

"I know it doesn't look like much," he commented, "but my father loved this place. Always tried to convince Mother to retire here full time."

"Hard to imagine why she objected," I replied sarcastically.

He smirked. "It serves its purpose just fine." He glanced about the living room briefly and added, "You want a tour, or you just want to wait here while I check the bedrooms?"

"I'm good here," I said, stifling my reaction to the odor.

When Georg went to check the back rooms, I stepped out onto the porch to escape the smell. As pleasant as the solitude was, it was almost too remote for my liking. Sort of a *Deliverance* kind of vibe. The type of place where you hear banjos in the distance and your blood curdles.

Suddenly, a loud crash sounded from inside the house and my heart nearly shot out of my chest in fright.

I turned abruptly and called, "Everything good?"

Another crash came from the back, soon followed by an agitated grumble from Georg.

"You alright?" I asked, making my way through the living room and into the narrow hallway toward the bedrooms.

"Don't come back here," Georg finally said, his voice strained.

I ignored his request, continuing back to the room that his voice was coming from.

"What happened?" I said as I came to the open doorway.

My senses were immediately struck by the smell of human waste, and I covered my nose and mouth with my hand to keep from gagging.

"Jesus Christ, what is that?" I asked.

The room was dark from the windows being partially boarded up, but enough light crept through so that I could see Georg's shadowed form struggling with something on the ground.

271

"Goddammit, Sharon, what the fuck did I say?" Georg barked, turning to me with the pistol pointed in my direction.

"Whoa... relax," I said, my hands rising defensively. "What's wrong? Let me help."

"I can promise you," he scoffed, "you don't want to help. Just wait outside."

"Ge—"

"Now!"

His anger made me freeze, and as I stared dumbfoundedly at him, I realized that he was struggling to tie someone up on the ground.

"Did you find someone in here?" I breathed.

"Are you deaf!?" he growled. "Get the fuck out!"

I was trying to come to grips with the fact that he had actually found a squatter in the cabin. I couldn't think of anything else to do, so I said, "Stay here. I'll go get the police."

As I turned to hurry out, a gunshot rocketed into the ceiling above us and I nearly jumped out of my skin it startled me so much. When I turned back, Georg was right in front of me with the pistol aimed just a few feet away from my face.

"Do not get the police," he muttered. "You understand me?"

"Y-yes," I stammered in a panic. "Just calm down, we'll figure this out."

He snickered at me. "No, *we* are not figuring this out, Sharon."

The shadow of the pistol disappeared before a blinding flash of light exploded in my eyes and a searing pain tore through my forehead as if I had been struck by lightning. I instantly crumpled to the floor, too dazed to yelp or realize what had happened.

"Nosy bitch," I heard Georg hiss at me.

I was trapped in a fog of disorientation, blinded to everything but the pain that engulfed my entire head. I put my hand to my forehead and felt the blood as it slowly seeped out.

"You shot me?" I breathed in a confused panic. Adrenaline instantly surged through my body and I vomited on the floor.

"I didn't fucking shoot you," Georg scoffed. "I barely touched you. Quit being so goddamn dramatic."

I touched the back of my head, certain that I would feel a gaping exit wound. I felt nothing though and a wave of relief washed over me.

I remained stunned for several moments. All the while Georg worked to restrain whomever he had found in the room. When he was done, he returned his attention to me.

"Can you get up on your own?" he asked.

My head hurt too badly to really comprehend what he had said, so I didn't answer.

He grumbled with irritation and proceeded to grab me by the wrists and drag me along the floor out of the room.

"What are you doing?" I mumbled dazedly.

"Well, I'm not going to have you stay in that room with *her*," he replied.

He dragged me down the hallway and stopped in the middle of the living room. He knelt beside me and lifted me so that I was sitting up on the floor.

"Let me check your head..." He inspected my forehead briefly before adding, "You might have a small concussion, but other than that, you'll be alright."

He took my hands and forced them behind my back.

"What are you doing?" I retorted as I tried to resist.

He jerked my arms back so hard that it felt like he dislocated both of my shoulders.

"Move again and I'll snap them in half," he hissed.

Panic shot through me, but I didn't dare move. I soon felt a rope wrap around my wrists, and the braids cut into my skin as Georg tightened and knotted the ends. Then suddenly, the reality struck me with the weight of an anvil. *He* had brought that girl here. *He* had abducted her. And whatever he was planning on doing with her, he had also done to others. The first girl they found in Del Norte. Maddie...

"You fucking monster," I breathed. "What have you done?"

"What have *I* done?" he retorted as he knotted the rope around my wrists. "The better question is what have *you* done, Dr. Stevenson? Better yet, what were you planning on doing with that poor girl back there? Sodomizing her so it looked like she was raped? Strangling her to death the exact same way the Blue River Strangler did? Dumping her body so that it looked like someone else was responsible for all those murders and not that simpleton Blackford? All for the sake of saving him from death row? You certainly wouldn't be the first copycat to try to exonerate the original, but that's crazy even by your standards."

My mind raced as I tried to comprehend what he was talking about.

"Nobody's going to believe that," I said.

"Sure they will," he replied, helping me to my feet and sitting me on the sofa. "You got so wrapped up in Kevin's case that you were willing to sacrifice your reputation and your career for him. You don't think people would believe that he manipulated you so badly that it caused you to have a psychotic breakdown? Forced you to come down here to mimic his crimes?"

"What about Maddie?" I said, emotion overwhelming me. "Who's going to believe that I would do that to my own daughter?"

"Yeah..." he responded ruminatively, "I'll admit, I wasn't expecting that one. If it makes you feel any better, I didn't know it was her until you told me. Until that point, I thought she was just another piece of trash drifting along the highway."

Tears formed in my eyes and I had to fight every urge to not throw myself at him.

"She fit the criteria all the same," he added, "so it wouldn't have made a difference one way or the other. But to answer your question about why *you* did it, I think it's possible that you've always resented Maddie for being what she was. I imagine that when you stumbled upon her down here, it was a perfect way to kill two whores with one stone. So to speak, of course."

"Shut your goddamn mouth," I hissed. "I didn't kill anyone. *You* did."

"Now, that's not the way to speak to an old friend, is it?" he replied.

And there was the phrase: *old friend*. It echoed within the cabin. Reverberated off of every wall back onto itself. Sounding exactly the way it sounded when Edward said it to me months before.

Our old friend.

That bastard Edward knew the whole time. Kept the truth trapped in Kevin's fragmented mind. Even if he *had* said it, who would have believed it? Not me. I *still* wasn't believing it. But somehow it was true. Georg wasn't just the copycat; he was the Blue River Strangler.

The realization must have shown on my face because Georg smiled wide. A big, shit-eating grin given by someone who's just pulled off the prank of the century.

"It wasn't Wayne that Kevin was talking about, was it?" I said. "It was *you*. *You* are Edward. *You* are the Strangler."

Georg winked at me, exactly the way Edward would.

I shook my head in disbelief, stammering, "H-h-how...?"

"Unlike *you*, Sharon, I kept much of my life to myself."

"I... I don't understand... How did you even know him?"

"Who? Kevin?" he asked. "He and I go *way* back. Remember when I was working in Denver for a time? Probably twenty-five years ago? Perhaps I never told you. I worked in Denver and I did some work at Wadsworth Center when I could. Volunteering and what not. They needed a psychiatrist and I needed a hobby. Mind you, this was before my—what should I call it?—*work with the homeless*. My *real* hobby. As I was saying, I worked with Kevin there when he was a little guy. Tormented as shit, my God. Twice as fucked up as some of our worst inmates, I'd bet. Sweet kid, though. He couldn't pronounce my last name, so I let him call me Dr. Eddie. Talk about transference? Shit, that kid took every ounce of his anger and confusion out on me. It was only fair that I took *something* back from him. An eye for an eye, you could say."

Voices echoed in my mind from a thousand directions. Jackie's and Robbie's and Russell's and Kevin's. All distinctive entities, yet identical at the same time. Voices that were inspired by Georg himself.

"To be honest," added Georg, "I had kind of forgotten about the little bastard until I ran into him in Park City about ten years ago when I was finishing one of my weekend projects. That was when I was working in Wind River. Stressful job really. Those weekend projects really kept me going, if you know what I mean. When I ran into Kevin again, I could tell that he remembered me but didn't *really* remember me. You know what I'm talking about? The eyes recognize the face and the ears recognize the voice, but the brain just can't pinpoint the association. Kevin's condition had really come into its own by that point, and even if he recognized something, he had repressed the memory so much that it might as well have not happened at all. I didn't think it was multiple personality disorder like you, but certainly some type of repressive disorder. You see, my craft with my weekend projects was really evolving, and frankly I needed more. That's where Kevin came into play. I started meeting up with him on occasion, and when I did, I harvested bits of his hair to garnish my projects with. Little breadcrumbs of DNA to give people hope. That's all they need, right? It doesn't matter if it's *false* hope, just as long as it looks and smells like the real thing. Then, when it was time to really toy with everyone, I mailed the sample of Kevin's DNA to the

Peak Courier. That was a thing of beauty, if you ask me. The police thought he did it, and there was no way for him to dispute it. The perfect scapegoat for the perfect crimes."

My brain was spinning so far into oblivion that I couldn't even discern which way was up or down. I saw Georg before me, and yet at the same time I saw nothing but a phantom.

"Now, I need a new scapegoat," he added, grabbing me by my arms and hoisting me off the couch.

"Don't do this," I pleaded.

"Me?" he replied with a laugh. "*I* am not going to do anything. *You* on the other hand? We'll just have to wait and see."

FORTY-FOUR

I've never thought of killing someone before, yet there I was, enveloped by the darkness of that foul-smelling room, straddling that poor girl's unconscious form with my hands hovering over her throat.

I could feel her abdomen rise and fall beneath me as she breathed. Shallow, but perceptible all the same. And I was going to be the one who stopped that. The one who took the air out of her lungs and the life out of her soul.

Georg was standing behind me, the gun pointed at the back of my head.

"You'll want both thumbs squeezing down on the trachea," he told me. "Wrap your other fingers behind the neck. Keep your arms straight and push your body weight down as you squeeze. Just like you're giving CPR."

I was too mortified to catch the irony of the analogy at the time. My hands trembled over the girl's throat, and tears streamed from my eyes and dripped from my cheeks.

"I drugged her for you," he added, "so she won't struggle. Just close your eyes and go for it."

Through the darkness, all I could see beneath me was

Maddie. Her pure eyes. Her vibrant smile. My own flesh and blood. It wasn't an innocent stranger I was killing; it was Maddie.

I whimpered. Helpless. Terrified. I couldn't control myself. Floodgates burst open and tears flowed even harder from my eyes.

"You'll do fine," Georg assured me.

I felt his hand press against my back, and as much as I wanted to shirk away from him, his touch was gentle and compassionate. As if he was trying to comfort me through a terrible loss.

I shook my head as I wept. "I. Can't. Do. This," I murmured, my throat catching on every syllable.

"Yes, you can," he said. "Think of it as one of those cadavers we used in med school. Just get a nice, tight grip and lean as hard as you can against the floor. It'll go quick. Trust me."

I choked for air as I sobbed. I couldn't do it. My body wouldn't even allow me to place my hands over her throat. I was paralyzed with terror.

"I-I can't..." I sputtered.

"Your DNA is going to end up on her one way or the other," he said. "Besides, there's no greater feeling than taking a life. Once you taste that kind of omnipotence, you'll be hooked."

I felt the muzzle of the pistol press against the back of my head and I screamed, "Please! Don't make me do this!"

"You insisted," he said. "You wanted to be involved in this, so now you are."

He pushed the gun against me harder, causing me to lose my balance and tip forward. My outstretched hands pushed against the girl's throat, but the feel of her skin startled me and I crumpled forward onto her.

"For fuck's sake," Georg grumbled.

He grabbed me by the hair and yanked me off of the

ground. Seating me on top of her again, he seized one of my hands and shoved it onto the girl's throat.

"See," he added forcefully. "She's not going to bite." He grabbed my other hand and placed it below. "There. Now all you have to do is squeeze and push."

He put the gun against my temple and used his other hand to press against my back.

I resisted, my body overcoming my paralyzed brain subconsciously.

"You're not going to make this easy, are you?" he remarked.

He pulled the gun away from my head and stuck it in the back of his waistband. "Fine," he sighed. "We'll do it together then."

Straddling the girl from behind me, he pressed his chest against my back and wrapped his arms around me with his hands on top of mine.

"Look at us..." he whispered, his breath tickling my ear and chills needling my spine. "Working together again."

I trembled within his grasp. A mouse quivering within the coils of a python.

"On the count of three," he muttered. "One... two..."

On impulse, I threw my head backward as hard as I could and my skull connected with the bridge of his nose. A hollow crack filled the darkness.

"Goddammit!" he barked, and the pressure of his body fell away from me.

Stars burst into my vision, but I had enough wherewithal to scramble away from him and scurry out of the room. A gunshot soon went off behind me, but the bullet rocketed into the wall nearby. I didn't stop. I didn't think. My instinct to run had overcome me too much to do anything else. Better to be shot in the back than to do what he had wanted me to do to her.

"Get back here!" he yelled, his footsteps thundering on the plank floor.

I raced into the living room and a second bullet tore past me and into a boarded window. I skirted through the front entryway as he fired a third shot, and I bolted off of the porch and ran toward the surrounding wilderness. Several gunshots sounded from behind me, but I kept running as fast as I could.

The trees and undergrowth soon enveloped me. I scrambled through the brush and wove around the tree trunks with no other thought than getting as far away from him as possible. I figured the more distance I could put between us, the less accurate his shots would be.

I assumed he was chasing after me, but I couldn't hear him over the sounds of my own scrambling through the wilderness. I heard no gunshots though, so I knew if nothing else that I had to be out of his shooting range.

I raced through the forest like that until my lungs were burning and my heart felt like it was going to beat through my chest. I stopped and crouched down in the brush, scanning my surroundings in every direction for a sign of movement.

I searched for several minutes, but I neither saw nor heard anything. Not a tree limb sway or a leaf rustle. Just raw silence.

Maybe he went back to deal with the girl, I wondered? He knew how remote we were, so he probably figured it would be a while before I could find help. Do what he was planning on doing with her, then come back for me later.

Of course, she wasn't going anywhere anytime soon, and I was the only one who knew who he truly was. His decades-long secret was scrambling around the wilderness, and my better judgment told me he would stop at nothing to squelch the truth. That included murdering one of his closest friends.

I had to keep going but, looking around, I didn't have a clue where I was or what direction to go in. I could easily scramble deeper into the wilderness and away from any chance of help, or worse, back in the direction of the cabin and into his crosshairs.

I wanted to scream for help, but as remote as the area was, I doubted it would serve any other purpose than giving my location away to Georg.

A new wave of panic overcame me. I was lost and trapped with no way of fixing either. But I couldn't just sit there. Night would fall in a few hours, and who knew what kind of predators were roaming those woods. I had to keep moving. Take a chance and pick a direction, I told myself.

I remembered when I first got to Del Norte that I had looked at maps of the areas surrounding Sugarloaf and Buffalo Creek because I was trying to figure out where the Strangler might strike next. I recalled the highway running along the northern edge of Buffalo Creek before it ascended the pass west of town. Despite the convoluted path we took to get out to the cabin, it seemed like our general direction was southeast of town. Going south or east would only take me deeper into the forest, so north and west seemed like my best option.

I looked upward, and through the canopy of the pine trees, I could see splotches of the sun as it made its descent toward the western horizon. That's my compass, I thought. As long as I had the sun to guide me, I would have a general idea of where I was going.

I scrambled through the wilderness for several hours before I finally stumbled upon a forestry service road. Tire treads were pressed into the loose dirt, and a few crumpled beer cans rested in the brush alongside the road. Not much of a sign of civilization, but something.

My feet felt like they weighed eight tons as I walked along the road. I figured if Georg was going to hunt me down in the wilderness, he would've found me by that point. The panic and adrenaline that had fueled me up to that point finally wore off, and exhaustion soon overcame me.

I just wanted to stop and rest, but I knew I couldn't. I clung to the hope that Georg hadn't killed that girl yet and there was still a chance to save her. I just had to find help.

I made my way down the road for half a mile or so before I came upon a massive fifth-wheel camper and pick-up truck parked in a clearing. The rig looked relatively new and well-kept, and when I saw an older man and woman sitting in lawn chairs nearby, I had to do everything within my power to not fall to the ground with relief.

"Help!" I called out, stumbling as I tried to hurry over to them with weakened legs. "Help!"

They were startled at first, but the man soon rushed over to me.

"Are you alright?" he asked. "What happened?"

"I need the sheriff," I said in heavy gasps. "Now!"

"There's a ranger station not far from here," he told me. "We'll take you."

FORTY-FIVE

I was lying in a hospital bed at Taos County General when Detective Luna knocked on the open door.

"How you holding up?" he asked.

"Fine, I guess. Considering the circumstances, of course."

He nodded. "You mind if I come in?"

"Not at all," I said, motioning to the chair near my bed. "I hope you're not here just to see how I'm doing. Not that I don't appreciate the sentiment."

He smirked. "No offense taken." He took a seat, his expression hardening as he added, "I just got word that they found Georg. He made it about a hundred miles north of Las Cruces before they finally caught up to him."

"Is he dead?" I asked, assuming that he didn't give himself up without a fight.

"No, he's alive and well," Luna replied. "Didn't even lift a finger at the troopers. Maybe he figured if he resisted that it would be the last thing he did on this earth."

"Maybe so..." I muttered. "What about the girl?"

Luna shook his head. "Still haven't found her body. When we didn't find her at the cabin, we were wondering if he took her in the car with him, but State Patrol didn't find her either. They asked him where she was, but he won't say anything other than 'lawyer'."

"Coward," I scoffed.

"Smart, though," Luna retorted. "The prosecution could very well waive the death penalty in exchange for the location of her body. He'll still get life without parole. Just not the needle."

"His punishment means nothing," I said firmly. "They could torture him and crucify him and it wouldn't make any difference to me. It's not going to bring back Maddie or any of the other girls."

"I understand..." he said. "But there *is* something to be said for justice."

"*Justice...*" I muttered with disgust. "After everything that's happened, I'm not sure I know what that even means. There was nothing just about Maddie's fate. Nothing just about Kevin's either. He's sitting on death row right now because of that monster."

"Maybe he'll make it right," Luna suggested. "I can get the prosecution to make it part of the plea bargain. Life without parole if he discloses the location of this recent girl and confesses to all of the Blue River Strangler murders."

I eyed Luna skeptically. "You never struck me as an idealist."

"I'm not," he replied. "But I do believe in man's self-serving nature, and given the chance to save his own ass, he might actually take the deal."

"Maybe..." I said, although I had my doubts. Everything I thought I knew about Georg was a lie. I didn't have a clue what —if anything—would motivate him to confess. Even self-preservation. A man like that does not fear death; he conquers it.

Over the course of the next few days, Detective Luna kept me in the loop on the investigation as much as he could. Georg didn't utter a word until he consulted with his lawyer for most of that first day in custody. Investigators and prosecutors alike were dreading what was to come. They expected the terms of Georg's plea to be outlandish, requiring a painfully drawn-out process of negotiation and leveraging.

Quite the opposite came to bear.

Georg promised to fully cooperate with the prosecution by leading them to the last victim's remains and confessing to all three of the New Mexico murders in exchange for a life sentence.

What was not part of Georg's deal, however, was confessing to the murders that Kevin had been wrongfully convicted for. Apparently, when Detective Luna brought this up to the prosecution, they told him that Blackford was Wyoming's problem, not theirs. Justice for New Mexico was all they cared about.

My heart sank when I heard this. As if everything else wasn't difficult enough, Kevin's exoneration would have at least been a slight glimmer of hope in an otherwise awful situation.

I wasn't going to give up that easily though.

I don't know if it was my sorrow for losing Maddie or the professional duties I felt toward Kevin that were fueling me, but I drove back up to Wyoming to meet with Arlo and plead Kevin's case to Kim Matthews in person.

Eight hours of nothing but flat pavement and intense rumination. Confusion. Regret. Anger. Bitterness. The whole gamut of emotions becoming one roiling torrent in my brain.

What happens at the neurological level when things like this occur, I wonder? Certainly it can't just be a handful of neurotransmitters rocketing back and forth between synapses. Certainly there has to be something else, right? Something monumental. Something catastrophic. Something to explain the complexity and the cacophony and the chaos.

But I know there isn't. Despite its intricacy, the human psyche is driven by nothing more than simplicity.

I tried to make sense of everything as I made my way to Wyoming, but how could I possibly understand something so unbelievable? Maddie's death. Georg's crimes. His bizarre connection to Kevin. The surreality compounded upon itself like layers of molten rock, sealing the truth beneath an impenetrable crust.

When I eventually arrived in Wind River, I called Arlo from my hotel to see if he had reviewed Georg's case file yet.

"Yeah..." he said dejectedly. "It's an awful story. I'm so sorry about Maddie."

"Thanks. I'm still in shock myself to tell you the truth."

"How long have you known Dr. Edmund?" he asked.

"Over twenty years."

"Shit. Just when you think you know someone..."

Silence overcame us for several moments before I asked, "So what do you think? Is it enough to reverse Kevin's sentence, or at least start an appeal?"

"Sharon..." Arlo said, "he pleaded guilty to twenty-eight counts of murder. The only way he can appeal a plea is if we have new DNA evidence that conclusively proves Georg actually committed those murders instead of Kevin."

"Well, I don't know if we have that," I said. "But the fact that Georg admitted to these ones in New Mexico should be enough, shouldn't it?"

"You know we can't use evidence from a separate case as proof for another," he replied. "As the law sees it, Georg is only guilty of the crimes in New Mexico, regardless of how circumstantial everything is."

"What about his connections to Kevin?" I demanded.

"Coincidence," he said. "But unfortunately it's irrelevant to Kevin's case. We need hard evidence to even consider an appeal. All we know for sure is that he is guilty of the copycat murders in New Mexico."

"But Kevin—"

"—is guilty as far as anyone can prove," Arlo interjected. "Look, I'm sorry that things have turned out the way that they have for you. With your daughter. With your career. With your friend. I can't begin to imagine what you're going through. But you've got to find another way to vent that. You might be able to flood the appellate court to get Kevin's execution date pushed back, but unless he gets a presidential pardon or some other miracle, Kevin's fate has been sealed. He's stuck on death row."

As much as I wanted to argue with him, there was no disputing logic. Arlo was right. If we presented what we had, a judge would laugh us out of the courtroom.

"Besides," Arlo added, "Kevin has no money. Do you know how expensive an appeal is going to be? Who's going to put that money up? You?"

"You shouldn't have to be a millionaire to appeal a death sentence," I said.

"Well, that's the reality of it, and unless Kevin is stashing that kind of money away in his uncle's shack, an appeal is going to go nowhere."

"Aren't there pro bono lawyers who specifically deal with these types of cases, though? Non-profits maybe?"

"Yeah..." he said, his voice trailing off. "The odds of them taking his case are slim to none. Do you know if Kevin even *wants* to appeal this?"

"Why wouldn't he want to?" I asked.

"I don't know," he said. "It's just that the last couple of times I spoke with him, he seemed like he had come to terms with it in some weird way."

"I doubt that," I replied. "Do you know what learned help-lessness is?"

"Sort of..."

"It's when people or animals essentially give up when there appears to be no way out of an aversive situation. Kevin has been living his *entire life* in a state of learned helplessness.

Rolling over and taking the beating because he knows he has no way of escaping it. Why would he treat this situation any differently?"

"Maybe you're right," he muttered. "Have *you* tried talking to him yet?"

"No," I said. "I've only spoken to Dr. Moneta at the prison. She said he's completely unresponsive. Catatonic practically."

"Well, there's only so much you can do," he said. "At the end of the day, he has to want to fight, not just you or me."

I understood what Arlo was saying, but for whatever reason I just couldn't give up on Kevin. Not yet at least.

The following morning, I called Carla and asked if I could stop by the prison to speak with Kevin. She said she wasn't sure if he would be up for it, but I could drop by anyway.

Aside from convincing him to pursue an appeal, I wanted to know if what Georg had said would match up with Kevin's recollection of events.

"They can't get him to come out of his cell," Carla told me when I arrived later that morning. "He hasn't left it in over a month actually. I've had to sit back there with him for our sessions."

"Is it okay if I go back there then?" I asked. "If nothing else, just to see if I can get him to talk."

"Sure," she said.

Along with several guards, Carla guided me from the main building across the prison complex to the southwest building that was designated for death row inmates. It was a lowly building to begin with, but because Kevin was the only inmate on death row at that time, it was eerily quiet save for the white noise provided by the HVAC system.

One of the death row guards led me and Carla down the hollow corridor to Kevin's cell.

Unlike the open-air bars of the Peak County Jail cells, Kevin's cell was steel-reinforced with only a narrow, triple-plated window in the doorway. Peering through the window, I could see Kevin was curled feebly on the concrete bed.

"Have you been trying to talk to him through the door?" I asked Carla.

"Yes," she said. "I certainly wasn't going to sit in there with him."

"I don't blame you," I said, "but it's no wonder you can't get him to talk."

"What are you suggesting?" she asked.

"Let me sit in the cell with him," I said. "The door open, of course."

"You're insane," she scoffed. "No way."

"Look at him," I said. "He's not getting up from that bed anytime soon. You and the guard can stay in the hallway just in case."

Carla and the guard glanced at each other warily.

"Only if he has handcuffs on," said the guard.

"Seriously?" I said.

"Yes," agreed Carla. "Either he wears handcuffs or the door stays shut."

"Alright, fine," I said.

The guard pounded his fist against the door. "Blackford," he ordered. "You got a visitor. Get up and come to the door so I can put the cuffs on you."

Kevin shook his head slowly, not moving from the bed.

"Blackford," the guard said with another heavy knock, "I'm not going to tell you again. Get your ass up and come to the door."

Again, he didn't budge.

"Kevin," I said, "it's Dr. Stevenson."

He still did not respond.

"Jackie?" I asked.

Kevin rolled over slowly and glanced at me. "What are you doing here?" he asked.

"I want to talk to you," I said. "I haven't seen you in a while and thought we could catch up."

"Why'd you leave me?" he asked.

"Something came up and I had to go home."

"I don't believe you," he said.

"That's the truth, Jackie. Now will you come to the door so I can sit in there with you?"

He turned his head away, and I thought he was going to shut me out for good, but he slowly got up from the bed and came over to the door.

"Hands behind your back," said the guard. "Turn and put your hands through the slot in the door."

Kevin did as instructed and the guard snapped the handcuffs onto his wrists. Kevin returned to the bed and took a seat on the floor.

The guard threw the door open and a sickly odor spilled out of the cell.

"Geez," I coughed.

"Yeah..." said Carla, "he hasn't showered in a while."

I gave her a look and entered the cell. I took a seat on the floor across the cell from Kevin. He was in a shambles, hardly able to hold himself up against the bed frame.

"When can I go home?" he mumbled.

"Not for a while," I said.

"Why not? I hate it here."

"I know you do," I said.

"What if I say I'm sorry? Can I go home then?"

"It's more complicated than that, Jackie."

"My mommy says when you do something bad, you say sorry to make it better."

"Sometimes we do things that sorry *can't* fix though. Do you understand?"

He shook his head.

"Jackie," I said, "I could really use your help with something. Will you help me?"

He glanced up at me. "Okay..."

One thing I had learned about Kevin's condition was that each persona was the compartmentalization of trauma from his past. As a result, he used each as a means of avoidance and repression. I figured if I confronted Jackie with the abuse from his childhood, I might be able to get him to switch personas.

"I need you to tell me more about Eddie," I said.

"I don't want to talk about him."

"I know you don't, but it's really important that you do."

"No," he said.

"Jackie, how can I make sure he doesn't do it again if you don't talk about it?"

He shook his head, stifling tears.

"Please?"

"No," he said more firmly.

"Jackie—"

"Just leave me alone!" he sobbed, jumping to his feet. "I hate you!"

I stood quickly and backed toward the entrance of the cell.

"Blackford, sit down," commanded the guard from the doorway.

"No!" Kevin screamed, tears streaming down his face.

"Jackie?" I said as calmly as I could. "I need you to sit down—"

Before I realized what was happening, Kevin rushed at me and crashed his bulk into my chest. I fell to the ground in a breathless heap, and in the moments before the guard seized him and pinned him against the cell wall, I saw Kevin loom over me with hollow, black eyes glowering down at me.

"NO!" he wailed, crying and writhing under the bulk of the guard.

I was choking for breath when Carla grabbed me under the arm and dragged me out of the cell.

"Go get back-up," the guard ordered Carla.

"NO! NO! NO!" Kevin screamed, crashing his head into the wall with each syllable. "NO! NO—"

Kevin's body suddenly went limp, and an eerie silence fell over death row once again.

I couldn't see Kevin's face, but I figured he had cracked his head open because blood was dripping all over the floor at his feet.

"Goddammit," the guard grunted, dragging Kevin over to the concrete bed.

I was watching from the hallway, still choking for breath.

The guard unlocked the handcuffs and left Kevin's unconscious form on the bed.

After the guard walked out of the cell and slammed the door shut, he turned and looked at me.

"Still want to sit in there by yourself?" he asked.

FORTY-SIX

After the incident, Carla refused to let me sit in the cell with Kevin again. I tried speaking to him the following day through the closed cell door, but he never uttered a word.

It wasn't until early that next morning the phone in my hotel rang and startled me awake.

"Hello?" I said, disoriented from sleep.

"Sharon, it's Carla," she replied, exasperated. "Something's happened at the prison."

"What?" I asked, the sleepiness leaching from my body. "What do you mean, something's happened?"

"Kevin attempted suicide late last night," she said.

"*What?* How?"

"He tried to strangle himself," she said gravely. "I guess he tied one of his pant legs around his neck and the other around his ankle from behind his back and used the force of his own leg to choke himself. When he fell unconscious, the pant leg must have loosened around his neck and allowed him to breathe again."

"Where is he now?" I asked, rushing out of bed and grabbing my clothes from the ground.

"He's at the prison infirmary right now," she said. "He should be okay. As okay as he can be, I suppose... I'm keeping him there more as a self-harm precaution than anything else."

"I'm coming over," I said.

"No, Sharon. I only called because I knew you would want to know, but I'm not sure seeing you is the best thing for him—"

"Don't be ridiculous," I interjected. "I'll be there in fifteen minutes."

And before Carla could tell me otherwise, I hung up.

As I got dressed, this feeling of intense dread overcame me, not only because I felt Kevin's suicide attempt was partially my fault, but also because it was a sobering reality that even his own self-destruction was completely out of his control. He was helpless beyond measure.

I raced over to the prison where Carla was waiting for me at the entry. She looked exhausted.

When we reached the infirmary, the glow of the day's first light was beginning to pour through the barred windows. Kevin was the only prisoner in there and the room was quiet. Tranquil, even. He was laying on one of the far beds. He was on his back, arms spread outward with each hand shackled to the frame of the bed. He looked strung out and haggard, but when I approached the bed, he turned his head toward me and smiled.

"Hey, Doc," he said, his voice dry and raspy.

Without realizing what I was doing, I put my hand on his shoulder and asked, "How are you feeling?"

"Throat's on fire..." he said, "but other than that, I'm alright."

"Can you tell us what happened?"

He swallowed and shook his head. "Not really... I just remember I was having a nightmare and then this terrible feeling that I couldn't breathe. I tried to wake up, but I couldn't. You ever have dreams like that, Doc?"

I nodded.

"I was so scared," he added. "I struggled to wake myself up, but the more I struggled the more I couldn't breathe. It was awful..."

"What were you dreaming about?" I asked.

"Some girl," he said, his eyes a little glossy.

"Did you recognize her?"

He shook his head before saying, "No. She was pretty young though. Like one of the girls from the community college."

"What else do you remember about this dream?" I asked.

I could see the glossiness in Kevin's eyes fade and his gaze became more intense. "I was kneeling down next to her and I had my hands around her throat," he said, his tone very matter-of-fact. "She had no pulse as far as I could tell, but her skin was still warm."

"Yes..." I breathed, a lump forming in my throat. "And what then?"

"Someone was standing behind me with their hand on my shoulder. It was dark so I didn't recognize him when I looked up at him, but I felt like I knew him from somewhere..." He trailed off briefly before adding, "I asked him what happened to her, but he just patted me on the shoulder and said, 'Be a good boy and help me carry her.' He grabbed her legs and made me grab her by the arms. She wasn't a big girl, but she was so heavy. We carried her into the woods for what felt like an eternity until we finally reached a small stream. 'Drag her into the water,' the man told me, and even though I didn't want to, something about the way he said that made me do it anyway. 'Into the main current,' he said, and I did as he told me..." Kevin paused and closed his eyes as if to compose himself.

After a moment, he sighed, but of all things, a grin slowly appeared on his face. That grin that I had come to know so well as that of Edward.

"You had no clue what you were doing," he murmured

slyly, "asking Dr. Edmund to help you out, did you? You didn't realize you were bringing a couple of friends back together to reminisce about old times? Well, let me tell you, we did. He relived every single one of them. *All thirty-six.*"

Carla and I simply stared at him. Stunned. My mind was racing and my entire body felt paralyzed. His retelling of the dream was startling enough, but to hear him implicate Georg made it that much more astonishing. Then the last part of what he said struck me to the core, and the realization brought me to the brink of nausea.

"Thirty-six?" I muttered. "Only twenty-nine bodies were found, Edward. Thirty-two if you count the three in New Mexico..."

Kevin smiled and shrugged. "Well, I guess you've got some digging to do, don't you?"

"There are four more bodies?" I said, as much an affirmation to myself as it was a question to him. "Is that what Dr. Edmund told you?"

Kevin nodded and snickered briefly.

"Where are they, Edward?" I asked. "Tell us where they are."

"Oh..." he breathed, "they're around here somewhere."

"Tell us where they are, Edward," I urged.

He grinned, answering, "Eighty-six, nine, one, one."

"What?"

"Eight—six—nine—one—one," he repeated empathically, as if it was the most obvious answer in the world.

"Quit screwing with me," I retorted. "Where are the other four bodies?"

Kevin sighed and rolled his eyes. "I'm trying to tell you, Doc, but you're not listening."

I muttered the number to myself, racking my brain for anything that would make it relevant. A location or an identifier of some kind?

"The numbers are the letters, Doc," he added.

I glared at him quizzically. "What did you say?"

"Christ, are you deaf?" he replied, agitated now. "The numbers *are* the letters."

Then suddenly, images of the Strangler case file swarmed into my mind. The photos of the victims. Kevin's driver's license. And the two letters sent by the Strangler to the *Peak Courier*. Edward's signature at the bottom of each. And the enigmatic number that followed. 8-6-9-1-1.

My eyes widened with the realization, and Kevin grinned in response.

"What do the numbers mean, Edward?" I muttered.

"Oh, come on now," he said, "that would ruin all the fun, Doc."

"What do they mean?" I added, practically begging him.

He shrugged. Just as his shoulders relaxed, the glossiness returned to his eyes and his brow furrowed with confusion.

"Doc..." he asked, his tone clearly that of Jackie. "What are you talking about? Where am I?"

"Jackie?" I said, frantic. "I need to talk to Edward."

"You're scaring me," he said, shirking away from me until he realized he was handcuffed to the bed. "Where am I?!" he screamed.

"Let me talk to Edward, dammit," I retorted.

Kevin ignored me, writhing against the shackles and shaking the bed frame. "Let me go!" he yelped. "HELP!"

"I need to sedate him," Carla said, grabbing a syringe and vial from a locked cabinet.

"No," I said to her, turning back to Kevin and adding, "Come back out here, Edward!"

"No! No! No!" Kevin screamed, his body convulsing on the bed as he struggled against the restraints to no avail.

"Edward!"

"Stop it, Sharon," urged Carla, hurrying over to the bed and grabbing hold of Kevin's arm.

Kevin tried to squirm away from her and released an ear-piercing shriek when she plunged the needle into his arm.

"GET OFF OF ME!" he screamed as she pushed the sedative into his bloodstream.

Within a matter of moments, Kevin's body calmed and the sedative knocked him unconscious. An eerie silence fell over the infirmary once again.

FORTY-SEVEN

Eight. Six. Nine. One. One.

I must've repeated the number to myself a thousand times as I drove from the Wyoming State Penitentiary to Park City. Investigators and forensic analysts had combed through all of the obvious possibilities for the five-digit number signed on the letters years ago, and nothing had come of it. The closer I got to Park City, the more I wondered if the number hadn't been a smoke screen to screw with police then, and me now. It angered me, despite the fact that I knew it wasn't Kevin who was doing it; it was Edward.

Then there was the confession about the four victims that had yet to be discovered. Supposedly. Was Edward just trying to play me with that too, I wondered? I had to push the doubt out of my head. I had to believe that he was telling the truth because it was the only chance that Kevin still had to be exonerated. I clung to the notion that if we found at least one of the still-missing bodies, there'd be evidence linking the Strangler murders to Georg, not Kevin. It was foolishly optimistic, yet it was the only option that remained.

Stepping through the entry of the Peak County courthouse

brought me an overwhelming sense of déjà-vu, and the negative memories caused me to second-guess what I had come there to do. I was probably the last person that Kim Matthews wanted to see, and I doubted she would even believe what I was going to tell her.

I didn't know what to expect as I walked down the corridor toward her office and stopped in front of her administrative assistant's desk.

"Can I help you?" asked the young woman, glancing at me briefly.

"I was hoping to speak with Kim Matthews," I said. "It's urgent."

The young woman looked up at me again, and when her eyes met mine, her expression changed. "You're Dr. Sharon Stevenson, aren't you?" she asked, her tone hesitant.

"Yes," I said.

She rose from her chair and headed for Matthews' closed office door. "What's the reason for your visit?" she asked.

I considered being vague, but I didn't want Matthews to dismiss me because she didn't think it was worth her time. "The Blue River Strangler. There are more bodies."

Shock overcame the young woman's expression and she hurriedly opened the door and disappeared. A moment later, Kim Matthews stepped out of her office. She was dressed more professionally than I remembered. She also looked as if she was averaging only a few hours of sleep most nights.

"What's this about more bodies?" she asked, impatient and skeptical.

"Can we talk in your office?" I said. "I assure you, you're going to want to hear this."

She crossed her arms and glowered at me. A few seconds passed before she said, "I have a meeting soon. You've got ten minutes."

I followed her into her office and took a seat. Most of her

belongings had been removed from shelves and walls and piled into legal boxes that were scattered throughout the room.

"You leaving Park City?" I asked.

"I am," she said, her tone neutral.

Sarcastically, I added, "Moving on up the ladder, huh?"

She nodded, but said nothing.

"Where are you headed?"

"Cheyenne," she answered. "I'll be the new State Attorney General in a few weeks."

"Congratulations," I said, although my tone betrayed my true feelings. If I had to guess, her conviction of Kevin had put her on the short list for a number of promotions.

She glanced at her watch and sighed. "Why are you here, Sharon?"

"I spoke to Kevin this morning," I said. "*Edward* actually. He told me that there are four more bodies that haven't been found."

Matthews' face remained impassive. "And where did Blackford say they are?"

"He didn't," I answered. "He just said there's four more and he referenced the five-digit number from the letters sent to the *Courier*."

Her eyes narrowed. "And you *believe* him?" she scoffed. "How long are you going to allow yourself to be led around by the nose by that monster?"

"Four more bodies," I interjected. "Doesn't that mean anything to you, or are the problems of Peak County no longer a concern of yours?"

"I think it's time you left," she said, moving toward her phone to call security.

"Dammit, wait," I pleaded. "What if he *is* telling the truth? Four more victims are out there somewhere. Four more young women whose lives were cut short. Four more families who have no idea what happened to their loved ones. Think about it."

She stopped, her hand hovering over the phone.

FORTY-EIGHT

I stopped the car at the end of the dirt forestry service road and glanced about the dense wilderness that surrounded me in all directions. I had sifted through the Blue River Strangler case file earlier, finding the map of the Griffith's Peak Wilderness that had the location of each victim's remains marked with a yellow number. The areas where bodies had already been found had been covered thoroughly by investigators at those times, so I figured the most likely areas to find the remaining four victims would be on the edges. The forestry service road that I had driven down came to a dead end just shy of that border.

Looking at the map alone in Park City, it didn't seem like too daunting a task to drive out there and begin the search myself, but now that I was in the heart of the forest, I realized just how expansive the area was.

"What am I doing?" I said to myself, my better judgment reminding me that I wasn't much of a hiker, let alone an experienced outdoorsman.

I looked at the map again, trying to figure out where to even begin my search.

I made a note of each of the victim's locations, but the only pattern I noticed was the obvious spiraling of the yellow dots.

I thought about some of the victims specifically. Denise Chapman. Tracy Malvar. All found along a section of the Blue River. Even the victims in New Mexico were found near waterways of some kind. Looking at the map, though, the Blue River was several miles to the east, making a sharp bend northward and out of the Griffith's Peak Wilderness. That's when I noticed the little blue lines on the map, etched finely into the wilderness like varicose veins. Some of the lines were thicker than the others and labeled in print so small that I had to squint to read them. Red Tail Creek. Eleven Mile Creek. They were all tiny bodies of water that fed into the Blue River at one point or another. Some so small probably that they weren't even denoted on the map. Every single yellow dot was on or near one of those little blue lines.

With the map in hand, I walked into the forest, heading for the nearest blue line that I could see. If there were more victims, chances were that their bodies were near some body of water. Why the Strangler had done that was beyond me. Maybe the wildlife activity was higher near water and he needed them to help destroy the bodies? Maybe he used the water to clean the bodies and himself before leaving them for good?

I plodded through the undergrowth of the forest, trying to keep my bearings so that I wouldn't get lost out in the middle of nowhere. My heart was racing at first; not so much from excitement, but from anticipation. I was almost desperate to find something out there. Searching for a microscopic needle that may or may not be in that giant haystack.

The further I hiked, though, the more massive the forest felt around me. The anticipation waned and left doubt in its wake. I looked at the map again and figured I should've reached the creek by that point. I was worried that I somehow got lost in my haste.

Stopping caused me to hear the ambient noise of the forest. The rustling of the branches. The caw of an occasional crow. The cutting of the wind over the tops of the pines, or what sounded like the wind at least. I listened closer, the sound originating to my left specifically. The rhythm didn't pulse the way gusts usually did. It was a constant whirring noise like that of an industrial fan. I immediately hurried toward the noise, realizing that what I was hearing was the sound of moving water.

I came upon a small brook in a matter of minutes, and in my eagerness, I half expected to see the rotting remains of a young woman right in front of me.

But I didn't. I simply saw a picturesque landscape. Clear water cutting in, out, and around the contours of the forest floor. Pine trees that towered over the entire thing like a fortress.

I followed the brook downstream, knowing if nothing else that it would lead me to one of the creeks that eventually dumped into the Blue River. I figured it was as good of a place as any for a body to be disposed of.

I honestly lost track of the time as I followed the rushing water. I was staring at the ground for quite some time, hypnotically watching my feet so as not to trip on anything.

When I first saw it, I thought it was a rock protruding from the ground. Roughly the size of a bowling ball with dirt and moss covering it. I almost fell to the ground when I realized that the moss wasn't actually moss. It was human hair, decayed and matted with filth. Attached to the rock that wasn't actually a rock. I couldn't bring myself to dig around it to get a better look, simply because I was paralyzed with fear. I didn't need to anyway. It was clear that I had almost stumbled over the partially decomposed remains of a young woman's head.

FORTY-NINE

I don't think the emergency dispatcher believed me when I told him I had found another dead body in the Griffith's Peak Wilderness. Rather, I don't think he *wanted* to believe me.

The Peak County Sheriff himself came out, and after I led him and a deputy to the body, he ordered for a search party immediately.

Over the course of the week, investigators discovered the partially decomposed remains of three more bodies. The medical examiner had determined that at least two had been killed shortly before Maddie was killed in New Mexico. Despite the decomposition, the medical examiner was able to extract partial DNA from one of the victim's mouths. Although I hoped the DNA would be a match to Georg, I had a terrible feeling that it would match Kevin instead.

Waiting to hear the results was agonizing, but I distracted myself by convincing Arlo to head up Kevin's appeals in the event that the DNA matched Georg. He agreed reluctantly, probably to get me to leave him alone more than anything else. Certainly not because he believed beyond a shadow of a doubt that Kevin was innocent. I think the previous defeats had made him less optimistic than I was. Even *I* had my doubts the longer we waited for the results.

The Peak County Sheriff notified me when the results did finally come in.

"It's an eighty percent match," he told me, "to Georg Edmund."

Stunned doesn't even begin to describe what I felt in that moment. When I told Arlo about the results, he was in as much disbelief as I was.

"I know this doesn't exactly exonerate Kevin for the other victims," I said to him, "but combined with Georg's confession in New Mexico, do you think it at least gives us enough to appeal the death penalty?"

He stared at me for a while until he finally said, "Absolutely."

There was still a glaring question in my mind, though: what was the meaning of the five-digit number that Kevin had emphasized so much?

I stumbled upon that answer by accident really. Arlo and I were working on Kevin's death penalty appeal when I was going through the case file for the New Mexico copycat murders and came across Georg's psychiatry license. Near the top of the document was where I saw the heading: *License No. 19618*. Despite doing everything he could to set Kevin up, the son of a bitch couldn't help himself; he had to take credit for his work somehow, even if that was a scrambled version of his psychiatry license number.

But explaining the enigmatic signature wasn't going to be enough to exonerate Kevin entirely. Not by itself at least. We needed a full confession to make that a reality.

Convicted for the murders in New Mexico already, Georg had been extradited to Wyoming to stand trial for the four victims found in the Griffith's Peak Wilderness. Even though he was being held a few hours away at the Peak County Prison,

Arlo and I were not allowed to meet with him or speak to him. Not only would his lawyer not have it, but Kim Matthews, who had recently been sworn in as the State Attorney General, had also given the new Peak County prosecuting attorney strict instructions to forbid anyone from speaking to Georg until the trial was over.

The trial itself was highly publicized, and the news outlets provided updates on the proceedings after each day. Arlo and I watched the updates religiously. The prosecuting attorney appeared to be extremely thorough in his presentation of the evidence, making it clear that he was aggressively seeking the death penalty. Because of the indisputable physical evidence facing Georg, his defense team tried to plead insanity to dodge the sentence. They even went so far as to put Georg on the witness stand to testify. From what I heard on the news, his initial testimony was more convincing than expected, so I waited anxiously to hear how the prosecuting attorney's cross-examination would turn out. When the stories broke the evening afterward, I couldn't believe what they reported:

"The courtroom in Peak County was left speechless today as the murder trial of Georg Edmund continued with the cross-examination of the accused. In an unprecedented twist during cross-examination, Edmund not only confessed to the three murders for which he is being charged, but he also indicated that he was responsible for the murders of dozens of other women in Wyoming over the last two decades, including those attributed to the Blue River Strangler, Kevin Blackford. When asked by the prosecuting attorney why he was finally coming clean, Edmund responded, 'Calling Kevin Blackford the Blue River Strangler is an insult to my work. Give credit where credit is due.'"

FIFTY

The witnesses who don't know any better think that Dr. Georg Edmund is dead shortly after he winks at me and shuts his eyes. Like a flick of a light switch. Instant darkness.

If only it worked that way.

I imagine he has at least a minute of subconscious lucidity. Sixty seconds of chaotic brain activity that his psyche will try to frantically interpret and unravel before his life is forever seized from him.

It makes me wonder what he's dreaming about in those moments before the pancuronium bromide paralyzes him and the potassium chloride puts him into cardiac arrest. Do the faces of those thirty-six women flash before his mind's eye? Does he relive the torment and trauma he inflicted upon Kevin? Does he wonder what ultimately caused him to be the way he was? Whenever people tried to ask him why he did what he did, he told them it was simply who he was. An instinct. Nothing more and nothing less.

I refuse to believe that. Something must have happened to shape what he became. Maybe it was the trauma he experienced in the Stanford Prison study? Or maybe it was abuse so far back in his childhood that he repressed it beyond his own recognition?

The drugs work as they are intended to work. Georg shows no signs of struggle or pain throughout the process. The movement of his chest as he breathes just slows until the peaceful rising and falling simply ceases.

After a few minutes, once the technicians are confident that the potassium chloride has done its work, the doctor enters the room and pronounces Georg Edmund, the Blue River Strangler, dead for good.

All of the witnesses stare soberly at his body regardless of our connections to him. For those who awaited this day with vengeful anticipation, I imagine they don't feel the sweetness of justice on their tongues like they hoped. I simply feel sadness, not because he is dead, but because I lost a friend.

Yet humans have done this for thousands of years. An eye for an eye. A tooth for a tooth. Retributive justice that neither prevents future evil nor satisfies our need for revenge.

And we will continue to do this, I imagine. If there's one thing I've learned about human nature, it's that we can't help but make the same mistakes over and over again.

I'm the last to leave the room, lingering long after the technicians unstrap Georg's lifeless body from the padded crucifix.

As I exit the foyer of the main building, I see Kim Matthews, the Wyoming State Attorney General. I try to walk past her unnoticed, but I hear her call my name out.

I turn and answer, "Hello, Kim... Excuse me, Ms. Attorney General."

She sneers, despite her attempt to not react to my sarcasm. "I guess you're pretty happy," she says.

"Happy?" I answer quizzically. "What about today would make me happy?"

She grins slightly. "Blackford is still alive," she says. "For now, at least."

I roll my eyes and answer, "So you still think Kevin is guilty?"

Her grin disappears. "Of being an accessory to murder?" she responds. "Absolutely."

"The governor seems to think differently," I retort.

"Against my advice," she adds. "If it was up to me, Blackford would have been on that table right after Edmund."

"Ironic that the man who appointed you was the same one who commuted him."

"Well," she says, "the governor is an impressionable man. I still have more than enough time to change his mind."

"Good luck with that," I say. "Just know that I'll do everything I can to prevent it."

I turn and walk away as she says something in response. I ignore it though. There's no point in listening anymore, nor is there any point in arguing with her. I've been doing this long enough to know that people like her won't change their minds, and that's why there have to be people like me who won't stop getting in their way.

A LETTER FROM THE AUTHOR

Huge thanks for reading *The Patient's Secret*. I hope you were hooked on Sharon's and Kevin's journeys from start to finish. If you want to join other readers in hearing all about my new releases and bonus content, you can sign up for my newsletter!

www.stormpublishing.co/sa-falk

If you enjoyed this book and could spare a few moments to leave a review, I would greatly appreciate it. Even a short review can make all the difference in encouraging a reader to discover my book for the first time. Thank you so much!

Inspired largely by my studies of psychology and criminology in college, *The Patient's Secret* as a concept came together almost four years ago. Initially, my goal was to subvert the typical crime novel by telling the serial killer's story after he has been convicted, focusing less on his crimes and more on what caused him to commit them in the first place. Subsequently, I wanted to explore the phenomenon that has intrigued me since I started studying psychology: what is more powerful in determining who we are and how we behave – our genetics or our experiences? Are people simply born evil, or do they become monsters over time?

As the narrative grew in complexity though, the novel became more than just an exploration of the criminal mind. I began to challenge my own perceptions of the justice system, specifically the feasibility of criminal rehabilitation and the ethics of capital punishment. One element I would like to specifically note is the implied correlation between mental dysfunction and criminality. People suffering from common disorders like bipolar disorder, borderline personality disorder, and schizophrenia are no more likely to exhibit violent or criminal behavior than those who do not have a mental illness. However, research shows that inmates are twice as likely to suffer from mental illness than those who are not incarcerated. I offer this correlation as another point of reflection for the reader on the justice system at large: should the goal of incarceration focus more on punishment or rehabilitation? Mind you, I do not seek to convince readers of certain attitudes or agendas within these areas. Instead, I want to invite readers into their own reflections on their beliefs and challenge them within the confines of the story. We may not draw the same conclusions, but what matters more is opening the door to thoughtful, mindful dialogue.

Something I personally cherish in a book is its ability to remain in my thoughts long after I have finished it, and it is my hope that *The Patient's Secret* has a similar effect on you.

Thanks again for being part of this amazing journey with me, and I hope you'll stay in touch – I have so many more stories and ideas to entertain you with!

S.A. Falk

facebook.com/SAFALKauthor
instagram.com/safalkauthor

ACKNOWLEDGMENTS

First and foremost, I am so grateful for the guidance and patience of my literary agent, Liza Fleissig. This project has improved dramatically over the past three years, and I owe so much of that to the time she spent advising and brainstorming with me.

Thank you to Emily Gowers and the entire editorial team at Storm Publishing for their expertise and constructive feedback. They have been monumental in polishing this manuscript and making it the best that it could possibly be.

I also must express my appreciation for the psychology department at Regis University, specifically Dr. Rona McCall and the late Dr. Charlie Shelton. Dr. McCall sparked my interest in developmental and criminal psychology, and Dr. Shelton taught me everything I know about clinical and abnormal psychology. Their mentorship outside of the class-room also helped me discover my calling as an educator, and for that I owe a debt that can never be repaid.

Printed in Great Britain
by Amazon